THE DAWN OF ALL

CLUNY CLASSICS

THE DAWN OF ALL

A Novel

Robert Hugh Benson

CLUNY
Providence, Rhode Island

Cluny Media edition, 2017

For information regarding this title
or any other Cluny Media publication,
please write to info@clunymedia.com, or to
Cluny Media, P.O. Box 1664, Providence, RI 02901

❦ VISIT US ONLINE AT WWW.CLUNYMEDIA.COM ❦

ISBN: 978-1944418465

Cover design by Clarke & Clarke
Cover image: Caspar David Friedrich, *The Cross Beside the Baltic,*
circa 1815, oil on canvas
Courtesy of Wikimedia Commons

CONTENTS

✳ PART ONE ✳

PROLOGUE

GRADUALLY memory and consciousness once more reasserted themselves, and he became aware that he was lying in bed. But this was a sad process of intense mental effort, and was as laboriously and logically built up of premises and deductions as were his theological theses learned twenty years before in his seminary. There was the sheet below his chin; there was a red coverlet (seen at first as a blood-colored landscape of hills and valleys); there was a ceiling overhead, at first as remote as the vault of heaven.

Then, little by little, the confused roaring in his ears sank to a murmur. It had been just now as the sound of brazen hammers clanging in reverberating caves, the rolling of wheels, the tramp of countless myriads of men. But it had become now a soothing murmur, not unlike the coming in of a tide at the foot of high cliffs—just one gentle continuous note, overlaid with light, shrill sounds. This too required long argument and reasoning before any conclusion could be reached; but it was attained at last, and he became certain that he lay somewhere within sound of busy streets. Then rashly he leapt to the belief that he must be in his own lodgings in Bloomsbury; but another long slow stare upwards showed him that the white ceiling was too far away.

The effort of thought seemed too much for him; it gave him a sense of inexplicable discomfort. He determined to think no more, for fear that the noises should roar again to the crash of hammers in his hollow head....

He was next conscious of a pressure on his lips, and a kind of shadow of a taste of something. But it was no more than a shadow: it was as if he were watching someone else drink and perceiving someone else to swallow.... Then with a rush the ceiling came back into view: he was aware that he was lying in bed under a red coverlet; that the room was large and airy above him; and that two persons, a doctor in white and a nurse, were watching him. He rested in that knowledge for a long time, watching memory reassert itself. Detail after detail sprang into view: farther and farther back into his experience, far down into the childhood he had forgotten. He remembered now who he was, his story, his friends, his life up to a certain blank day or set of days, between him and which there was nothing. Then he saw the faces again, and it occurred to him, with a flash as of illumination, to ask. So he began to ask, and he considered carefully each answer, turning it over and reflecting upon it with what seemed to him an amazing degree of concentration.

"So I am in Westminster Hospital," he considered. "That is extraordinarily interesting and affecting. I have often seen the outside of it. It is of discolored brick. And I have been here how long? How long, did they say? Oh, that is a long time! Five days! And what in the world can have happened to my work? They will be looking out for me in the Museum. How can Dr. Waterman's history get on without me? I must see about that at once. He'll understand that it's not my fault.

"What's that? I mustn't trouble myself about that! But—oh, Dr. Waterman has been here, has he? That's very kind—very kind and thoughtful indeed. And I'm to take my time, am I? Very well. Please thank Dr. Waterman for his kindness and his thoughtfulness in inquiring.... And tell him I'll be with him again in a day or two at any rate. Oh, tell him that he'll find the references to the thirteenth-century papers in the black notebook—the thick one—on the right of the fireplace. They're all verified. Thank you. Thank you very much.... And...and...by the way...just tell him I'm not sure yet about the

Piccolomini matter. What's that? I'm not to trouble myself? But…oh, very well! Thank you. Thank you very much."

There followed a long pause. He was thinking still very hard about the thirteenth-century Popes. It was really very tiresome that he could not explain to Dr. Waterman himself. He was certain that some of the pages in his thick black notebook were loose; and how terrible it would be if the book were taken out carelessly, and some of the pages fell into the fire. They easily might! And then there'd be all the work to do again. And that would mean weeks and weeks.

Then there came a grave, quiet voice of a woman speaking in his ear; but for a long time he could not understand. He wished it would let him alone. He wanted to think about the Popes. He tried nodding and murmuring a general sort of assent, as if he wished to go to sleep; but it was useless: the voice went on and on. And then suddenly he understood and a kind of fury seized him.

How did they know he had once been a priest? Spying and badgering, as usual! No: he did *not* want a priest sent for. He was not a priest anymore; not even a Catholic. It was all lies—lies from the beginning to the end—all that they had taught him in the seminary. It was all lies! There! Was that plain enough?

Ah! Why would not the voice be quiet?

He was in great danger, was he? He would be unconscious again soon, would he? Well, he didn't know what they meant by that; but what had it to do with him? No, he did *not* want a priest. Was that clear enough? He was perfectly clear-headed; he knew what he was saying.

Yes; even if he were in great danger, even if he were practically certain to die. That, by the way, was impossible; because he had to finish the notes for Dr. Waterman's new *History of the Popes*; and it would take months. Anyhow, he didn't want a priest. He knew all about that: he had faced it all, and he wasn't afraid. Science had knocked all that religious nonsense on the head. There wasn't any religion. All religions were the same. There wasn't any truth in any of them. Physical science had settled one-half of the matter, and psychology the other half. It was all accounted for. So he didn't want a priest anyhow. Damn priests! There! Would they let him alone after that?

And now as to the Piccolomini affair. It was certain that when Aeneas was first raised to the Sacred College…

Why, what was happening to the ceiling? How could he attend to Aeneas while the ceiling behaved like that? He had no idea that ceilings in the Westminster Hospital could go up like lifts. How very ingenious! It must be to give him more air. Certainly he wanted more air.

The walls too. Ought not they also to revolve? They could change the whole air in the room in a moment. What an extraordinarily ingenious. Ah, and he wanted air. He wanted more air. Why don't those doctors know their business better? What was the good of catching hold of him like that? He wanted air. He must get to the window! Air…air!

CHAPTER I

I

THE first objects of which he became aware were his own hands clasped on his lap before him, and the cloth cuffs from which they emerged; and it was these latter that puzzled him. So engrossed was he, that at first he could not pay attention to the strange sounds in the air about him; for these cuffs, though black, were marked at their upper edges with a purple-red line such as prelates wear. He mechanically turned the backs of his hands upwards; but there was no ring on his finger. Then he lifted his eyes and looked.

He was seated on some kind of raised chair beneath a canopy. A carpet ran down over a couple of steps beneath his feet, and beyond stood the backs of a company of ecclesiastics—secular priests in cotta, cassock, and biretta, with three or four bare-footed Franciscans and a couple of Benedictines. Ten yards away there was a temporary pulpit with a back and a sounding-board beneath the open sky; and in it was the tall figure of a young friar, preaching, it seemed, with extraordinary fervor. Around the pulpit, beyond it, and on all sides to an immense distance, so far as he could see, stretched the heads of an incalculable multitude, dead silent, and beyond them again trees, green against a blue summer sky.

He looked on all this, but it meant nothing to him. It fitted in nowhere with his experience; he knew neither where he was, nor at what he was assisting, nor who these people were, nor who the friar was, nor who he was himself. He simply looked at his surroundings, then back at his hands and down his figure.

He gained no knowledge there, for he was dressed as he had never been dressed before. His caped cassock was black, with purple buttons and a purple cincture. He noticed that his shoes shone with gold buckles; he glanced at his breast, but no cross hung there. He took off his biretta, nervously, lest someone should notice, and perceived that it was black with a purple tassel. He was dressed then, it seemed, in the costume of a Domestic Prelate. He put on his biretta again.

Then he closed his eyes and tried to think; but he could remember nothing. There was, it seemed, no continuity anywhere. But it suddenly struck him that if he knew that he was a Domestic Prelate, and if he could recognize a Franciscan, he must have seen those phenomena before. Where? When?

Little pictures began to form before him as a result of his intense mental effort, but they were far away and minute, like figures seen through the wrong end of a telescope; and they afforded no explanation. But, as he bent his whole mind upon it, he remembered that he had been a priest—he had distinct memories of saying mass. But he could not remember where or when; he could not even remember his own name.

This last horror struck him alert again. *He did not know who he was.* He opened his eyes widely, terrified, and caught the eye of an old priest in cotta and cassock who was looking back at him over his shoulder. Something in the frightened face must have disturbed the old man, for he detached himself from the group and came up the two steps to his side.

"What is it, Monsignor?" he whispered.

"I am ill…I am ill, Father," he stammered.

The priest looked at him doubtfully for an instant.

"Can you…can you hold out for a little? The sermon must be nearly—"

Then the other recovered. He understood that at whatever cost he must not attract attention.

He nodded sharply.

"Yes, I can hold out, Father; if he isn't too long. But you must take me home afterwards."

The priest still looked at him doubtfully.

"Go back to your place, Father. I'm all right. Don't attract attention. Only come to me afterwards."

The priest went back, but he still glanced at him once or twice.

Then the man who did not know himself set his teeth and resolved to remember. The thing was too absurd. He said to himself he would begin by identifying where he was. If he knew so much as to his own position and the dresses of those priests, his memory could not be wholly gone.

In front of him and to the right there were trees, beyond the heads of the crowd. There was something vaguely familiar to him about the arrangement of these, but not enough to tell him anything. He craned forward and stared as far to the right as he could. There were more trees. Then to the left; and here, for the first time, he caught sight of buildings. But these seemed very odd buildings neither houses nor arches—but something between the two. They were of the nature of an elaborate gateway.

And then in a flash he recognized where he was. He was sitting, under this canopy, just to the right as one enters through Hyde Park Corner; these trees were the trees of the Park; that open space in front was the beginning of Rotten Row; and Something Lane—Park Lane—(that was it!)—was behind him.

Impressions and questions crowded upon him quickly now—yet in none of them was there a hint as to how he got here, nor who he was, nor what in the world was going on. This friar—What was he doing, preaching in Hyde Park? It was ridiculous—ridiculous and very dangerous. It would cause trouble.

He leaned forward to listen, as the friar with a wide gesture swept his hand around the horizon.

"Brethren," he cried, "look around you! Fifty years ago this was a Protestant country, and the Church of God a sect among the sects. And today—today God is vindicated and the truth is known. Fifty years ago we were but a handful among the thousands that knew not God, and today we rule the world. 'Son of man, can these dry bones live?' So cried the voice of God to the prophet. And behold! they stood up upon their feet, an exceedingly great army. If then He has done such things for us, what shall He not do for those for whom I speak? Yet He works through man. 'And shall they hear without a preacher?'

"Do *you* see to it then that there are not wanting laborers in that vineyard of which you have heard. Already the grapes hang ready to pluck, and it is but we that are wanting… Send forth then laborers into My vineyard, cries the Lord of all."

The words were ill-chosen and commonplace enough, and uttered in an accent indefinably strange to the bewildered listener, but the force of the man was tremendous, as he sent out his personality over the enormous crowd, on that high vibrant voice that controlled, it seemed, even those on the outskirts far up the woods on either side. Then with a swift sign of the cross, answered generally by those about the pulpit, he ended his sermon and disappeared down the steps, and a great murmur of talk began.

But what in the world was it all about, wondered the man under the canopy. What was this vineyard? And why did he appeal to English people in such words as these? Everyone knew that the Catholic Church was but a handful still in this country. Certainly, progress had been made, but…

He broke off his meditations as he saw the group of ecclesiastics coming towards him, and noticed that on all sides the crowd was beginning to disperse. He gripped the arms of his chair fiercely, trying to gain self-command. He must not make a fool of himself before all these people, he must be discreet and say as little as possible.

But there was no great need for caution at present. The old priest who had spoken to him before stepped a little in advance of the rest, and turning, said a low sentence or two to the Benedictines; and the group stopped, though one or two still eyed, it seemed, with sympathy, the man who awaited him. Then the priest came up alone and put his hand on the arm of the chair.

"Come out this way," he whispered. "There's a path behind, Monsignor, and I've sent orders for the car to be there."

The man rose obediently (he could do nothing else), passed down the steps and behind the canopy. A couple of police stood there in the familiar old uniform, and these drew themselves up and saluted. They went on down the little pathway and out through a side-gate. Here again the crowd was tremendous, but barriers kept them away, and the two passed on together across the pavement, saluted by half a dozen men who were pressed against the barriers—(it was here, for the first time, that the bewildered man noticed that the dresses seemed altogether unfamiliar)—and up to a car of a peculiar and unknown shape, that waited in the roadway, with a bare-headed servant, in some strange purple livery, holding the door open.

"After you, Monsignor," said the old priest. The other stepped in and sat down. The priest hesitated for an instant, and then leaned forward into the car.

"You have an appointment in Dean's Yard, Monsignor, you remember. It's important, you know. Are you too ill?"

"I can't…I can't," the man stammered.

"Well, at least, we can go around that way. I think we ought, you know. I can go in and see him for you, if you wish; and we can at any rate leave the papers."

"Anything, anything. Very well."

The priest got in instantly; the door closed; and the next moment, through crowds, held back by the police, the great car, with no driver visible in front, through the clear-glass windows, moved off southward.

II

I⊤ was a moment before either spoke. The old priest broke the silence. He was a gentle-faced old man, not unlike a very shrewd and wide-awake dormouse; and his white hair stood out in a mass beneath his biretta. But the words he used were unintelligible, though not altogether unfamiliar.

"I don't understand, Father," stammered the man.

The priest looked at him sharply.

"I was saying," he said slowly and distinctly, "I was saying that you looked very well, and I was asking you what was the matter."

The other was silent a moment. How to explain the thing? Then he determined on making a clean breast of it. This old man looked kindly and discreet.

"I…I think it's a lapse of memory," he said. "I've heard of such things. I…I don't know where I am nor what I'm doing. Are you…are you sure you're not making a mistake? Have I got any right—?"

The priest looked at him as if puzzled.

"I don't quite understand, Monsignor. What can't you remember?"

"I can't remember anything," wailed the man, suddenly broken down. "Nothing at all. Not who I am, nor where I'm going, or where I come from. What am I? Who am I? Father, for God's sake tell me."

"Monsignor, be quiet, please. You mustn't give way. Surely—"

"I tell you I can remember nothing. It's all gone. I don't know who you are. I don't know what day it is, or what year it is, or anything—"

He felt a hand on his arm, and his eyes met a look of a very peculiar power and concentration.

He sank back into his seat strangely quieted and soothed.

"Now, Monsignor, listen to me. You know who I am—" (he broke off). "I'm Father Jervis. I know about these things. You'll be all right presently, I hope. But you must be perfectly quiet—"

"Tell me who I am," stammered the man.

"Listen, then. You are Monsignor Masterman, secretary to the Cardinal. You are going back to Westminster now, in your own car—"

"What's been going on? What was all that crowd about?"

Still the eyes were on him, compelling and penetrating.

"You have been presiding at the usual midday Saturday sermon in Hyde Park, on behalf of the Missions to the East. Do you remember now? No! Well, it doesn't matter in the least. That was Father Anthony who was preaching. He was a little nervous, you noticed. It was his first sermon in Hyde Park."

"I saw he was a friar," murmured the other.

"Oh! You recognized his habit then? There, you see; your memory's not really gone. And what's the answer to *Dominus vobiscum?*"

"*Et cum spiritu tuo.*"

The priest smiled, and the pressure on the man's arm relaxed.

"That's excellent. It's only a partial obscurity. Why didn't you understand me when I spoke to you in Latin then?"

"That was Latin? I thought so. But you spoke too fast; and I'm not accustomed to speak it."

The old man looked at him with grave humor. "Not accustomed to speak it, Monsignor! Why—" (He broke off again.) "Look out of the window, please. Where are we?"

The other looked out. (He felt greatly elated and comforted. It was quite true; his memory was not altogether gone then. Surely he would soon be well again!) Out of the windows in front, but seeming to wheel swiftly to the left as the car whisked around to the right, was the Victoria Tower. He noticed that the hour pointed to five minutes before one.

"Those are the Houses of Parliament," he said. "And what's that tall pillar in the middle of Parliament Square?"

"That's the image of the Immaculate Conception. But what did you call those buildings just now?"

"Houses of Parliament, aren't they?" faltered the man, terrified that his brain was really going.

"Why do you call them that?"

"It is their name, isn't it?"

"It used to be; but it isn't the usual name now."

"Good God! Father, am I mad? Tell me. What year is it?"

The eyes looked again into his.

"Monsignor, think. Think hard."

"I don't know. I don't know. Oh, for God's sake!"

"Quietly then. It's the year nineteen hundred and seventy-three."

"It can't be; it can't be," gasped the other. "Why, I remember the beginning of the century."

"Monsignor, attend to me, please…. That's better. It's the year nineteen hundred and seventy-three. You were born in the year—in the year nineteen hundred and thirty. You are just forty years old. You are secretary and chaplain to the Cardinal—Cardinal Bellairs. Before that you were Rector of St. Mary's in the West. Do you remember now?"

"I remember nothing."

"You remember your ordination?"

"No. Once I remember saying Mass somewhere. I don't know where."

"Stay, we're just there." (The car wheeled in swiftly under an archway, whisked to the left, and drew up before an archway.) "Now, Monsignor, I'm going in to see the Prior myself and give him the papers. You have them?"

"I…I don't know."

The priest dived forward and extracted a small dispatch-box from some unseen receptacle.

"Your keys, please, Monsignor."

The other felt wildly about his person. He saw the steady eyes of the old priest upon him.

"You keep them in your left-hand breast pocket," said the priest slowly and distinctly.

The man felt there, fetched out a bundle of thin, flat keys, and handed them over helplessly. While the priest turned them over, examining each, the other stared hopelessly out of the window, past the motionless servant in purple who waited with his hand on the car door. Surely he knew this place…. Yes, it was Dean's Yard. And this was the entrance to the cloister of the Abbey. But who was the Prior, and what was it all about?

He turned to the other, who by now was bending over the box and extracting a few papers laid neatly at the top.

"What are you doing, Father? Who are you going to see?"

"I am going to take these papers of yours to the Prior—the Prior of Westminster. The Abbot isn't here yet. Only a few of the monks have come."

"Monks! Prior! Father!"

The old man looked him in the eyes again.

"Yes," he said quietly. "The Abbey was made over again to the Benedictines last year, but they haven't yet formally taken possession. And these papers concern business connected with the whole affair—the relations of seculars and regulars. I'll tell you afterwards. I must go in now, and you must just remain here quietly. Tell me again. What is your name? Who are you?"

"I…I am Monsignor Masterman, secretary to Cardinal Bellairs."

The priest smiled as he laid his hand on the door. "Quite right," he said. "And please sit here quietly, Monsignor, till I come back."

III

HE sat in perfect silence, waiting, leaning back in his corner with closed eyes, compelling himself to keep his composure.

It was, at any rate, good luck that he had fallen in with such a friend as this—Father Jervis, was it not?—who knew all about him, and, obviously, could be trusted to be discreet. He must just attend to his instructions quietly then, and do what he was told. No doubt things would come back soon. But how very curious this all was about Hyde Park and Westminster! He could have sworn that England was a Protestant country, and the Church just a tiny fragment of its population. Why, it was only recently that Westminster Cathedral was built, was it not? But then this was the year seventy-three and…and… he could not remember what year the Cathedral was built in. Then again the horror and bewilderment seized him. He gripped his knees with his hands in an agony of consternation. He would go mad if he could not remember. Or at least—Ah! Here was Father Jervis coming back again.

The two sat quite silent again for a moment, as the car moved off.

"Tell me," said the priest suddenly, "don't you remember faces, or people's names?"

The other concentrated his mind fiercely for a moment or two.

"I remember some faces—yes," he said. "And I remember some names. But I cannot remember which faces belong to which names. I remember the name Archbishop Bourne; and…and a priest called Farquharson—"

"What have you been reading lately? Ah! I forgot. Well, but can't you remember the Cardinal—Cardinal Bellairs?"

"I've never heard of him."

"Nor what he looks like?"

"I haven't a notion."

The priest again was silent.

"Look here, Monsignor," he said suddenly, "I'd better take you straight up to your rooms as soon as we arrive; and I'll have a notice put up on your confessional that you are unable to attend there today. You'll have the whole afternoon—after four at least—to yourself, and the rest of the evening. We needn't tell a soul until we're certain that it can't be helped, not even the Cardinal. But I'm afraid you'll have to preside at lunch today."

"Eh?"

"Mr. Manners is coming, you know, to consult with the Cardinal; and I think if you weren't there to entertain him—"

Monsignor nodded sharply, with compressed lips. "I understand. But just tell me who Mr. Manners is?"

The priest answered without any sign of discomposure.

"He's a member of the Government. He's the great political economist. And he's coming to consult with the Cardinal about certain measures that affect the Church. Do you remember now?"

The other shook his head.

"No."

"Well, just talk to him vaguely. I'll sit opposite and take care that you don't make any mistakes. Just talk to him generally. Talk about the sermon in Hyde Park, and the Abbey. He won't expect you to talk politics publicly."

"I'll try."

The car drew up as the conversation ended; and the man who had lost his memory glanced out. To his intense relief, he recognized where he was. It was the door of Archbishop's House, in Ambrosden Avenue; and beyond he perceived the long northern side of the Cathedral.

"I know this," he said.

"Of course you do, my dear Monsignor," said the priest reassuringly. "Now follow me: bow to anyone who salutes you; but don't speak a word." They passed in together through the door, past a couple of liveried servants who held it open, up the staircase and beyond up the further flight. The old priest drew out a key and unlocked the door before them; and together they turned to the left up the corridor, and passed into a large, pleasant room looking out onto the street, with a further door communicating with a bedroom beyond. Fortunately they had met no one on the way.

"Here we are," said Father Jervis cheerfully. "Now, Monsignor, do you know where you are?"

The other shook his head dolorously.

"Come, come; this is your own room. Look at your writing-table, Monsignor; where you sit every day."

The other looked at it eagerly and yet vaguely. A half-written letter, certainly in his own handwriting, lay there on the blotting-pad, but the name of his correspondent meant nothing to him; nor did the few words which he read. He looked around the room—at the bookcases, the curtains, the *prie-dieu*. And again terror seized him.

"I know nothing, Father, nothing at all. It's all new! For God's sake!"

"Quietly then, Monsignor. It's all perfectly right. Now I'm going to leave you for ten minutes, to arrange about the places at lunch. You'd better lock your door and admit no one. Just look around the rooms when I'm gone—Ah!" Father Jervis broke off suddenly and darted at an armchair, where a book lay face downwards on the seat. He snatched up the book, glanced at the pages, looked at the title, and laughed aloud.

"I knew it," he said; "I was certain of it. You've got hold of Manners' *History*. Look! You're at the very page."

He held it up for the other to see. Monsignor looked at it, still only half-comprehending, and just noticing that the paper had a peculiar look, and saw that the running dates at the top of the pages contained the years 1904–1912. The priest shook the book in gentle triumph. A sheet of paper fell out of it, which he picked up and glanced at. Then he laughed again.

"See," he said, "you've been taking notes of the very period—no doubt in order to be able to talk to Manners. That's the time he knows more about than any living soul. He calls it the 'crest of the wave,' you know. Everything dated from then, in his opinion."

"I don't understand a word—"

"See here, Monsignor," interrupted the priest in mild glee, "here's a subject to talk about at lunch. Just get Manners onto it, and you'll have no trouble. Tell him you've been reading his *History* and want a bird's-eye view."

Monsignor started.

"Why, yes," he said, "and that'll tell me the facts, too."

"Excellent. Now, Monsignor, I must go. Just look around the rooms well and get to know where things are kept. I'll be back in ten minutes, and we'll have a good talk before lunch as to all who'll be there. It'll all go perfectly smoothly, I promise you."

IV

WHEN the door closed Monsignor Masterman looked around him slowly and carefully. He had an idea that the mist must break sooner or later and that all would become familiar once again. It was perfectly plain, by now, to his mind, what had happened to him; and the fact there were certain things which he recognized, such as the Cathedral, and Hyde Park, and a friar's habit, and Archbishop's House all this helped him to keep his head. If he remembered so much, there seemed no intrinsic reason why he should not remember more.

But his inspection was disappointing. Not only was there not one article in the room which he knew, but he did not even understand the use of some of the things which he saw. There was a row of what looked like small black boxes fastened to the right-hand wall, about the height of a man's head; and there was some kind of a machine, all wheels and handles, in the corner by the nearer window, which was completely mysterious to him.

He glanced through into the bedroom, and this was not much better. Certainly there was a bed; there was no mistake about that;

and there seemed to be wardrobes sunk to the level of the walls on all sides; but although in this room he thought he recognized the use of everything which he saw, there was no single thing that wore a familiar aspect.

He came back to his writing-table and sat down before it in despair. But that did not reassure him. He took out one or two of the books that stood there in a row—directories and address-books they appeared chiefly to be—and found his name written in each, with here and there a note or a correction, all in his own handwriting. He took up the half-written letter again and glanced through it once more, but it brought no relief. He could not even conjecture how the interrupted sentence on the third page ought to end.

Again and again he tried to tear up from his inner consciousness something which he could remember, closing his eyes and sinking his head upon his hands, but nothing except fragments and glimpses of vision rose before him. It was now a face or a scene to which he could give no name; now a sentence or a thought that owned no context. There was no frame at all—no unified scheme in which those fragments found cohesion. It was like regarding the pieces of a shattered jar whose shape even could not be conjectured.

Then a sudden thought struck him; he sprang up quickly and ran into his bedroom. A tall mirror, he remembered, hung between the windows. He ran straight up to this and stood staring at his own reflection. It was himself that he saw there—there was no doubt of that—every line and feature of that keen, pale, clear-cut face was familiar, though it seemed to him that his hair was a little grayer than it ought to be.

CHAPTER II

I

"I shall be delighted, Monsignor," said the thin, professional-looking statesman, in his high, dry voice. "I shall be delighted to sketch out what seem to be the principal points in the century's development."

A profound silence fell upon all the table. Really, Monsignor Masterman thought to himself, as he settled down to listen, he had done very well so far. He had noticed the old priest opposite smiling more than once, contentedly, as their eyes met.

Father Jervis had come to him as he had promised, for half an hour's good talk before lunch; and they had spent a very earnest thirty minutes together. First they had discussed with great care all the persons who would be present at lunch—not more than eight, besides themselves; the priest had given him a little plan of the table, showing where each would sit, and had described their personal appearance and recounted a salient fact or two about every one. These were all priests except Mr. Manners himself and his secretary. The rest of the time had been occupied in information being given to the man who had lost his memory, with regard to a few very ordinary subjects of conversation the extraordinary fairness of the weather; a new opera produced with unparalleled success by a "well-known" composer of whom Monsignor had never heard; a recent Eucharistic congress in Tokyo, from which the Cardinal had just returned; and the scheme for re-decorating the interior of Archbishop's House.

There had not been time for more; but these subjects, under the adroit handling of Father Jervis, had proved sufficient; and up to the preconcerted moment when Monsignor had uttered the sentence about his study of Mr. Manners' *History of Twentieth Century*

Development which had drawn from the author the words recorded above, all had gone perfectly smoothly.

There had been a few minor hitches; for example, the food and the manner of serving it and the proper method of consuming it had furnished a bad moment or two; and once Monsignor had been obliged to feign sudden deafness on being asked a question on a subject of which he knew nothing by a priest whose name he had forgotten, until Father Jervis slid in adroitly and saved him. Yet these were quite unnoticed, it appeared, and could easily be attributed to the habit of absent-mindedness for which, Monsignor Masterman was relieved to learn, he was almost notorious.

And now the crisis was past and Mr. Manners was launched. Monsignor glanced almost happily around the tall dining-room, from which the servants had already disappeared, and, with his glass in his hand, settled himself down to listen and remember. "The crisis, to my mind, in the religious situation," began the statesman, looking more professional than ever, with his closed eyes, thin, wrinkled face, and high forehead, "the real crisis is to be sought in the period from 1900 to 1920.

"This was the period, you remember, of tremendous social agitation. There was the widespread revolution of the Latin countries, beginning with France and Portugal, chiefly against Authority, and most of all against Monarchy (since Monarchy is the most vivid and the most ornate embodiment of authority); and in Teutonic and Anglo-Saxon countries against Capital and Aristocracy. It was in these years that Socialism came most near to dominating the civilized world; and, indeed, you will remember that for long after that date it did dominate civilization in certain places.

"Now the real trouble at the bottom of all this was the state in which religion found itself. And you will find, gentlemen," said the quasi-lecturer in parenthesis, glancing around the attentive faces, "that religion always is and always has been at the root of every world-movement. In fact it must be so. The deepest instinct in man is his religion, that is, his attitude to eternal issues; and on that attitude must depend his relation to temporal things. This is so, largely, even in the case of the individual; it must therefore be infinitely more so in large bodies or nations; since every crowd is moved by principles that are the least common multiple of the principles of the units which compose it. Of course this is universally recognized now; but it was not always so. There was a time, particularly at this period of which I am now speaking, when men attempted to treat religion as if it were one department of life, instead of being the whole foundation of every and all life. To treat it so is, of course, to proclaim oneself as fundamentally irreligious—and, indeed, very ignorant and uneducated.

"To resume, however: religion at this period was at a very strange crisis. That it could possibly be treated in the way I have mentioned shows how very deeply irreligion had spread. There is no such thing, of course, really as irreligion—except by a purely conventional use of the word: the 'irreligious' man is one who has made up his mind either that there is no future world, or that it is so remote, as regards effectivity, as to have no bearing upon this. And that is a religion—at least it is a dogmatic creed—as much as any other.

"The causes of this state of affairs I take to have been as follows: religion up to the Reformation had been a matter of authority, as it is again now; but the enormous development of various sciences and the wide spread of popular 'knowledge' had, in the first flush, distracted attention from that which is now, in all civilized countries, simply an axiom of thought, viz., that a Revelation of God must be embodied in a living authority safeguarded by God. Further, at that time science and exact knowledge generally had not reached the point which they reached a little later—of corroborating in particular after particular, so far as they are capable of doing so, the Revelation of God known as Catholicism; and of knowing their limitations when they cannot. Many sciences, at this time, had gone no further than to establish certain facts which appeared, to the very imperfectly educated persons of that period, to challenge and even to refute certain facts or deductions of Revelation. Psychology, for example, strange as it now appears in our own day, actually seemed to afford other explanations of the

Universe than that of Revelation. (We will discuss details presently.) Social Science, at that time, too, moved in the direction of Democracy and even Socialism. I know it appears monstrous, and indeed almost incredible, that men who really had some claim to be called educated seriously maintained that the most stable and the most reasonable method of government lay in the extension of the franchise—that is, in reversing the whole eternal and logical order of things, and permitting the inexpert to rule the expert, and the uneducated and the ill-informed to control by their votes—that is, by sheer weight of numbers—the educated and the well-informed. Yet such was the case. And the result was—since all these matters act and react—that the idea of authority from above in matters of religion was thought to be as 'undemocratic,' as in matters of government and social life. Men had learnt, that is to say, something of the very real truth in the theory of the least common multiple, and, as in psychology and many other sciences, had presumed that the little fragment of truth that they had perceived was the whole truth."

Mr. Manners paused to draw breath. Assuredly he was enjoying himself enormously. He was a born lecturer, and somehow the rather pompous sentences were strangely alive and strangely interesting. Above all, they fascinated and amazed the prelate at the head of the table, for they revealed to him an advance of thought and an assurance in the position they described that seemed wholly inexplicable. Such phrases as "all educated men," "the well-informed," and the rest—these were vaguely familiar to him, yet surely in a very different connection. He had at the back of his mind a kind of idea that these were the phrases that the irreligious or the agnostics applied to themselves; yet here was a man, obviously a student, and a statesman as he knew, calmly assuming (scarcely even giving himself the trouble to state) that all educated and well-informed persons were Catholic Christians!

He settled himself down with renewed interest to listen again, as Mr. Manners began once more.

"Well," he said, "to come more directly to our point; let us next consider what were those steps and processes by which Catholic truth once more became the religion of the civilized world, as it had been five centuries earlier.

"And first we must remark that even at the very beginning of this century popular thought—in England as elsewhere—had retraced its steps so far as to acknowledge that if Christianity were true, really and actually—the Catholic Church was the only possible embodiment of it. Not only did the shrewdest agnostic minds of the time acknowledge this, such men as Huxley in the previous century, Sir Leslie Stephen, Mallock, and scores of others—but even popular Christianity itself began to turn in that direction. Of course there were survivals and reactions, as we should expect. There was a small body of Christians in England called Anglicans, who attempted to hold another view; there was that short-lived movement called Modernism, that held yet a third position. But, for the rest, it was as I say.

"It was the Catholic Church or nothing. And just for a few years it seemed humanly possible that it might be nothing.

"And now for the causes of the revival. Briefly, I should say they were all included under one head—the correlation of sciences and their coincidence into one point. Let us take them one by one. We have only time to glance very superficially at each.

"First there was Psychology. Even at the end of the nineteenth century it was beginning to be perceived that there was an inexplicable force working behind mere matter. This force was given a number of names—the 'subliminal consciousness,' in man, and 'nature' in the animal, vegetable, and even mineral creation; and it gave birth to a series of absurd superstitions such as that now wholly extinct sect called 'Christian Science,' or the Mental Healers; and among the less educated of the Materialists, to Pantheism. But the force was acknowledged, and it was perceived to move along definite lines of law. Further, in the great outburst of Spiritualism it began gradually to be evident to the world that this force occasionally manifested itself in a personal, though always a malevolent manner. Now it must be remembered that even this marked an immense advance in the circles called scientific; since in the middle of the nineteenth century, even the

phenomena so carefully recorded by the Church were denied. These
were now no longer denied, since phenomena, at least closely resembling them, were matters of common occurrence under the eyes of the
most sceptical. Of course, since the inquiries were made along purely
'scientific' lines—lines which in those days were nothing other than
materialistic—an attempt was made to account for the phenomena
by new anti-spiritual theories hastily put together to meet the emer-
gency. But, little by little, an uneasy sense began to manifest itself that
the Church had already been familiar with the phenomena for about
two thousand years, and that a body which had marked and recorded
facts with greater accuracy than all the 'scientists' put together at least
had some claim to consideration with regard to her hypothesis concerning them. Further, it began to be seen (what is perfectly familiar
to us all now) that religion contributed an element which nothing
else could contribute—that, for example, 'Religious Suggestion,' as it
was called in the jargon of the time, could accomplish things that
ordinary 'Suggestion' could not. Finally the researches of psychologists
into what was then called the phenomenon of 'Alternating Personality' prepared the way for a frank acceptance of the Catholic teaching
concerning Possession and Exorcism—a teaching which half a century before would have been laughed out of court by all who claimed
the name of Scientist. Psychology, then, up to this point, had redis-
covered that a force was working behind physical phenomena, itself
not physical; that this force occasionally exhibited characteristics of
personality; and finally that the despised Catholic Church had been
more scientific than scientists in her observation of facts; and that this
force, dealt with along Christian lines, could accomplish what it was
unable to accomplish along any other.

"The next advance lay along the lines of Comparative Religion.
The study of Comparative Religion was practically a new science at
the end of the nineteenth century, and like all new sciences, claimed
at once, before it had constructed its own, to destroy the schemes
of others. For instance, there were actually educated persons who
advanced as an argument against Christianity the fact that many

Christian dogmas and ceremonies were to be found in other religions.
It is exceedingly difficult for us now, even in imagination, to sympathize with such a mentality as this; but it must be remembered that
the science was very youthful, and had all the inexperience and the
arrogance of youth. As time went on, however, this argument began
to disappear, except in very elementary rationalistic manuals, as the
fact became evident that while this or that particular religion had one
or more identities with Christian doctrines, Christianity possessed
them all; that Christianity, in short, had all the principal doctrines
of all religions—or at least all doctrines that were of any strength
to other religions, as well as several others necessary to weld these
detached dogmas into a coherent whole—that, to use a simple met-
aphor, Christianity stood in the world like a light upon a hill, and
that partial and imperfect reflections of this light were thrown back,
with more or less clearness, from the various human systems of belief
that surrounded it. And at last it became evident, even to the most
unintelligent, that the only scientific explanation of this phenomenon
lay in the theory that Christianity was indeed unique, and, at the very
least, was the most perfect human system of faith—perfectly human,
I mean, in that it embodied and answered adequately all the religious
aspirations of the human race—the most perfect system of faith the
world had ever seen.

"A third cause was to be found in the new philosophy of evidence
that began to prevail soon after the dawn of the century. Up to that
period, so-called Physical Science had so far tyrannized over men's
minds as to persuade them to accept her claim that evidence that
could not be reduced to her terms was not, properly speaking, evidence at all. Men demanded that purely spiritual matters should be, as
they said, 'proved,' by which they meant should be reduced to physical
terms. Little by little, however, the preposterous nature of this claim
was understood. People began to perceive that each order of life had
evidence proper to itself—that there were such things, for instance, as
moral proofs, artistic proofs, and philosophical proofs; and that these
proofs were not interchangeable. To demand physical proof for every

article of belief was as fantastic as to demand, let us say, a chemical proof of the beauty of a picture, or evidence in terms of light or sound for the moral character of a friend, or mathematical proof for the love of a mother for her child. This very elementary idea seems to have come like a thunderclap upon many who claimed the name of 'thinkers'; for it entirely destroyed a whole artillery of arguments previously employed against Revealed Religion.

"For a time, Pragmatism came to the rescue from the philosophical camp; but the assault was but a very short one; since tested by pragmatic methods (that is, the testing of the truth of a religion by its appeal to human consciousness) if one fact stood out luminous and undisputed, it was that the Catholic religion, with its eternal appeal in every century and to every type of temperament, was utterly supreme.

"Let us turn to another point—"

(Mr. Manners lifted the glass he had been twirling between his fingers, and drank it off with an appearance of enjoyment. Then he continued.)

"Let us turn to the realm of politics—even to the realm of trade. Socialism, in its purely economic aspect, was a well-meant attempt to abolish the law of competition—that is, the natural law of the Survival of the Fittest. It was an attempt, I say; and it ended, as we know, in disaster; for it established instead, so far as it was successful, the law of the Survival of the Majority, and tyrannized first over the minority and then over the individual. But it was a well-meant attempt; since its instinct was perfectly right, that competition is not the highest law of the Universe. And there were several other ideals in Socialism that were most commendable in theory: for example, the idea that the society sanctifies and safeguards the individual, not the individual the society; that obedience is a much neglected virtue, and so forth.

"Then, suddenly almost, it seems to have dawned upon the world that all the *ideals* of Socialism (apart from its methods and its dogmas) had been the ideals of Christianity; and that the Church had, in her promulgation of the law of love, anticipated the Socialist's discovery by about two thousand years. Further, that in the Religious Orders these ideals had been actually incarnate; and that by the doctrine of vocation—that is by the freedom of the individual to submit himself to a superior—the rights of the individual were respected and the rights of the society simultaneously vindicated.

"A very good example of all this is to be found in the Poor-law system. You remember that before the Reformation, and in Catholic countries long after, there was no Poor-law system, because the Religious Houses looked after the sick and needy. Well, when the Religious Houses were destroyed in England the State had to do their work. You could not simply flog beggars out of existence, as Elizabeth tried to do. Then the inevitable happened, and it began to be a mark of disgrace to be helped by the State in a workhouse: people often preferred to starve. Then at the beginning of the twentieth century a well-meant attempt was made, in the Old-Age Pensions, to remedy this and to keep the poor in a manner that would not injure their self-respect. Of course that failed too. It is incredible that statesmen did not see it must be so. Old-Age Pensions, too, began to be considered a mark of disgrace—for the simple cause that it is not the giving of money that is resented, but the motive for which the money is given and the position of the giver. The State can only give for economic reasons, however conscientious and individually charitable statesmen may be; while the Church gives for the love of God, and the love of God never yet destroyed any man's self-respect. Well, you know the end. The Church came forward once more and, under certain conditions, offered to relieve the State of the entire burden. Two results followed: first, all grievances vanished; and second, the whole pauper population of England within ten years was Catholic in sympathies. And yet all this is only a reversion to medieval times—a reversion made absolutely necessary by the failure of every attempt to supplant divine methods by human.

"Now look at it all in another way, the general situation, I mean. The Socialist saw plainly the rights of the society; the Anarchist saw the rights of the individual. How therefore were these to be reconciled? The Church stepped in at that crucial point and answered, "By the family"—whether domestic or religious. For in the family you have both claims recognized: there is authority and yet there is liberty. For the union of the family lies in love; and love is the only reconciliation of authority and liberty.

"Now, as I have put it—and as we all now see it—the argument is simplicity itself. But it took a long time to be recognized; and it was not until after the appalling events of the first twenty years of the century, and the discrediting of the absurd Socialistic attempt to preach the law of love by methods of force, that civilization as a whole saw the point. Yet for all that it was beginning to mold popular opinion even as early as 1910.

"Turn now to a completely different plane. Turn to art. This, too, drove men back to the Church."

(Mr. Manners' air was becoming now less professional and more vivid. He glanced quickly from face to face with a kind of sharp triumph; his long, thin hands waved a slight gesture now and again.)

"Art, you remember, in the end of the Victorian era had attempted to become realistic—had attempted, that is, the absurdly impossible; and photography exposed the absurdity. For no man can be truly a realist, since it is literally impossible to paint or to describe all that the eye sees. When photography became general, this began to be understood; since it was soon seen that the only photographer who could lay any claim to artistic work was the man who selected and altered and posed—arranged his subject, that is to say, in more or less symbolic form. Then people began to see again that symbolism was the underlying spirit of art—as they had known perfectly well, of course, in medieval days: that art consisted in going beneath the material surfaces that reflected light, or the material events that happened, in painting and literature respectively, and, by a process of selection, of symbolizing (not photographically representing) the ideas beneath the things—the substance beneath the accidents—the thought beneath the expression (you can call it what you like). Zola in literature, Strauss in music, the French school of painting—these reduced Realism *ad absurdum*. Thus once more the Catholic Church, in this as in everything else, was discovered to have possessed the secret all along. The symbolic reaction therefore began, and all our music, all our painting, and all our literature today are frankly and confessedly symbolic, that is, Catholic. And this too, you see, pointed to the same lesson as Psychology, that beneath phenomena there was a force which transcended phenomena; and that the Church had dealt with this force, knowing it to be personal, through all her history.

"Finally—and this was the crowning argument of all, that correlated all the rest—there was the growing scientific and popular perception of the recuperative power of the Church—that which our divine Lord Himself called the Sign of the Prophet Jonas, or Resurrection.

"There were of course countless other lines of advance, in practically every science, and they all pointed in the same direction, and met, so to speak, from every quarter of the compass the end of the tunnel which the Church had been boring through all the heaped-up stupidities and ignorances of man. Psychology tunneled, and presently heard the voices of the exorcists and the echoes of Lourdes through the darkness. Human religions tunneled—Hinduism with its idea of a divine incarnation, Buddhism with its coarse apprehension of the eternal peace of a beatific vision, North American Religion with its guesses at Sacramentalism, Savage Religion with its caricature of a bloody sacrifice; all from various points; and presently heard through the tumult the historical dogma of the Incarnation of Christ, the dogma of Eternal Life, the Sacramental System, and the Sacrifice of the Cross—all proclaimed in one coherent and perfectly philosophical Creed. Ideals of social reform met with the same experiences. The Socialist with his dream of a divine society, the Anarchist with his passionate nightmare of complete individual liberty, both ran up together, in the heart of the black darkness, against the vast outline of a divine family that was a fact and not a far-off ambition—a family that fell in Eden and became a competitive State; a Holy Family that redeemed Nazareth and all the world; a Catholic family in whom was neither Jew nor Greek, nor masters against men—in whom the doctrine of vocation secured the rights and the dignities of the society on one side and the individual on the other. Finally, art, wandering hither and thither in the mazes of Realism, saw light ahead, and found in Catholic art and symbolism the secret of her life.

"This, then, was the result—that the Church was found to be eternally right in every plane. In plane after plane she had been condemned. Pilate—the law of separate nations—had found her guilty of sedition; Herod—the miracle-monger at one instant and the skeptic at the next—the Scientist, in fact—had declared her guilty of fraud; Caiaphas had condemned her in the name of national religion. Or, again, she had been thought the enemy of art by the Greek-spirited; the enemy of law by the Latins; the enemy of religion by the Hebraic Pharisee. She had borne her title written in Greek and Latin and Hebrew. She had been crucified, and taunted as she hung there; she had seemed to die; and, lo and behold! when the Third Day dawned she was alive again for evermore. From every single point she had been justified and vindicated. Men had thought to invent a new religion, a new art, a new social order, a new philosophy; they had burrowed and explored and dug in every direction; and, at the end, when they had worked out their theories and found, as they thought, the reward of their labors, they found themselves looking once more into the serene, smiling face of Catholicism. She was risen from the dead once more, and was seen to be the Daughter of God, with power."

There was a moment's silence.

"There, gentlemen," said Mr. Manners, dropping back again into the quiet professor, "that, I think, in a few words, is the outline for which Monsignor asked. I hope I have not detained you too long."

II

"It is the most extraordinary story I have ever heard," said Monsignor Masterman ten minutes later, as he threw himself down in his chair upstairs, with Father Jervis sitting opposite.

"Certainly he puts it very well," said the old priest, smiling. "I think every one was interested. It's not often that we can hear such a clear analysis of events. Of course Manners is an expert—"

"But the amazing thing to me," interrupted the other, "is that this isn't just a dream or a prophecy, but a relation of facts. Do you mean to tell me that the whole world is Christian?"

The priest looked at him doubtfully.

"Monsignor, surely your memory isn't—" Monsignor made an impatient gesture.

"Father," he said, "it's exactly as I told you before lunch. I'll promise to tell you if my memory comes back. At present I remember practically nothing at all, except instinctively. All I know is that this story we have heard simply astounds me. I had a sort of idea that Christianity was ebbing from the world; that most thinking men had given up all belief in it; and now I find it's exactly the other way. Please treat me as if I had stepped straight out of the beginning of the century. Just tell me the facts as if for the first time. Is it really true that practically the whole world is Christian?"

The priest hesitated.

"You mean that, Monsignor?"

"Certainly."

"Very well then." He paused again. "But it's extraordinarily hard to know where to begin."

"Begin anywhere. It's all new to me."

"Very good. Well, yes: roughly we may say that the world is Christian, in the same sort of way, at least, in which Europe was Christian, say in the twelfth century. There are survivals, of course, particularly in the East, where large districts still cling to their old superstitions; and there are even eminent men here and there who are not explicitly Catholics; but, as a whole, the world is Christian."

"Do you mean Catholic?"

The priest stared a moment. "Why, yes. What else?"

"All right; go on."

"Well then, to begin with England. Catholicism is not yet established as the State religion; but it'll only be a question of time, and it may be said that all the laws are Christian."

"Divorce?"

"Divorce was abolished thirty years ago, and fornication was made a felony ten years later," said the priest quietly. "Benefit of clergy also was restored three years ago; and we have our own courts for heresy, with power to hand over convicted criminals to the secular arm."

"What?"

"Certainly. It has been in force now for three years."

"Then what do you mean by saying that the Church isn't established?"

"I mean that no religious test is demanded of officers of state and that bishops and abbots have no seat in Parliament. It was the enfranchisement of women that turned the tide once and for all."

"Do you mean that all women have the vote?"

"They are under the same conditions as men. There's a severe educational test now, of course. Not more than about one in seventy adults ever get the vote at all. But the result is that we're governed by educated persons."

"Stop. Is it a Monarchy?"

"Certainly. Edward IX—a young man—is on the throne."

"Go on."

"Christianity, then, holds the field. Of course there are infidels left, who write letters to the newspapers sometimes, and hold meetings, and so on. But they are practically negligible. As regards Church property, practically everything has finally been given back to us. I mean in the way of buildings, and, very largely, revenues too. All the cathedrals are ours, and all parish churches built before the Reformation, as well as all other churches in parishes where there was not organized Protestant resistance."

"I thought you said there were no Protestants."

Father Jervis suddenly laughed aloud.

"Monsignor, are you really serious? Do you really mean you wish me to go on?"

"Good God, man! I'm not playing a game. Go on, please. Tell me about the Protestants."

"Well, of course there are some Protestants left. I think they've got four or five churches in London, and yes, I'm sure of it, they've got some kind of bishop. But really I scarcely know. I shall have to look it up."

"Well, go on."

"Well, that's the state of England. Practically everybody is a Catholic—from the King downwards. The last remains of Church property was only actually given back to us last year. That's why the monks haven't come back to Westminster yet."

"What about the rest of the world?"

"Well, first Rome. Austria drove out the House of Savoy nearly twenty-five years ago; and the Holy Father—"

"What's his name?"

"Gregory the Nineteenth. He's a Frenchman. Well, the Holy Father is Temporal Ruler of the whole of Italy; but the Emperor of Austria administers it. Then France is, of course, a very small country."

"Why small?"

"Well, you know the Emperor War of 1914?"

Monsignor interrupted by a large sigh.

"Good heavens!" he said. "How I shall have to read. I'm sorry. Go on, please."

"Well, France is a very small country, but intensely Catholic. The Church is re-established there."

"Is it a monarchy too?"

"Certainly. The Orleans line came back after the war. Louis XXII is king. I was saying that the Church is re-established there, and is practically supreme. That is traceable entirely to Pius X's policy."

"Pius X! Why—"

"Yes, Monsignor."

"I know all about that. But I thought Pius X simply ruined everything."

"So they said at the time. His policy was to draw the lines tight and to make no concessions. He drove out every half-hearted Catholic by his regulations, and the result was a small but extraordinarily pure body. The result has been that the country was re-evangelized, and has become almost a land of saints. They say that Our Lady—"

"Well, go on with the other countries."

"Spain and Portugal, are, of course, entirely Catholic, like France. The Monarchy was re-established in both of them in about 1935. But Germany—Germany's the weak spot."

"Well?"

"You see the Emperor isn't a Christian yet; and Socialism lingers on there with extraordinary pertinacity. Practically Berlin is the Holy City of Freemasonry. It's all organized from there—such as it is. And no one is quite comfortable about Germany. The Emperor Frederick is a perfectly sincere man, but really rather uneducated; he still holds onto some sort of materialism; and the result is—"

"I see."

"But there are hopes of his conversion. He's to be at Versailles next week; and that's a good sign."

"Well, what about America?"

"Oh! America's chiefly English; and very like England."

"You mean she isn't republican?"

"Of course not. My dear Monsignor—"

"Please go on, as I asked you. Tell me when she ceased to be republican."

"Why, I scarcely know," murmured the priest. "It must have been about 1930, I suppose. I know there was a lot of trouble before that—civil wars and so forth. But at any rate that was the end. Japan got a good deal of the Far West; but the Eastern States came in with Canada and formed the American Colonies; and the South of course became Latinized, largely through ecclesiastical influence. Well, then America asked England—"

"Stop, please. I shall get bewildered. What about the religion?"

"Well, the Empire of Mexico—"

"Eh?"

"The Empire of Mexico."

"Who's Emperor?"

"The King of Spain, Monsignor," said the priest patiently. "Well, that used to be called South America. It's all the Empire of Mexico now, and belongs to Spain. That's solidly Catholic, of course. And the American Colonies—old North America—that's like England. It's practically Catholic, of course; but there are a few infidels and Socialists."

"Australia?"

"Australia's entirely Irish, and Catholic."

"And Ireland itself?"

"Ireland developed enormously as soon as she had gained independence, but emigration continued, and the Irish strength really lies abroad. Then an odd thing happened. Ireland continued to empty, obeying some social law we don't even yet understand properly; and the Religious began to get possession of the country in an extraordinary way, until they owned all the large estates, and even most of the towns. You may say that Ireland is practically one religious enclosure now. Of course she's a part of the British Empire; but her real social life lies in her colonies. Australia succeeded in getting Home Rule from Ireland about twenty-five years ago."

Monsignor pressed his hands to his head.

"It sounds like the wildest dream," he said.

"Hadn't I better—?"

"No, go on. I only want an outline. What about the East?"

Well, old superstitions still linger on in the East, especially in China. But the end is quite certain. It is simply a matter of time—"

"But…but…I don't understand. If the whole world is practically Christian, what is there left to do?"

The priest smiled.

"Ah! But you must remember Germany. There are great forces in Germany. It's there that the danger lies. And you must remember too that there is no Universal Arbitrator yet. Nationalism is still pretty strong. There might easily be another big European war."

"Then you hope—"

"Yes. We're all working for the recognition of the Pope as Universal Arbitrator, as he was practically in Europe in the Middle Ages. Of course, as soon as the sovereigns acknowledge officially that they hold all their rights at the will of Rome, the thing will be done. But it's not done yet, except—"

"Good God!"

"Look here, Monsignor, you've had enough," said the priest, rising. "Though I must say you have followed it closely enough. Are you certain that it is quite new to you? Don't you remember—"

"It's not only new; it's inconceivable! I understand it perfectly; but—"

"Well, you've had enough. Now what about coming to see the Cardinal? I feel sure he'll insist upon your taking a rest instantly. I feel rather guilty—"

"Stop. Tell me about languages. Why did you talk to me in Latin this morning?"

"Ecclesiastics generally do. And so do the laity a good deal. Europe is practically bilingual. Each country keeps up its own tongue, and learns Latin as well. You must rub up your Latin, Monsignor."

"Wait a moment. What are you going to say to the Cardinal?"

"Well, hadn't I better tell him the whole thing, just as it happened? Then you needn't explain."

The other pondered a moment.

"Thanks very much, Father. Stop. Do I talk English all right?"

"Perfectly."

"But—Oh well. And I did I do all right at lunch? Did anyone suspect anything?"

"You did perfectly. You seemed a little absentminded once or twice; but that was quite in keeping."

The two smiled at one another pleasantly.

"Then I'll be going," said the priest. "Will you wait here till I come for you?"

CHAPTER III

I

"Just be natural," whispered Father Jervis a quarter of an hour later, as they passed through the big ante-room. "You needn't explain a word. I've told him everything."

He tapped; and a voice answered.

Sitting in a big armchair drawn up to the writing-table, the man who had lost his memory saw a tall, thin figure, in black with scarlet buttons, and a small scarlet skull-cap crowning his iron-gray hair. It was a little hard to make out the face at first, as the window was immediately beyond it; but he saw almost immediately that, although the face smiled at him reassuringly and welcomingly, it was entirely unfamiliar.

The Cardinal stood up as the two approached, pushing back his chair, and held out both his hands. "My dear Monsignor," he said; and grasped the other's hands firmly and kindly.

"I...your Eminence..." stammered the man.

"Now, now; not one word till I've done. I've heard everything. Come and sit down."

He led him to a chair on the hearth-rug, placed him in it, and himself sat down in his own, facing him. The priest remained standing.

"Now, I'm going to begin with an order, on holy obedience," smiled the Cardinal. "You and Father Jervis—if the doctor approves—are to start for a little European tour by the midnight volor."

"The...?"

"The volor," said the Cardinal. "It'll do you good. Father Jervis will undertake all responsibility, and you needn't worry yourself at all. I shall telegraph to Versailles in my own name, and make one or two arrangements, and a couple of my servants will attend you. You will have nothing to do but get better. You can't be spared. It'll all come perfectly right, I have no manner of doubt. Father Jervis, just ask the doctor to step here."

The Cardinal talked a minute or two longer, still with that soothing, peaceful air; and Monsignor, as he listened, watched the priest go up to a row of black boxes, resembling those in his own room, and take down a shutter from one of them. He then said a rapid sentence or two in a whisper, reclosed the shutter, and came back.

"If things don't clear themselves, you will just have to learn your business over again, Monsignor," went on the Cardinal, still smiling. "Father Jervis has told me how well you did at lunch; and Mr. Manners said nothing, except that you were a very good host and a very graceful listener. So you need not fear that anyone will notice. So please put out of your mind any thought that anyone else will take your place here. I shall expect you back in a month or two, and not a soul will be any the wiser. I shall just let it be known that you've gone for a holiday. You have always worked hard enough, anyhow, to deserve one."

At that moment, somewhere out of the air, from the direction of the boxes on the wall, a very deferential, quiet voice uttered a few words in Latin.

The Cardinal nodded. Father Jervis went to the door and opened it, and there came through a man in a black cloak, resembling a gown, followed by a servant carrying a bag. The bag was set down, the servant went out, and the doctor came forward to kiss the Cardinal's ring.

"I want you just to examine Monsignor Masterman," said the Cardinal. "And, doctor, please observe absolute silence afterwards. Just say that you have found him a little run down."

Monsignor made a movement to stand up, but the Cardinal restrained him.

"Do you remember this gentleman?" he asked.

Monsignor stared blankly at the doctor.

"I have never seen him in my life," he said.

The doctor smiled, simply and frankly. "Well, well, Monsignor," he said.

"It seems just a loss of memory," went on the Cardinal. "Just tell the doctor how it happened."

The invalid made an effort; he shut his eyes for an instant to recover himself; and then he related at length his first apparent consciousness in Hyde Park, and all that had followed. Father Jervis put a question from time to time, which he answered quite rationally; and at the close the doctor, who was sitting opposite, watching every movement of his face, leaned back, smiling.

"Well, Monsignor," he said, "it seems to me that your memory is sufficiently good. Just put another question, Father—a really difficult one—about something that has happened since noon."

"Can you remember the points of Mr. Manners' speech?" asked the priest doubtfully.

The other paused for a moment.

"Psychology, Comparative Religion, the Philosophy of Evidence, Pragmatism, Art, Politics, and finally Recuperation. These were the—"

"Now that's astonishing!" said the priest. "I could only remember four myself."

"When did you see the Cardinal last?" asked the doctor suddenly.

"I have never seen him before, to my knowledge," faltered the sick man.

The Cardinal leaned forward and patted him gently on the knee. "Never mind," he said. "Then, doctor—"

"Would your Eminence put a question to him on some very important matter? Something that would make a deep impression?"

The Cardinal considered.

"Well," he said, "yes. Do you remember the message brought by special messenger from Windsor yesterday evening?"

Monsignor shook his head.

"That'll do," said the doctor. "Don't attempt to strain yourself."

He rose from his chair, fetched his bag and opened it. Out of it he took an instrument faintly resembling a small camera, but with a bundle of minute wires of some very pliable material, each ending in a tiny disk.

"Do you know what this is, Monsignor?" asked the doctor, busying himself with the wires.

"I have no idea."

"Well, well. Now, Monsignor, kindly loosen your waistcoat, so that I can get at your breast and back."

"Is it a stethoscope?"

"Something like it," smiled the doctor. "But how did you know that name? Never mind. Now then, please."

He placed the camera affair on the corner of the table near the armchair; and then, very rapidly, began to affix the disk—it seemed by some process of air-exhaustion—all over the head, breast, and back of the amazed man. No sensation followed this at all, except the very faint feeling of skin-contraction at each point of contact.

"May I have that blind down, your Eminence? Ah, that's better. Now then." He bent closely over the square box on the table, and seemed to peer at something inside. The others kept silence.

"Well?" asked the Cardinal at last.

"Perfectly satisfactory, your Eminence. There is a very faint discoloration, but no more than is usual in a man of Monsignor's temperament at any excitement. There is absolutely nothing wrong, and—Monsignor," he continued, looking straight at the wire-bedecked invalid, "not the very faintest indication of anything even approaching insanity or imbecility."

The man who had lost his memory drew a swift breath.

"May I see, doctor?" asked the Cardinal suavely.

"Certainly, your Eminence; and Monsignor can look himself, if he likes."

When the other two had looked, the sick man himself was given the box.

"(Carefully with that wire, please.) There!" said the doctor. "Look down there."

In the center of the box, shielded by a little plate of glass, there appeared a small semi-luminous globe. This globe seemed tinted with slightly wavering colors, in which a grayish blue predominated; but, almost like a pulse, there moved across it from time to time a very pale red tint, suffusing it, and then dying away again.

"What is it?" asked the man in the chair hoarsely, lifting his head.

"That, my dear Monsignor," explained the doctor carefully, "is a reflection of your physical condition. It is an exceedingly simple, though of course very delicate instrument. The method was discovered—"

"Is it anything to do with magnetism?"

"They used to call it that, I think. It's got several names now. All mental disturbance has, of course, a physical side to it, and that is how we are able to record it physically. It was discovered by a monk, of course."

"But...but...it's marvelous."

"Everything is marvelous, Monsignor. Certainly this, however, caused a revolution. It became the symbol of the whole modern method of medicine."

"What's that?" The doctor laughed.

"That's a large question," he said.

"But...but..."

"Well, in a word, it's the old system turned upside down. A century ago when a man was ill they began by doctoring his body. Now, when a man's ill, they begin by doctoring his mind. You see the mind is much more the man than the body is, as Theology always taught us. Therefore by dealing with the mind—"

"But that's Christian Science!" The doctor looked bewildered.

"It was an old heresy, doctor," put in the Cardinal, smiling, "that denied the reality of matter. No, Monsignor, we don't deny the reality of matter. It's perfectly real. Only, as the doctor says, we prefer to attack the real root of the disease, rather than its physical results. We still use drugs; but only to remove painful symptoms."

"That...that sounds all right," stammered the man, bewildered by the simplicity of it. "Then...then do you mean, your Eminence, that physical diseases are located—?"

"There are no physical diseases left," put in the doctor. "Of course there are accidents and external physical injuries; but practically all the rest have disappeared. Very nearly all of them had their seat in the state of the blood; and, by injection, the blood is made immune."

"But…but…are there no diseases then?"

"Why, yes, Monsignor," interrupted the Cardinal, with the patient air of one talking to a child; "there are hundreds of those; and they are very real indeed; but they are almost entirely mental—or psychical, as some call them. And there are specialists on all of these. Bad habits of thought, for example, always set up some kind of disease; and there are hospitals for these; and even isolation homes."

"Forgive me, your Eminence," put in the doctor, with a certain imperiousness, "but I think we ought not to talk to Monsignor too much on this subject. May I put a question or two?"

"I beg your pardon, doctor. Certainly. Put any question you wish."

The doctor sat down again.

"Have you been in the habit of saying Mass every day, Monsignor?"

"I…I don't know," said the invalid.

"Yes, doctor," put in Father Jervis.

"And confession once a week?"

"Twice a week," said Father Jervis. "I am Monsignor's confessor."

"Very good," said the doctor. "For the present, as far as I am concerned, I should recommend confession only once a fortnight as a general rule. Mass can be as before. Then Monsignor may say half of his office every day, or the rosary; but not both. And no other devotions of any kind, except the particular Examen. If Monsignor and Father Jervis both consent, I should like the Examen to be forwarded to a priest-doctor for a few weeks."

An exclamation broke from the invalid.

"Well, Monsignor?"

"I don't understand. What are you talking about?"

The Cardinal leaned forward.

"Monsignor, listen to me. In those cases the doctor always gives his advice. You see even the sacraments have their mental side; and

on this mental side the doctor speaks. But the whole decision rests
entirely with the patient and his confessor; or they can call in an
expert priest-doctor. Only a priest can possibly decide finally the relations between the grace of the sacraments and their purely mental
effect. A lay doctor only recommends. Are you satisfied?"

The man nodded. It seemed very simple, so stated.

"For the rest," continued the doctor, with a certain stateliness of
manner, "I order a complete change of scene. This must be for a fortnight at least, if not longer. If the priest-doctor's report to whom the
Examen may be sent is not satisfactory, it will have to be for longer.
The patient must engage in no business that does not honestly interest
him."

"May he travel tonight?" asked the Cardinal.

"The sooner the better," said the doctor, rising.

"What is the matter with me?" asked the invalid hoarsely.

"It is a small mental explosion that has affected a certain spot in
the brain. There is not, as I have said, a trace of insanity or of loss of
balance. I cannot promise that the injury will be repaired; but defects
that may follow from this can easily be remedied by study. It simply
depends upon yourself, Monsignor, as to how long before you can be
at your post again here. As soon as you have learned the threads of
business, you will be able to apply yourself as before. I shall look for a
report in a fortnight's time at the latest. Good day, your Eminence."

II

THE clocks of London were all striking the single stroke of midnight
as the two priests stood on the wind-sheltered platform of the volor,
waiting for the start.

To Monsignor Masterman the scene was simply overwhelming. There was hardly a detail that was not new and unfamiliar. From
where he stood on the upper deck, grasping the rail before him, his
eyes looked out over a luminous city as lovely as fairyland. There were
no chimneys, of course (these, he had just learnt, had altogether disappeared more than fifty years ago), but spires and towers and pinnacles

rose before him like a dream, glowing against the dark sky, lit by the soft radiance of the streets beneath. To the right, not a hundred yards away, rose Saint Edward's tower, mellowed now to clear orange by the lapse of three-quarters of a century; to the left a flight of buildings, of an architectural design which he did not understand, but which gave him a sense of extreme satisfaction; in front towered the masses of Buckingham Palace as he seemed always to have known it.

The platform of the flying ship on which he stood hung in dock at least a hundred and fifty feet high above the roads beneath. He had examined the whole vessel just now from stem to stern, and had found it vaguely familiar; he determined to examine it again presently. There was no gas-bag to sustain it—so much he had noticed—though he could not say whence he had the idea that gas-bags were usual. But it seemed to him as if the notion of air-ships did carry some faint association to his mind, although far less distinct than that of motorcars and even trains. He had inquired of his companion an hour or two earlier as they had discussed their journey as to whether they would not go by train and steamer, and had received the answer that these were never used except for very short journeys.

Here, then, he stood and stared.

It was very quiet up here; but he listened with considerable curiosity to the strange humming sound that filled the air, rising and falling, as of a beehive. At first he thought it was the working of engines in the ship; but he presently perceived it to be the noise of the streets rising from below; and it was then that he saw for the first time that foot-passengers were almost entirely absent, and that practically the whole roadway, so far as he could make out from the high elevation at which he stood, was occupied by cars of all descriptions going this way and that. They sounded soft horns as they went, but they bore no lights, for the streets were as light as day with a radiance that seemed to fall from beneath the eaves of all the buildings that lined them. This effect of lighting had a curious result of making the city look as if it were seen through glass or water—a beautifully finished, clean picture, moving within itself like some precise and elaborate mechanism.

He turned around at a touch on his arm.

"You would like to see the start, perhaps," said the old priest. "We are a little late tonight. The country mails have only just arrived. But we shall be off directly now. Come this way."

The upper deck, as the two turned inwards, presented an extremely pleasant and comfortable picture. From stem to stern it ran clear, set out, however, with groups of tables and chairs clamped to the floor, at which sat a dozen parties or so, settling themselves down comfortably. There were no funnels, no bridge, no break at all to the delightful vista. The whole was lighted by the same device as were the streets, for around the upper edges of the transparent walls that held out the wind shone a steady, even glow from invisible lights.

In the very center of the deck, however, was a low railing that protected the head of a staircase, and down this well the two looked.

"Shall I explain?" asked the old priest, smiling. "This is the latest model, you know. It has not been in use for more than a few months."

The other nodded.

"Tell me everything, please."

"Well, look right down there, below the second flight. The first flight leads to the second-class deck, and the flight below to the work-ing parts of the ship. Now do you see that man's head, straight in the middle, in the bright light?—yes, immediately under. Well, that's the first engineer. He's in a glass compartment, you see, and can look down passages in every direction. The gas arrangements are all in front of him, and the—"

"Stop, please. What power is it that drives the ship? Is it lighter than air, or what?"

"Well, you see the entire framework of the ship is hollow. Every single thing you see—even the chairs and tables—they're all made of the metal *aerolite* (as it's generally called). It's almost as thin as paper, and it's far stronger than any steel. Now it's the framework of the ship that takes the place of the old balloon. It's infinitely safer, too, for it's divided by automatically closing stops into tens of thou-sands of compartments, so a leak here or there makes practically no difference. Well, when the ship's at rest, as it is now, there's simply air in all these tubes; but when it's going to start, there is forced into these tubes, from the magazine below, the most volatile gas that has been discovered—"

"What's it called?"

"I forget the real name. It's generally called *aeroline*. Well, this is forced in, until the specific gravity of the whole affair, passengers and all, is as nearly as possible the same as the specific gravity of the air."

"I see. Good Lord, how simple!"

"And the rest is done with planes and screws, driven by electricity. The tail of the boat is a recent development. (You'll see it when we've once started.) It's exactly like the tail of a bird, and contracts and expands in every direction. Then besides that there are two wings, one on each side, and these *can* be used, if necessary, in case the screws go wrong, as propellers. But usually they are simply for balancing and gliding. You see, barring collisions, there's hardly the possibility of an accident. If one set of things fails, there's always something else to take its place. At the very worst, we can but be blown about a bit."

"But it's exactly like a bird, then."

"Of course, Monsignor," said the priest, with twinkling eyes, "it isn't likely that we could improve upon Almighty God's design. We're very simple, you know. Look, he's signaling. We're going to start. Come to the prow. We shall see better from there."

The upper deck ended in a railing, below which protruded, from the level of the lower deck, the prow proper of the boat. Upon this prow, in a small compartment of which the roof, as well as the walls, was of hardened glass, stood the steersman amid his wheels. But the wheels were unlike anything that the bewildered man who looked down had ever dreamed of. First, they were not more than six inches in diameter; and next, they were arranged, like notes on a keyboard, with their edges towards him, with the whole set curved around him in a semi-circle.

"Those to right and left," explained the priest, "control the planes on either side; those in front, on the left, control the engines and the gas supply; and on the right, the tail of the boat. Watch him, and you'll see. We're just starting."

As he spoke three bells sounded from below, followed, after a pause, by a fourth. The steersman straightened himself as the first rang out and glanced around him; and upon the fourth, bent himself suddenly over the keyboard, like a musician addressing himself to a piano.

For the first instant Monsignor was conscious of a slight swaying motion, which resolved itself presently into a faint sensation of constriction on his temples, but no more. Then this passed, and as he glanced away again from the steersman, who was erect once more, his look happened to fall over the edge of the boat. He grasped his friend convulsively. "Look," he said, "what's happened?"

"Yes, we're off," said the priest sedately.

Beneath them, on either side, there now stretched itself an almost illimitable and amazingly beautiful bird's-eye view of a lighted city, separated from them by what seemed an immeasurable gulf. From the enormous height up to which they had soared the city looked like a complicated flat map, of which the patches were dark and the dividing lines rivers of soft fire. This stretched practically to the horizon on all sides; the light toned down at the edges into a misty luminosity, but as the bewildered watcher stared in front of him, he saw how directly in their course there slid towards them two great patches of dark, divided by a luminous stream in the middle.

"What is it? What is it?" he stammered.

The priest seemed not to notice his agitation; he just passed his hand quietly into the trembling man's elbow.

"Yes," he said, "there are houses all the way to Brighton now, of course, and we go straight down the track. We shall take in passengers at Brighton, I think."

There was a step behind them.

"Good evening, Monsignor," said a voice. "It's a lovely night."

The prelate turned around, covered with confusion, and saw a man in uniform saluting him deferentially.

"Ah! Captain," slipped in the priest. "So we're crossing with you, are we?"

"That's it, Father. The *Michael* line's running this week."

"It's a wonderful thing to me—" began Monsignor, but a sharp pressure on his arm checked him—"how you keep the whole organization going," he ended lamely.

The captain smiled.

"It's pretty straightforward," he said. "The *Michael* line runs the first week of every month; the *Gabriel* the second, and so on."

"Then—"

"Yes," put in Father Jervis. "Whose idea was it to dedicate the lines to the archangels? I forget."

"Ah! That's ancient history to me, Father. Excuse me, Monsignor; I think I hear my bell." He wheeled, saluting again, and was off.

"Do you mean—?" began Monsignor.

"Of course," said Father Jervis, "everything runs on those lines now. You see we're very matter-of-fact, and it's really rather obvious, when you think of it, to dedicate the volor lines to the angels. We've been becoming more and more obvious for the last fifty years. By the way, Monsignor, you must take care not to give yourself away. You'd better not ask many questions except of me."

Monsignor changed the subject.

"When shall we get to Paris?" he asked.

"We shall be a little late, I think, unless they make up time. We're due at three. I hope there won't be any delay at Brighton. Sometimes on windy nights—"

"I suppose the descending and the starting again take some time."

The priest laughed.

"We don't descend at places *en route*," he said. "The tender comes up to us. It'll probably be in its place by now. We aren't ten minutes away."

The other compressed his lips and was silent.

Presently, far away to the southward beneath the soft starlit sky, the luminous road down which they traveled seemed to expand once more almost abruptly into another vast spread of lights. But as they approached this did not extend any farther, but lay cut off sharp by a long, curving line of almost complete darkness.

"Brighton…the sea…and there's the tender waiting."

At first the prelate could not make it out against the radiance below, but an instant later, as they rushed on, it loomed up, sudden and enormous, itself blazing with lights against the dark sea. It looked to him something like a floating stage, outlined with fire; and there were glimmering, perpendicular lines beneath it which he could not understand, running down to lose themselves in the misty glow three hundred feet beneath.

"How's it done?" he asked.

"It's a platform, charged of course with *aeroline*. It runs on lines straight up from the stage beneath, and keeps itself steady with screws. You'll see it go down after we've left again. Come to the stern, we shall see better from there."

By the time that they had reached the other end of the ship, the pace had rapidly diminished almost to motionlessness; and as soon as Monsignor could attend again, he perceived that there was sliding at a footpace past their starboard side the edge of the huge platform that he had seen just now half a mile away. For a moment or two it swayed up and down; there was a slight vibration; and then he heard voices and the tramping of footsteps.

"The bridges are fixed," remarked the priest.

"They're on the lower deck, of course. Prompt, aren't they?"

The prelate stood, staring with all his eyes; now at the motionless platform that hung alongside, now at the gulf below with the fairy lights strewed like stars and *nebulae* at its bottom. It seemed impossible to realize that this station in the air was not the normal level, and the earth not a strange foreign body that attended on it. There came up on deck presently a dozen figures or so, carrying wraps, and talking. It was amazing to him that they could behave with such composure. Two were even quarreling in subdued voices.

It was hardly five minutes before the three bells rang again; and before the fourth sounded, suddenly he saw drop beneath, like a stone into a pit, the huge immovable platform that just now he had conceived of as solid as the earth from which it had risen. Down and down it went, swaying ever so slightly from side to side, diminishing as it went; but before the motion had ceased the fourth bell rang, and he clutched the rail to steady himself as the ship he was on soared again with a strange intoxicating motion. The next instant, as he glanced over the edge, he saw that they were far out over the blackness of the sea.

"I think we might go below for a bit," said the priest in his ear.

There was no kind of difficulty in descending the stairs; there was practically no oscillation of any kind in this still and windless summer night, and the two came down easily and looked around the lower deck. This was far more crowded with figures: there were padded seats fully occupied running around all the sides, beneath the enormous continuous windows. In the center, sternwards, ran a narrow refreshment bar, where a score of men were standing to refresh themselves. Forward of the farther stairs (down the well of which they had seen the engineer's head), by which they were standing, the deck was closed in, as with cabins.

"Like to see the shrine?" asked Father Jervis.

"The what?"

"Shrine. The long-journey boats, that have chaplains, carry the Blessed Sacrament, of course; but there is only a little oratory on these continental lines."

Monsignor followed him, unable to speak, up the central passage running forwards; through a pair of heavy curtains; and there, to his amazed eyes, appeared a small altar, a hanging lamp, and an image of St. Michael.

"But it's astounding!" whispered the prelate, watching a man and a woman at their prayers.

"It's common sense, isn't it?" smiled the priest. "Why, the custom began a hundred years ago."

"No!"

"Indeed it did! I learnt it from one of the little guide-books they give one on these boats. A company called the Great Western had mosaic pictures of the patron saint of each boat in the saloon. And their locomotives, too, were called after saints' names. It's only plain common sense, if you come to think of it."

"Are lines like this—and railways, and so on—owned by the State now? I suppose so."

The other shook his head. "That was tried under Socialism," he said. "It was one of their smaller failures. You see, when competition ceases, effort ceases. Human nature is human nature, after all. The Socialists forgot that. No; we encourage private enterprise as much as possible, under State restrictions."

They paused as they came out again.

"Care to lie down for a bit? We shan't be in till three. The Cardinal engaged a room for us."

He indicated a small cabin that bore his own name on a card.

Monsignor paused.

"Yes, I will, I think. I've a lot to think about…"

But he could not sleep. The priest promised to awaken him in plenty of time, and he slipped off his buckled shoes and tried to compose his mind. But it was useless. His mind whirled with wonder.

Once he slipped to a sitting position, drew back the little curtain over the porthole, and stared out. There was little to be seen; but by the sight of a lake of soft light that slid past at some incalculable depth a dozen miles away, he perceived that they had left the sea far behind and were spinning over the land of France. He looked out long, revolving thoughts and conjectures, striving to find some glimmer of memory by which he might adjust these new experiences; but there was none. He was like a child, with the brain of a man, plunged into a new mode of existence, where everything seemed reversed, and yet astonishingly obvious; it was the very simplicity that baffled him. The Christian religion was true down (or up) even to the archangels that stand before God and control the powers of the air.

The priesthood was the priesthood; the Blessed Sacrament was the God-Man tabernacling with men. Then where was the cause for amazement that the world recognized these facts and acted upon them; that men should salute the priest of God as His representative and agent on earth; that air-ships (themselves constructed on the model of the sea-gull—hollow feathers and all) should carry the Blessed Sacrament on long journeys, that communicants might not be deprived of their Daily Bread, and even raise altars on board to the honor of those Powers under whose protection they placed themselves. It was curious, too, he reflected, that those who insist most upon the claims of divinity insist also upon the claims of humanity. It seemed suggestive that it was the Catholics who were most aware of the competitive passions of men and reckoned with them, while the Socialists ignored them and failed.

So he sat—this poor man bewildered by simplicity and almost shocked by the obvious—listening with unheeding ears to the steady rush of air past the ship, voices talking naturally and easily, heard through the roof above his head, an occasional footstep, and once or twice a bell as the steersman communicated some message to one of his subordinates. Here he sat—John Masterman, Domestic Prelate to His Holiness Gregory XXII, Secretary to His Eminence Gabriel Cardinal Bellairs, and priest of the Holy Roman Church, trying to assimilate the fact that he was on an air-ship, bound to the court of the Catholic French King, and that practically the whole civilized world believed and acted on the belief that he, as a priest, naturally also had taught and was accustomed to teach.

A tap on his door roused him at last.

"It's time to be moving, Monsignor," said Father Jervis through the half-open door. "We're in communication with St. Germain."

CHAPTER IV

I

"Tell me a little about the costumes," said Monsignor, as the two set out on foot from their lodgings in Versailles after breakfast next morning, to present their letters of introduction. "They seem to me rather fantastic, somehow."

Their lodgings were situated in one of the great palaces on the vast road that runs straight from the gates of the royal palace itself into Paris. They had come straight on by car from St. Germain, had been received with immense respect by the proprietor, who, it appeared, had received very particular instructions from the English Cardinal; and had been conducted straight upstairs to a little suite of rooms, decorated in eighteenth-century fashion, and consisting of a couple of bedrooms for themselves, opening to a central sitting-room and oratory; the two men-servants they had brought with them were lodged immediately across the landing outside.

"Fantastic?" asked Father Jervis, smiling. "Don't you think they're attractive?"

"Oh, yes; but—"

"Remember human nature, Monsignor. After all, it was only intense self-importance that used to make men say that they were independent of exterior beauty. It's far more natural and simple to like beauty. Every child does, after all."

"Yes, yes; I see that, I suppose. But I didn't mean only that. I was on the point of asking you yesterday, again and again, but something marvelous distracted me each time," said the prelate, smiling. "They're extraordinarily picturesque, of course; but I can't help thinking that they must all mean something."

"Of course they do. And I never can imagine how people ever got on without the system. Why, even less than a hundred years ago, I understand that everyone dressed, or tried to dress alike. How in the world could they tell who they were talking to?"

"I…I expect that was deliberate," faltered the other. "You see, I think people used to be ashamed of their trades sometimes, and wanted to be thought gentlemen."

Father Jervis shrugged his shoulders.

"Well, I don't understand it," he said. "If a man was ashamed of his trade, why did he follow it?"

"I've been thinking," said Monsignor animatedly, "that perhaps it's the new teaching on vocation that has made the difference. Once a man understands that his vocation is the most honorable thing he can do, I suppose—There! who's that man," he interrupted suddenly, "in blue with the badge?"

A tremendous figure was crossing the road just in front of them. He wore a short, full blue cloak, with a silver badge on the left breast, a tight-fitting cap of the same color repeating the same badge and, from beneath his cloak in front hung a tunic, with enormous legs in tight blue hose and shoes moving underneath.

"Ah! that's a great man," said the priest. "He's a butcher, of course—"

"A butcher!"

"Yes; that's obvious—it's the blue, for one thing, and the cut, for another. Wait an instant. I shall see his badge directly."

As the great man came past them he saluted deferentially. The priests bowed with equal deference, lifting their hands to their broad-leaved hats.

"Yes: he's very high up," said the priest quietly. "A member of the Council of the National Guild, at least."

"Do you mean that man kills oxen?"

"Not now, of course; he's worked his way up. He probably represents the Guild in the Assembly."

"Do all the trades have guilds, and are they all represented in the Assembly?"

"Why of course! How else could you be certain that the trade was treated fairly? If all the citizens voted as citizens, there's simply no fair representation at all. Look; there's a goldsmith—he has probably been to the King; that's a journeyman with him."

An open car sped past them. Two men were seated in it; both in clothes of some really beautiful metallic color; but the cap of one was plain, while the cap of the other blazed with some device.

"And the women? I can't see any system among them."

"Ah, but there is, though it is harder to detect. They have much more liberty than the men; but, as a rule, each woman has as a predominating color the color of the head of her family, and all, of course, wear badges. There are sumptuary laws, I needn't say."

"I shouldn't have guessed it!"

"Well, not as regards price or material, certainly—only size. There are certain absolute limits on both sides; and fashions have to manage between the two. You see it's the same thing as in trades and professions, as I told you yesterday. We encourage the individual to be as individualistic as possible, and draw the limits very widely, beyond which he mustn't go. *But* those limits are imperative. We try to develop both extremes at once—liberty and law. We had enough of the *via media*—the mediocrity of the average—under Socialism."

"But do you mean to say that people submit to all this?"

"Submit! Why it's perfectly obvious to everyone that it's simply human—besides being very convenient practically. Of course in Germany they still go in for what they call liberty; and the result is simple chaos."

"Do you mean to say there's no envy or jealousy between the trades?"

"Not in the social sense, in the very least, though there's tremendous competition. Why, every one under royalty has to be a member of some trade. Of course only those who practice the trade wear the full costume; but even the dukes have to wear the badges. It's perfectly simple, you know."

"Tell me an English duke who's a butcher."

"Butcher? I can't think of one this minute. Southminster's a baker, though." Monsignor was silent. But it certainly seemed simple. They were passing up now between the sentry-guarded gates of the enormous and exquisite palace of Versailles; and beyond the great expanse of gravel on which they had just set foot rose up the myriad windows, pinnacles, and walls where the Kings of France lived again as they had lived two hundred years before. Far up against the tender summer sky flapped the Royal Standard; and the lilies of France, once more on their blue ground, indicated that the King was in residence. Even as they looked, however, the banner seemed to waver a little; and simultaneously a sudden ringing sound from a shadowed portico a couple of hundred yards away brought Father Jervis to a sudden stop.

"We'd better step aside," he said. "We're right in the way."

"What's the matter?"

"Someone's coming out. Look."

From out of the shadow into the full sunlight with a flash of silver lightning whirled a body of cuirassiers, wheeled into line, and came on, re-forming as they came, at a canter.

A couple of heralds rode in front; and a long trumpet-cry pealed out, was caught, echoed, and thrown back by the walls of the palace.

Behind, as Father Jervis drew him to one side, Monsignor caught a glimpse of white horses and a gleam of gold. He glanced hastily back at the gates through which they had just come, and, as if sprung out of the ground, there was the crowd standing respectfully on either side of the avenue to see its Sovereign. (It was up this avenue to Paris, Monsignor reflected, that the women had come on their appalling march to the Queen who ruled them then.) As he glanced back again the heralds were upon them, and the thunder of hoofs followed close behind. But beyond the line of galloping guards, in the midst, drawn by white horses, ran the great gilded coach with glass windows, and the crown of France atop.

Two men were seated in the coach, bowing mechanically as they came—one a small, young, vivacious-looking man with a pointed dark beard; the other a heavy, fair-haired, sanguine-featured, clean-shaven man. Both alike were in robes in which red and gold predominated; and both wore broad feathered hats, shaped like a priest's.

Then the coach was gone through the tall gilded gates, and a cloud of dust, beaten up by the galloping hoofs on all sides, hid even the cuirassiers who closed the company.

"The King and the German Emperor," observed Father Jervis, replacing his hat. "Now there's the other side of the picture for you."

"I don't understand."

"Why, we treat our kings like kings," smiled the other. "And, at the same time, we encourage our butchers to be really butchers and to glory in it. Law and liberty, you see. Absolute discipline and the cultivation of individualism. No republican stew-pot, you see, in which everything tastes alike."

II

THEY had to wait a few minutes in an ante-room before presenting their letters, as the official was engaged, and Father Jervis occupied the time in running over again the names and histories of three or four important personages to whom they would probably have to speak. He had given an outline of these at breakfast.

There were three in particular about whom Monsignor must be informed.

First, the King; and Monsignor learned again thoroughly of the sensational reaction which, after the humiliation of France in the war of 1914—the logical result of a conflict between a republicanism worked out to mediocrity and a real and vivid monarchy—had placed this man's father—the undoubted legitimate heir—upon the throne. He had died only two years ago, when the Dauphin, who had ascended the throne, was only eighteen years old. The present King was not yet married, but there were rumors of a love-match with a Spanish princess. He was a boyish king, it seemed, but he played his royal part with intense enjoyment and dignity, and had restored, to the delight of this essentially romantic and imaginative people, most of the glories of the eighteenth-century court, without its scandals. Certainly France was returning to its old chivalry, and thence to its old power.

Next there was the Cardinal Archbishop of Paris, Monsignor Guinet, a very old ecclesiastic, very high in the counsels of the Church, who would almost certainly have been elected Pope at the last vacancy if it had not been for his age. He was an "intellectual," it seemed, and, among other things, was one of the first physicists of Europe. He had been ordained comparatively late in life.

Thirdly there was the Archbishop's secretary—Monsignor Allet—a rising man and an excellent diplomatist.

There were two or three more, but Father Jervis was content with scarcely more than recounting their names. The King's brother, and the heir-presumptive, was something of a recluse and seldom appeared at court. Of the German Emperor, Monsignor had already learned, it seemed, sufficient.

In the middle of these instructions, the door suddenly opened, and an ecclesiastic hurried in with outstretched hands, and apologies in a torrent of Latin.

("Monsignor Allet," whispered Father Jervis, as he appeared.)

Monsignor Masterman stood bewildered. The dilemma had not occurred to him; but Father Jervis, it seemed, was prepared. He said a rapid sentence to the secretary, who turned, bowing, and immediately began in English without the trace of any accent.

"I perfectly understand—perfectly indeed. These doctors rule us with a rod of iron, don't they? It'll be arranged directly. We all talk English here; and I'll say a word to His Eminence. The very same thing happened to himself a year or two back. He was forbidden to talk in French. It is astonishing, is it not? The subtlety of those doctors! And yet how natural. No two languages have the same mental reaction, after all. They're perfectly right."

Monsignor caught a glimmering of what he was at. But he thought he had better be cautious.

"I'm afraid I shall give a lot of trouble," he murmured, looking doubtfully at this sparkling-eyed, blue-chinned young man, who spoke with such rapidity.

"Not in the least, I assure you." He turned to the older priest. "The Cardinal left here only half an hour ago. How unfortunate! He came over to arrange the final details of the disputation. You've heard of that?"

"Not a word."

The young prelate beamed.

"Well, you'll hear the finest wit in France! It's for this afternoon." (His face fell.) "But it's Latin. Perhaps Monsignor might not—"

"Ah! So long as he doesn't talk!" (Father Jervis turned to his friend.) "I was telling Monsignor here that the doctor ordered you to engage in no business that did not interest you; and that Latin was rather a strain to you just now—"

This seemed adroit enough. But Monsignor was determined to miss no new experience.

"It will simply delight me," he said. "And what is the subject?"

"Well," said the Frenchman, "it's for the benefit of the Emperor. Two of the Parisian theologians are disputing *De Ecclesia*. The thesis of the adversary, who opens, is that the Church is merely the representative of God on earth—a society that must, of course, be obeyed; but that infallibility is not necessary to her efficiency."

Father Jervis' eyes twinkled.

"Isn't that a little too pointed? Why, that's the Emperor's one difficulty! I understand that he allows, politically speaking, the need for the Church, but denies her divinity."

"I assure you," said the French priest solemnly, "that the thesis is his own selection. You see, he's sick of these Socialists. He understands perfectly that the one sanction of human authority must come from God, or from the people; and he's entirely on God's side! But he cannot see the infallibility, and therefore, as he's a sincere man—!" He ended with an eloquent shrug.

"Well," said Father Jervis, "if the Cardinal's not here—"

"Alas! He is back in Paris by now. But give me your letters! I'll see that they are presented properly; and you shall receive a royal command for the disputation in plenty of time."

They handed over their letters; they exchanged compliments once more; they were escorted as far as the door of the room by the prelate, across the next ante-chamber by an imposing man in black velvet with a chain, across the third by a cuirassier, and across the hall to the bottom of the steps by two tremendous footmen in the ancient royal livery.

Monsignor was silent for a few yards.

"Aren't you afraid of an anti-clerical reaction?" he asked suddenly.

"How do you mean? I don't understand."

Then Monsignor launched out. He had accepted by now the theory that he had had a lapse of memory, and that so far as his intellect was concerned, he was practically a man of a century ago, owing to the history he had happened to be reading shortly before his collapse; and he talked therefore from that standpoint.

He produced, that is to say, with astonishing fluency all those arguments that were common in the mouths of the more serious anti-clericals of the beginning of the century—the increase of Religious Orders, the domineering tendency of all ecclesiastics in the enjoyment of temporal power, the impossibility of combating supernatural arguments, the hostility of the Church to education—down even to the celibacy of the clergy. He paused for breath as they turned out of the great gateway.

Father Jervis laughed aloud and patted him on the arm.

"My dear Monsignor, I can't compete with you. You're too eloquent. Of course, I remember from reading history that those things used to be said, and I suppose Socialists say them now. But, you know, no educated man ever dreams of such arguments; nor indeed do the uneducated! It's the half-educated, as usual, who's the enemy. He always is. The Wise Men and the shepherds both knelt in Bethlehem. It was the bourgeois who stood apart."

"That's no answer," persisted the other.

"Well, let's see," said the priest good-humoredly. "We'll begin with celibacy. Now it's perfectly true that it's thought almost a disgrace for a man not to have a large family. The average is certainly not

less than ten in civilized nations. But for all that a priest is looked
upon without any contempt at all. Why? Because he's a spiritual
father; because he begets spiritual children to God, and feeds and
nourishes them. Of course to an atheist this is nonsense; and even to
an agnostic it's a very doubtful benefit. But, my dear Monsignor, you
must remember that these hardly exist amongst us. The entire civilized world of today is as absolutely convinced of Heaven and grace
and the Church, and the havoc that sin makes not only as regards
the next world but in this—so absolutely convinced that he understands perfectly that a priest is far more productive of general good
than a physical father possibly can be. It's the priest who keeps the
whole thing going. Don't you see? And then, in a Catholic world, the
instinct that the man who serves the altar should be without physical
ties—Well, that's simply natural."

"Go on. What about education?"

"My dear friend," said Father Jervis. "The Church controls the
whole of education, as she did, in fact, up to the very time when the
State first took it away from her and then abused her for neglecting
it. Practically all the scientists; all the specialists in medicine, chem-
istry, and mental health; nine-tenths of the musicians; three-quarters
of the artists—practically all those are religious. It's only the active
trades, which are incompatible with religion, that are in the hands of
the laity. It's been found by experience that no really fine work can
be done except by those who are familiar with divine things; because
it's only those who see things all around, who have, that is to say, a
really comprehensive intuition. Take history. Unless you have a really
close grasp of what Providence means—of not only the end, but the
means by which God works; unless you can see right through things
to their intention, how in the world can you interpret the past? Don't
you remember what Manners said about Realism? 'We don't want
misleading photographs of externals any more. We want ideas.' And
how can you correlate ideas, unless you have a real grasp of the central
idea? It's nonsense."

"Go on with the other things."

"There's a lot more about education. There's the graduated education we have now (entirely an ecclesiastical notion, by the way). We don't try to teach everybody everything. *We* teach a certain foundation to everyone—the Catechism, of course, two languages perfectly, the elements of physical science, and a great deal of history. (You can't understand the Catechism without history, and vice versa); but after that we specialize. Well, the world understands now—"

"That's enough, thank you. Go on with the other things."

Father Jervis laughed again.

"We're nearly home. Let's turn in here, and get into the gardens for a bit. Well, I think you'll find that the root of all your difficulties is that you seem not to be able to get into your head that the world is really and intelligently Christian. There are the Religious Orders you spoke of. Well, aren't the active Religious Orders the very finest form of association ever invented? Aren't they exactly what Socialists have always been crying for, with the blunders left out and the gaps filled up? As soon as the world understood finally that the active Religious Orders could beat all other forms of association at their own game—that they could teach and work more cheaply and effectively, and so on—well, the most foolish political economist had to confess that the Religious Orders made for the country's welfare. And as for the Contemplative Orders—"

Father Jervis' face grew grave and tender.

"Yes?"

"Why, they're the princes of the world! They are models of the Crucified. So long as there is sin in the world, so long must there be penance. The instant Christianity was accepted, the Cross stood up dominant once more. And then…then people understood. Why, they're the Holy Ones of the universe—higher than angels; for they suffer."

There was a moment's silence. "Yes," said Monsignor softly.

"My dear Monsignor, just force upon your mind the fact that the world is really and intelligently Christian. I think it'll all be plain then. You seem to me, if I may say so, to be falling into the old-fashioned way of looking at 'Clericalism,' as it used to be called, as a kind of department of life, like art or law. No wonder men resented its intrusion when they conceived of it like that. Well, there is no 'Clericalism' now, and therefore there is no anti-Clericalism. There's just religion— as a fact. Do you see? Shall we sit down for a few minutes? Aren't the gardens exquisite?"

III

Monsignor Masterman sat that night at his window, looking out at the stars and the night and the blotted glimmering gardens beneath; and it seemed to him as if the dream deepened every day. Things grew more, not less marvelous, with his appreciation of the simplicity of it all.

From three to seven he had sat in one of the seats on the right of the royal dais, reserved for prelates, almost immediately opposite the double-pulpited platform, itself set in the midst of the long outer side of the great gallery of Versailles, through which access was to be had to the little old private rooms of Marie Antoinette, and had listened spellbound to two of the greatest wits of France, respectively attacking and defending, with extraordinary subtlety and fire, the claim of the Church to infallibility. The disputation had been conducted on scholastic lines, all verbal etiquette being carefully observed; again and again he had heard, first on one side a string of arguments adduced against the doctrine; then on the other a torrent of answers, with the old half-remembered words "Distinguo," "Nego," "Concedo"; and the reasoning on both sides had appeared to him astonishingly brilliant. And all this before two sovereigns—the one keen, vivacious, and appreciative; the other heavy, patient, considerate—two sovereigns, treated, as the elaborate etiquette of the whole affair showed plainly enough, as kings indeed—men who stood for authority, and the grades and the differentiation of functions, as emphatically as the old democratic hand-shaking statesmen, dressed like their own servants, stood for the other complementary principle of the equality of men. For alongside of all this tremendous pomp there was a very practical recognition of the "People"; since the whole disputation was conducted in the presence of a crowd drawn, it seemed, from almost every class, who pressed behind the barriers, murmured, laughed gleefully, and now and again broke out into low thunders of applause, as the Catholic champion drove logic home, or turned aside the infidel shaft.

The very thesis amazed the man, for the absolute necessity of an authoritative supernatural Church, with supernatural sanctions, seemed assumed as an axiom of thought, not merely by these Catholics, but by the entire world, Christian and un-Christian alike. More than once the phrase "It is conceded by all men" flashed out, and passed unrebuked, in support of this claim. The only point of dispute between reasoning beings seemed to be not as to whether or not the Church must be treated practically as infallible, but whether dogmatically and actually she were so.

As he sat here now at his window, Father Jervis' words began to come back with new force. Was it indeed true that the only reason why he found these things strange was that he could not yet quite bring home to his imagination the fact that the world now was convincedly Christian as a whole? It began to appear so.

For somewhere in the back of his mind (why he knew not) there lurked a sort of only half-perceived assumption that the Catholic religion was but one aspect of truth—one point of view from which, with sufficient though not absolute truth, facts could be discerned. He could not understand this; yet there it was. And he understood, at any rate intellectually, that if he could once realize that the dogmas of the Church were the dogmas of the universe, and not only that, but that the world convincedly realized it too, why then the fact that the civilization of today was actually molded upon it would no longer bewilder him.

IV

It was on the following morning that he spoke with the King.

The two priests had said Mass in their oratory, and an hour later were walking in the park beneath the palace windows.

It was one more of that string of golden days, of which they had already enjoyed so many, and the splendor of that amazing landscape was complete.

They had passed below the enclosure known as the "King's Garden," and were going in the direction of the Trianon, which Monsignor had expressed a desire to see, and had just emerged into the immense central avenue which runs straight from the palace to the lake. Above them rose the forest trees, enormous now, yet tamed by Lenotre's marvelous art, resembling a regiment of giants perfectly drilled; the grass was like carpets on all sides; the sky blazed like a blue jewel overhead; the noise of singing birds and falling water was in the air. But above all there towered on their right, beyond the almost endless terraces, the splendid palace of the kings of France, royal at last once more. And there, as symbol of the restoration, there hung around the flagstaff as he had seen it yesterday the blue folds and the lilies of the monarchy.

It was no good trying to frame words as to what he felt. He had said all he could, and it was useless. Father Jervis seemed unable to understand the fierce enthusiasm of a man who now experienced all this, as it appeared, for the first time. He walked silently, exulting.

There seemed not many people abroad this morning. The two had presented an order, obtained through Monsignor Allet, at the gates below the Orange Gardens, and had learned from the sentry that until the afternoon this part of the park was closed to the public. Here and there, however, in the distance a single figure made its appearance, walking in the shade or hurrying on some errand.

The priests had just come out from the line of trees and had set foot in the avenue itself, when, twenty yards farther up, from the entrance to some other path parallel to their own, a group came out, and an instant later they heard themselves hailed and saw Monsignor Allet himself, in all his purple, hurrying towards them.

"You are the very men," he cried, again stretching out his hands in a welcoming French gesture. "His Majesty was speaking of you not five minutes ago. He is here, in the garden. Shall I present you now?"

Father Jervis glanced at his friend. "His Majesty is very kind—" he began.

"Not a word more! If you will follow me and wait an instant at the entrance, I will speak with His Majesty and bring you in."

"I have not my ferraiuolo—" began Monsignor.

"The King will excuse travelers," smiled the Frenchman.

The entrance to the King's Garden on this side passed beneath an arch of yew, and there the two waited.

Somewhere beyond the green walls they could hear talking, and now and again a burst of laughter. Then the talking ceased, and they heard a single voice.

"In what language—" began Monsignor Masterman nervously.

"Oh! English, no doubt. You can't talk French?"

Monsignor shook his head.

"Not a hundred words," he said.

Again came the quick footstep, and the French priest appeared, still gay, but with a certain solemnity. "Come this way, gentlemen," he said. "The King will see you." (He glanced at the prelate.) "You won't forget to kneel, Monsignor."

To the English prelate the scene that he saw, on emerging at last into the open space in the middle, protected by the ancient yews— even though he should have been prepared for it by all that he had already seen—simply once more dazed and stupefied him.

The center of the space was occupied by a around pond, perhaps thirty yards across, of absolutely still water, and in this mirror, shaded by the masses of foliage overhead, was reflected a picture that might have been taken straight from some painting two hundred years old. For, on the semicircle of marble seats that stood beyond the water, sat a company of figures dressed once more in all the bravery of real color and splendor, as from days when men were not ashamed to use publicly and commonly these glittering gifts of God.

Monsignor hardly noticed the rest (there were perhaps twelve or fifteen all told, with half a dozen women amongst them); he looked only, as he came around the pond, at the central figure that advanced to meet him. Twice he had seen him yesterday—yet those occasions had been public. But to see the King now, at ease amongst his friends, yet still royally dressed in his brilliant blue suit and feathered hat, with his tall cane—to see the whole company, gay and brilliant, talking and laughing, taking their pleasure in the air before breakfast—the thing somehow brought home to him the reality of what appeared to him as a change, more than had all the pomps and glories of the day before. Splendor seemed no longer ceremonial, but natural.

Monsignor Allet was explaining something in rapid French in the King's ear, and as the two came up, the face that listened smiled suddenly with intelligence.

"I give you welcome," he said in excellent English.

"Come, gentlemen" (he turned to the others, who had risen to their feet as he rose), "we must be getting homewards. Monsignor!" (And he beckoned to the two English priests to walk with him.)

That walk seemed like a dream.

They went leisurely upwards towards the palace, through yew alley after yew alley, French chattering sounding behind them as they went; and the King, still in fluent English, though with an accent that increased as he talked, questioned them courteously as to England, spoke of the disputation of yesterday, discussed frankly enough the situation in Germany, and listened with attention to the remarks of Father Jervis; for Monsignor Masterman was discreetly silent for the most part.

It was not until the great doors of the palace flew open at last, and the rows of liveried men showed within, that the King dismissed them. He turned on the steps and gave them his hand to kiss. Then he raised them from their knees with a courteous gesture.

"And you go to Rome, you say?"

"Almost immediately, sire. We shall be there for Sts. Peter and Paul."

"Present my homage at the feet of the Holy Father," smiled the King. "You are fortunate indeed. I have not seen His Holiness for three months. Good day, gentlemen."

The two passed again in silence down the terraces on their way to the Trianon.

"It is amazing," burst out Monsignor suddenly. "And the people. What of them? Is there no resentment?"

"Why should there be?" asked the other.

"But they are excluded from the palace and the park. It was not so a hundred years ago."

"Do you think they are any the less happy?" asked Father Jervis. "My dear Monsignor, surely you know human nature better than that! They have lost the vulgarity of Versailles, and they have regained its royalty. Don't you see that?"

"Well!" Monsignor paused. "It's simply medievalism back again, it seems to me."

"Exactly!" said the other. "You have hit it at last. It is medievalism—that is to say, human nature with faith and reverence, and without cant."

He paused again, and his eyes twinkled.

"You know honors and privileges are worth nothing if everyone has them. If we all wore crowns, the kings would go bareheaded."

CHAPTER V

I

HE awoke suddenly, at some movement, and for an instant did not remember where he was.

For nearly a week they had stayed on at Versailles; and each day that had passed had done its share in making this fairyland seem more like a reality. But that strange subconscious self of his, for which even now there seemed no accounting, was still obstinate; it still assured him that the world ought not to be like this, that religion ought not to be so concrete and effective—that he would awake soon and find himself in some desolate state of affairs where faith, hemmed in by enemies, still fought for very life against irresistible odds. It was at night and at morning that the mood came on him most forcibly; when instinct, free from facts, and ranging clear of the will's dominion, asserted itself most strongly, and as he awoke this night it was on him again.

He looked around the dark little room with bewildered eyes; then he fumbled with a button, and all was flooded with light.

He was lying in a little spring-bed, set within two padded sides, like a berth in a steamship. And beside him was the closed bureau which he perceived to be washing arrangements in disguise; overhead protruded a broad shelf; on the wall, above a little couch, hung silk curtains over a window—as they swayed slightly with some movement he caught sight of glass beyond. On the door, at the foot of his bed, hung his cassock, and the purple cincture that lay across it recalled him to at least a part of the facts. The cabin was upholstered and painted in clean white, and an electric globe emerged from the ceiling.

He was next conscious of cold, and instinctively leaned forward
to draw the quilt farther over his knees. Then, with a flash, he remembered, and, in spite of the cold, was out of bed in a moment, kneeling
on the couch and peering out through the curtains.

At first he could see nothing at all. There was but an unfathom-
able gulf beyond the glass. He stood up on the couch, and drawing
the curtains behind his head to shut out the light, he once more stared
out. Then he began to see.

Immediately opposite him glimmered a huge white outline—in
the incalculable night it might be a hundred yards or a mile away. It
was of irregular outline, for the star-strewn sky showed in patches and
rifts above it. And this white mass curved away beneath, under the
ship in which he traveled, till it met, at a point which he could but just
discern, a blackness that rose to meet it.

Then, as his eyes grew accustomed to the dark, he began to see
that the huge whiteness was flitting past, steadily and leisurely, from
right to left; that it was streaked with shadows or clefts; and that
following it, as in a sliding procession, came another, like it yet (it
seemed) more distant.

All this time, too, the silence was profound. There was but a soft
humming note somewhere in the air, and the faintest sense of vibration in the metal-work on which his hands were pressed. Once too
he heard a footstep pass softly and rhythmically overhead, as if some
watcher moved up and down the length of the upper deck.

The man dropped the curtains and sat back on his heels, trying
to force into his imagination the facts that he now perceived and
remembered.

They had left St. Germain last night, after dining at Versailles.
They were now crossing the Alps. They would be in Rome for Mass
and breakfast.

They were traversing at this moment, no doubt, only a thousand
feet high, one of those passes up which (he thought he remembered
from history) the old railway-trains had been accustomed to climb,
yard by yard and spiral by spiral, a hundred years before.

In a minute or two he leaned forward and stared again, once more closing the curtains behind his head.

The sky seemed a little brighter, he thought, than when he had looked just now. Perhaps the moon was rising somewhere. And certainly the sky was more in evidence. Far away to the left behind, passing even as he looked, moved those gigantic horns of white, as if the ship stood still and the earth turned beneath; and below now, sloping to the right, lay long lines of darkness, jutting here and there with a sudden crag against the blaze of stars. It was marvelous, he thought, how still all lay; there was a steady hiss, now heard for the first time, as the air tore past the glassy sides of the bird-shaped ship, as high as the cry of a bat.

He shifted on his knees a little, and staring forwards, saw far ahead and at what seemed an incalculable distance something that baffled him entirely, for it changed its aspect every instant that he watched.

At first it was no more than a patch of luminosity; and he thought it to be, perhaps, a lighted town. But the character of it was changed as he formulated his thought, and three brilliant spots like blue stars broke out on a sudden, and these three stars shifted their positions. He kept his eyes on these, marveling; and, with something very like fear, saw that they were approaching upwards and onwards with the swiftness of thought.

Up and on they came. He shrank back a little, instinctively; and then, as he leaned forward once more, determined to understand, shrank back with a sharp in-drawing of breath, as there whirled past, it appeared only a few yards away, a flare of brilliant blue lines, in the midst of which passed a phantom-like body in a mist, and accompanied by a musical sound (it seemed) of extraordinary charity and beauty, that rose from a deep organ-note to the shrill of a flute, and down again into a bass and a silence.

He smiled to himself as he climbed back into bed a minute or two later, when he had reconstructed the phenomena and interpreted them. It was but another volor, bound northwards, and it had probably passed at least half a mile away.

Well, he must sleep again if he could. They would be in Rome by morning.

They had delayed their departure from Versailles to the last possible moment, since France was, after all, under the circumstances, one of the best places in the world for Monsignor to pick up again the threads of life. For one thing, it was near to England—English was spoken there amongst the educated almost as frequently as French; yet it was not England, and Monsignor's plight would not cause him any great inconvenience. Further, France was at present the theater of the world's interest, since the Emperor was there, and on the Emperor's future depended largely the destinies of Europe: his conversion, it was thought, might be the final death-blow to Socialism in his dominions.

Monsignor had employed his time well. Not only had he learned accurately the general state of the world, but morning by morning he had familiarized himself with his own work, and felt, by now, very nearly competent to finish his lessons in England. Cardinal Bellairs communicated with him almost every day, and professed himself delighted with the progress made. Finally he had talked Latin continually with Father Jervis in preparation for Rome, and would have passed muster, at least, in general conversation.

The two motored into the city from the volor-station outside, and everywhere as they went through the streets and crossed the Tiber on their way to the Leonine City, where they were to lodge, were evidences of the feast.

For the whole route from Vatican to Lateran, which they crossed more than once, was one continual triumphal way. Masts had been erected, swathed in the Papal colors and crowned with garlands; barriers ran from mast to mast, behind which already the crowds were beginning to gather, though it was hardly past six o'clock in the morning; and from every window hung carpets, banners, and tapestries. The motor was stopped at least half a dozen times; but the prelate's insignia passed them through quickly; and it was just half-past six as they drew up before an old palace situated on the right in the road leading from the Tiber to the Vatican, and scarcely a quarter of a mile away from St. Peter's.

Monsignor glanced up at the arms above the doorway and smiled.

"I did not know you were bringing me here," he said.

"You know it?"

"Why, it's the old place where the kings of England lodged, isn't it?" Father Jervis smiled.

"Your memory's improving," he said.

Then a magnificent servant came out, bowed profoundly, and opened the door of the car.

"By the way," said Father Jervis as they went in, "I'd better go and inquire the details at the Vatican. You might give me your card. I'll go at once, and then come back and join you at breakfast."

It was a pleasant little suite of rooms, not unlike in arrangements to those of Versailles. The windows looked out on the central court, where a fountain played, and the rooms themselves were furnished in the usual Roman fashion—painted ceilings, stone floors, and a few damask hangings.

Monsignor turned to the servant who was superintending the two Englishmen they had brought.

"I've not been in Rome for some time," he said in Latin. "Tell me what this house is now?"

"Monsignor, it is the English palace. Monsignor is in the apartment of His Eminence Cardinal Bellairs."

"The King himself stays here?"

"It is His Majesty's palace," said the man. "The Prince George arrived two days ago. His Highness is in the apartment below."

Monsignor smiled. He understood now Father Jervis' evasion as to where they were to stay in Rome. Plainly it was determined that he should have a front seat at all ceremonies.

Ten minutes later, as he came out of his bedroom, Father Jervis himself came in.

"You have your choice, Monsignor," he said. "As a Domestic Prelate you have the right to walk in the procession (here is the permit), or as occupying rooms here we can, if you prefer, see the procession from the front windows."

"Tell me what the program is."

"At nine the procession leaves St. Peter's to go to the Lateran—at least they call it nine. There the Holy Father sings Mass, as bishop in his own cathedral. On the return of the procession, I suppose about midday, the Holy Father visits the tomb of St. Peter. Then this afternoon he is present at Vespers in St. Peter's; and afterwards gives the blessing *Urbi et Orbi* from the window as usual."

"What would you advise?"

"Well, I should advise your remaining here till midday. There's no use in overdoing it. We can see everything admirably. Then we can go into St. Peter's for the visit to the tomb, and come back here to dejeuner. After that we can arrange about the rest of the day."

"Very good. Then let us have something to eat at once."

"Who's Prince George of England?" demanded Monsignor presently as they sat over coffee.

Father Jervis laughed.

"You've found that out, have you? Yes, he's here, of course. Well, he's the second son; he's only a boy. He's over here to represent the King. Every sovereign sends a prince of the blood-royal for today. Even the German Emperor."

"Do you mean from Europe?"

"I mean from the whole world. You see the East is scarcely three days away by the fast volors; so even the Chinese—"

"Do you mean that China and Japan send representatives?"

"Certainly. Japan is Christian of course, anyhow; and China has at least one or two Christian princes of the blood."

"By the way, what about Russia?"

"Well, what about it?"

"Is it Catholic?"

"My dear Monsignor, it's been Catholic for thirty years."

"Oh, dear me! You must lend me some more histories. What made it Catholic?"

"Common sense, I suppose. How they could have stood out for so long is the only thing that puzzles me."

"But the Petrine claims—"

"Why, the Petrine claims were the very point. Facts were too strong. If you look back over history you can't help seeing that the only Christian body that was ever able to resist Erastianism on the one side and endless division on the other has been the Church built on Peter. They began to see it nearly a hundred years ago in Russia and Greece. Then the Emperor of Russia was secretly reconciled in 1930; and ten or twelve years later his people followed him."

"Then there's no more dispute? What about the *Filioque* clause?"

"Why, when Peter is accepted, the rest follows."

"Then you may say that the entire civilized world is represented in Rome today?"

"Certainly. You'll see the princes in the procession."

II

AN hour later they took their places at the central window of the long sala on the third floor, looking out immediately upon the narrow street, which, opposite, fell back into a tiny square, and further up to the right, upon the enormous piazza of St. Peter's and the basilica itself behind.

It was a real Roman day—not yet at its full heat, but intensely clear and bright; and Monsignor congratulated himself on having elected to remain as a spectator. The return journey from the Lateran about noon would be something of an ordeal.

The street and the piazza presented an astonishingly brilliant appearance. Beneath, the roadway was now one sheet of greenery— box, myrtle, and bay. The houses opposite, as well as within the little square, of which every window was packed with heads, were almost completely hidden under the tapestries, the carpets, the banners. Behind the barriers on either side of the garlanded masts was one mass of heads resembling a cobbled pavement. So much for sight. For sound, the air was filled with one steady low roar of voices; for down to where the street opened far away to the left into the space above the river, the same vista presented itself. The Campagna since twenty-four hours before had been emptying every living inhabitant into Rome; and there was not a town in Italy, and scarcely in Europe, whence special volors and trains had not carried the fervent to the Feast of the Apostles in Holy Rome. And, for scent, the air was sweet and fragrant with the aromatic herbs of the roadway, already bruised a little by the feet of the galloping horses of those that went up and down to guard the route or to carry messages.

It was a little hard to make out the arrangements of the vast circular piazza in front of St. Peter's. The front of the basilica was hung, in usual Roman fashion, with gigantic garlands and red cloth; and the carpet of greenery lined with troops ran straight up the center of the space, rippled over the steps, and ceased only beneath the towering portico of the church. But on either side of this, with spaces between, stood enormous groups of men and horses, marshaled, no doubt, in order to take their places at the proper moment in the procession.

At the right, immovable and tremendous, rose up the great palace of the Vatican itself, unadorned except where a glint of some color showed itself at the Bronze Doors; and above all, like a benediction in stone, against the vivid blue of the sky, hung the dome of the basilica.

Monsignor Masterman made a long, keen survey of all this. Then he leaned back and sighed.

"What was the first year that the Pope came out of the Vatican like this?"

"The year after the conquest of United Italy. It was Austria that—"

"I know all that. And you mean he never came out so long as the old state of affairs continued?"

"How could he? Don't you see that the one thing, humanly speaking, absolutely necessary for the world to have confidence in the Church, was that the Pope should be really supra-national? Of course for many years he had to be an Italian—that's obvious, since he was at the mercy of Italy, and the Romans would never have stood a foreigner; and that made it all the more essential that he should be cut clean off, in everything else, from Italian sympathies. He had to be two things simultaneously, so to speak—emphatically an Italian for the sake of Italy and indeed his own existence in Rome; and emphatically not an Italian for the sake of the rest of Christendom. And can you suggest any other way of accomplishing this paradox? I can't."

Monsignor sighed again and began to meditate.

For somewhere at the back of his mind there ran an undercurrent of thought, or as of someone talking, to the effect that the Pope's old method of remaining as a prisoner in the Vatican was a foolish and unhumble pose. (He supposed he must have read it all somewhere in history.) Surely even Catholics used to talk like that! They used to say how much more spiritual and Christian it would have been, had the Vicar of Christ acquiesced and been content to live as a simple Italian subject, neither claiming nor desiring a position such as Peter had never enjoyed. Why all this fuss, it used to be asked, about a temporal power on behalf of a "Kingdom that was not of this world"? Yet, somehow, now as he looked back on it all, with his friend's comment in his mind, he began to see, not how clever or diplomatic had been the old attitude, but how absolutely and obviously essential. It was possible indeed for Peter to be a subject of Nero in things pertaining to Caesar; but how could that be possible to Peter's successor when the Kingdom of Christ which he ruled on earth had become a supra-national society to which the nations of the earth looked for guidance?

The phrase he had just heard ran in his mind. "An Italian for the sake of Italy and his own existence in Rome. Not an Italian for the sake of the rest of Christendom."

It seemed simple, somehow, just like that.

He was roused by a touch on his knee, and simultaneously was aware of a new sound from the piazza.

"Look," said the old priest sharply. "They're beginning to move."

III

A curious seething movement had broken out in the piazza, resembling the stir of a troubled anthill, on either side of the broad green

way down which the Pope would come; and already into the head of
the street up which the priests looked figures were emerging. Simultaneously a crash of brazen music had filled the air. A movement of
attention, exactly like the lift of a swell along the foot of a cliff, passed
down the crowded street to the left and lost itself around the corner
towards S. Angelo.

Then they began to come, swinging over from the piazza to street
as if from a pool into a narrow channel. Troops came first—company
after company—each with a band leading. First the Austrian guard in
white and gold on white chargers—passing from the flash and dazzle
their uniforms threw back in the sunlight into the glow of the shadowed street. And then, by the time that the Austrians were passing
below the window, came troop after troop down from the piazza in all
the uniforms of the civilized world.

At first Father Jervis murmured a name or two; he even laid his
hand upon his friend's arm as the Life-guards of England came dash-
ing by with their imperturbable faces above their silver splendor; but
presently the amazing spectacle forming in the piazza, and, above all,
on the steps of St. Peter's, silenced them both. Monsignor Masterman
gave scarcely a glance even to the monstrous figures of the Chinese
imperial guard who went by presently in black armor and vizarded
helmets, like old Oriental gods. For in the piazza itself the procession
of princes was forming; and the steps of the basilica already began to
burn with purple and scarlet where the Cardinals and the Papal Court
were making ready for the coming of the Lord of them all.

And then, at last, he came.

Monsignor Masterman had begun to stare, almost with unintelligent eyes, at the thronged street beneath, watching the great carriages
come past, each surmounted by a crown with its proper supporters,
each surrounded by a small guard drawn from the troops that had rid-
den by just now. He identified a few here and there; and his heart gave
a strange leap as the Imperial Crown of England came in sight, held
up by the Lion and the Unicorn, and beneath it, within the gilded
couch, the face of a boy capped and robed in scarlet. And then he

looked up again, startled by a silence broken only by the footsteps of the horses and the wheels over the matted roadway, and the murmur of talking.

The piazza was now one sea of white and purple, with emblems, gold and silver and jeweled, shining here and there; the green strip was gone; for the Papal procession was begun; and then, on the instant, as he looked, there was a new group standing beneath the giant columns of the portico, and the cry of the silver trumpets told to the thousands that waited that the Vicar of Christ had come out into this city that was again the City of God.

Very slowly he came down the steps, a tiny white and gemmed figure, yet perfectly visible on the high throne on which he was borne, his hand swaying as he came, and the huge fans moving behind him like protecting deities. Down and down he came, while the trumpets cried, and the waves of color followed him, and then vanished for a time among the crowd beneath, as he reached the level ground.

Monsignor Masterman leaned back and closed his eyes.

He was disturbed by another touch on his arm; and, opening them, perceived that his friend was attracting his attention almost mechanically, and without looking at him.

"Look," murmured Father Jervis—"it's the white jennet."

Beneath, the street was now as wholly ecclesiastical as it had been military just before, except that the Papal zouaves marched in single file on either side of the procession. But within there was just one packed army, going eight abreast, of seminarians and clerics. These were just passing as the priest looked again, and close on their heels came the Count and the Cardinals; the latter an indescribable glory of scarlet, riding four abreast in broad hats and ample cloaks. But he gave scarcely more than a glance at these; for, full in sight for at least half a minute, advancing straight towards him down the weary roaring street, moved a canopy held by figures he could not clearly make out, and beneath it, detached and perfectly visible, on a white horse, a white figure, its shoulders just draped in scarlet and its head shadowed by a great scarlet hat, came slowly towards him.

IV

AND so the day went by like a dream; and the man who still seemed to himself as one risen from the dead into a new and wholly bewildering world, watched and gathered impressions and assimilated them. Once or twice during the day he found himself at meals with Father Jervis; he asked questions now and then and scarcely heard the answers; he talked with ecclesiastics a little who came and went; but, for the most part almost unknown to himself, he worked interiorly, busy as a bee, building up, not so much facts as realizations, into the new and strange world-edifice that was gradually forming about him. He was present at the visit of the Pope to the tomb of the Apostle, and watched from a tribune, even then so concentrated on observation that he was hardly conscious of connected thought, as the vast doors rolled back and a vision as of such a celestial troop as was dreamed of by the old Italian painters came up out of the vivid sunlight into the cool darkness of the basilica, as the roofs gave back the roaring of the fervent thousands and the clear cry of the silver trumpets; watched as the army of ecclesiastics deployed this way and that, and the Father of Princes and Kings came on between his royal children to the gates of the confession ringed by the golden lamps, and went down to kneel by the body of the first Fisherman-King.

And again at Vespers, from the same tribune, he heard the peal of the new great organs in the dome, and the psalm-melodies rocking from side to side between the massed choirs; he glanced now and again at the royal tribune opposite, where, each beneath a canopy, the rulers of the earth sat together to do honor to the Lord and His Anointed. And, above all, he watched, still with that steady set face that made Father Jervis look at him once or twice, the central figure of all, now on his throne, with his assistants beside him, now passing up to the altar to incense it, and finally passing out again on the *sedia gestatoria* to the palace where at last he ruled indeed.

Last of all, as the sun began to sink behind the monstrous dome, and Rome stood out like an Oriental city of dreams, and the purple lights came out on the low-lying hills, and the illuminations glowed

from every window, and blazed beneath the feet and around the heads
of the gigantic apostolic figures gathered around their Lord—there,
watching again from his window, he saw, in a sudden hush over the
heads of the countless crowds, the tiny white figure standing above
the tapestries, with the Papal triple cross glinting beside him like a
thread, and heard the thin voice, gnat-like and clear, declared the
"help of the Lord who," as the thunder of the square answered him,
"hath made heaven and earth," and then invoke upon the city and the
world, before the tremendous *Amen,* the blessing of God Almighty,
Father, Son, and Holy Spirit.

CHAPTER VI

I

It was a few minutes after they had finished their almost silent meal that evening, that Monsignor suddenly leaned forward from his chair in the great cool loggia and passed his hands over his eyes like a sleepy man. From the streets outside still came the murmur of innumerable footsteps and voices and snatches of music.

"Tired?" asked the other gently. (He had not spoken for some minutes, and remembering the long silence, had wondered if, after all, it had been wise to bring a man with such an experience behind him to such a rush and excitement as that through which they had passed today.)

Monsignor said nothing for an instant. He looked around the room, opened and closed his lips, and then, leaning back again, suddenly smiled. Then he took up the pipe he had laid aside just now and blew through it.

"No," he said. "Exactly the opposite. I feel awake at last."

"Eh?"

"It seems to have got into me at last. All this, all this very odd world. I have begun to see."

"Please explain."

Monsignor began to fill his pipe slowly.

"Well, Versailles, even, didn't quite do it," he said. "It seemed to me a kind of game—certainly a very pleasant one; but—" (He broke off.) "But what we've seen today seems somehow the real thing."

"I don't quite understand."

Well, I can see for myself now that all that you've told me is real—that the world's really Christian, and so on. It was those Chinese guards, I think, which as much as anything—"

"Chinese? I don't remember them."

The prelate smiled again.

"Well, I scarcely noticed them at the time, either. But I've been thinking about them. And then all the rest of it…and the Pope…. By the way, I couldn't make out his face very well. Is that a picture of him?"

He stood up suddenly and stepped across to where the portrait hung. There was nothing very startling about the picture. It showed just a very ordinary face with straight closed lips, of a man seated in an embossed chair, with the familiar white cap, cassock, and embroidered stole with spade-ends. "He looks quite ordinary," mused Monsignor aloud. "It's…it's like the face of a business man."

"Oh, yes, he's ordinary. He's an extremely good man and quite intelligent. He's never had any very great crisis to face, you know. They say he's a good financier. You look disappointed."

"I hadn't expected him to look like that," said the prelate, musing.

"Why not?"

"Well, he seems to have an extraordinary position in the world. I should have expected more of a—"

"More of a great man? Monsignor, don't you think that the average man makes the best ruler?"

"But that's rank Democracy!"

"Not at all. Democracy doesn't give the average man any real power at all. It swamps him among, under his friends—that is to say, it kills his individuality; and his individuality is the one thing he has which is worth anything."

Monsignor sat down again, sighing.

"Well, I think it's got into me at last," he repeated. "I mean, I think I really realize what the world's like now. But I want to see a great deal more, you know."

"What sort of things?"

"Well, I don't quite know. You might call it the waterline between faith and science. I see the faith side. I understand that the life of the world moves on Catholicism now; but I don't quite realize yet how all that joins onto science. In my day—" (He broke off.) "I mean I had a kind of idea that there was a gap between faith and science—if not actual contradictions. How do they join onto one another? What's the average scientific attitude towards religion? Do people on both sides just say that each must pursue its own line, even if they never meet?"

Father Jervis looked puzzled.

"I don't quite understand. There's no conflict between faith and science. A large proportion of the scientists are ecclesiastics."

"But what's the meeting-point? That's what I don't see."

The priest shook his head, smiling.

"I simply don't know what you mean, Monsignor. Give me an example."

"Well…er…what about faith-healing? The dispute used to be, I think, as to the explanation of certain cures. (Mr. Manners spoke of it, you know.) Psychologists used to say that cures happened by suggestion; and Catholics used to say that they were supernatural. How have they become reconciled?"

Farther Jervis considered a moment.

"I don't think I've ever thought of it like that," he said. "I think I should say—" (he hesitated) "I think I should say that everybody believes now that the power of God does everything; and that in some cases He works through suggestion, and in some through supernatural forces about which we don't know very much. But I don't think it matters much (does it?), if you believe in God."

"That doesn't explain what I mean."

The door opened abruptly and a servant came in.

He bowed.

"The Bishop of Sebaste inquires whether you are at home, Monsignor?"

Monsignor glanced at Father Jervis.

"He's come out as chaplain to Prince George," explained the priest in rapid Latin. "We'd better see him."

"Very good. Yes," said Monsignor. He turned to the priest again.

"Hadn't you better tell him about me?"

"You don't mind?"

"Of course not."

Father Jervis got up and slipped quickly out of the room. "I'm delighted to see you again, Monsignor," began the Bishop, coming in, followed by Father Jervis three minutes later.

Monsignor straightened himself after the kissing of the ring.

"You're very kind, my lord," he said.

As the Bishop sat down, he examined him carefully, noticing that there was nothing noticeable about him. He seemed a characteristic prelate—large, genial, ruddy, and smiling, with bright eyes and well-cut mouth. He was in his purple and ferraiuolo, and carried himself briskly and cheerfully.

"I came to see if you were going to the reception tonight. If so, we might go together. But it's rather late."

"We haven't heard about that."

"Oh! it's purely informal. The Holy Father probably won't appear himself, except perhaps for a moment."

"Oh! At the Vatican?"

"Yes. There will be an enormous crowd, of course. The Prince has gone to bed, poor little chap! He's done up altogether; and I thought of slipping over for a half-hour or so."

Monsignor glanced at his friend.

"I think it would be an excellent thing," observed the old priest.

"Well, there's a carriage waiting," said the Bishop, rising. "I think we'd better go, if we're going. We shall be back within the hour."

II

IT was within ten minutes of the time that the three had arranged to meet again at the foot of the Scala Regia that Monsignor suddenly realized that he had lost himself.

He had wandered for half an hour, after making his salutations to the Master of the Apostolic Palace, who, in the Pope's absence, was receiving the visitors; and, at first with Father Jervis and the Bishop,

who had pointed out to him the notabilities, and presently drifting
from them in the crowds, by himself, had gone up and down and
in and out through endless corridors, courts, loggia, and great recep-
tion-rooms of the enormous place, watching the amazing crowds, and
exchanging bows and nods with persons who had bowed and nodded
to him.

The whole system of the thing seemed new to him. He had imagined (he scarcely knew why) the Vatican to be a place of silence and
solemn dignity and darkness, with a few sentries here and there, a few
prelates, a cardinal or two—with occasionally a group of very particular visitors, or, on still rarer occasions, a troop of pilgrims being
escorted to some sight or some audience.

Certainly it was not at all like this tonight.

First, the whole place was illuminated in nearly every window.
Huge electric lights blazed behind screens in all the courts; bands
of music were stationed at discreet intervals one from another;
and through every station that he went, through corridors, recep-
tion-rooms, up and down stairways, seething in every court, streaming
through every passage and thoroughfare, moved a multitude of persons—largely ecclesiastics, but also very largely otherwise (though
there were no ladies present)—talking, questioning, laughing, wholly,
it seemed, at their ease, and appearing to find nothing unusual in the
entire affair. Here and there in some of the great rooms small courts
seemed to be in process—a company of perhaps twenty or forty would
be standing around two or three notabilities who sat. There was usually a cardinal here, sometimes two or three; and on three or four
occasions he saw what he imagined must be a royalty of some kind,
seated with a cardinal, while the rest stood.

It was to him a very extraordinary spectacle, in spite of his further initiation that day into this new world, so utterly unfamiliar to
him; and it seemed once more to drive home to his consciousness this
strange state of affairs of which his friend had tried to persuade him,
but which he yet found difficult wholly to take in. Certainly the world
and the Church seemed on very cordial terms.

But now he had lost himself altogether. He had wandered up a long corridor, thinking that it would lead him back to the Court of St. Damasus, whence he knew his way well enough; and he now paused, hesitating. For it seemed to him that every step he was taking led him farther from the lights and the din of voices and music.

He could see behind him, framed in a huge open doorway, as on an illuminated disc, a kaleidoscope of figures moving; and in front, as he stood, the corridor, although here the lights burned as brilliantly as elsewhere, seemed to lead away into comparative darkness. Yet he felt certain of his direction.

Then, as he stood, a door opened somewhere in front, and he thought he heard voices talking again. It reassured him, and he went on.

It was not until he found himself in a small lobby (comparatively small that is, for it was not less than forty feet square, and the painted coffered ceiling was twenty feet above his head), that he stopped again, completely bewildered. There was no longer any sound to guide him, for he had closed a couple of passage-doors behind him as he came; and he noticed that practically complete silence was on all sides; a single illuminated half-globe shone gently from the ceiling overhead.

He stood some time considering and listening to the silence, till he became aware that it was not silence. There was a very faint murmur of a voice behind one of the four doors that opened on this lobby; and beside the door there rested (he now noticed for the first time) the halberd of a Swiss, as if the soldier had just been called within. This decided him; he went to the door, laid his hand upon the handle, and immediately the murmur ceased. He pushed down the handle and opened the door.

For a moment as he stared within he could not understand: he had expected a passage—a guardroom—at least something secular. Yet it was some kind of a chapel or sacristy into which he was looking: he observed the outline of an altar with its crucifix; and two figures.

Then one of the figures—in the habit of a Franciscan, barefooted, with a purple stole across its shoulders—had sprung towards him, and half pushed, half waved him backwards again.

"What are you doing here? How dare you—I beg pardon, Monsignor, but—"

"I beg pardon, Father; I had lost my way. I am a stranger."

"Back—back that way, Monsignor," stammered the friar. "The guard should have told you."

The truth was dawning on the prelate little by little, helped by the flash of the other kneeling white figure he had seen within.

"Yes," stammered the friar again. "The Holy Father. Back that way, Monsignor. Yes, yes—that door straight opposite."

It was over; the two doors had closed almost simultaneously, behind the friar as he had gone back to his duty, and behind the priest who now stood again at the end of the long corridor down which he had come. He stood here now, strangely moved and affected.

He had seen nothing remarkable in itself—the Pope at confession. And yet in some manner, beyond the startling fact that he had groped his way, all unknowing, to the Pope's private apartments, and at such a moment, the dramatic contrast between the glare and noise of the reception outside—itself the climax of a series of brilliant external splendors and the silent, half-lighted chapel where the Lord of All knelt to confess his sins, caused a surprising disturbance in his soul.

Up to now he had been introduced step by step into a new set of experiences, Christian indeed, yet amazingly worldly in their aspect; he had begun to learn that religion could transform the outer world, and affect and use for its own purposes all the pomps and glories of outward existence; he had begun to realize that there was nothing akin to God, no line of division between the Creator and the creature; and now, in one instant, he had been brought face to face again with inner realities, and had seen, as it were, a glimpse of the secret core of all the splendor. The Pope attended by princes—the Pope on his knees before a barefooted friar.

These were the two magnetic points between which blazed religion.

He stood there, trembling a little, trying to steady his bewildered brain—even now, in spite of his years, not unlike the brain of a child. He passed his tongue over his suddenly dry lips. Then he began to move down the passage again, to find his friends.

CHAPTER VII

I

"What I can't yet quite understand," said Monsignor, "is that point I mentioned the other day about faith and science. I don't see where one ends and the other begins. It seems to me that the controversy must be unending. The materialist says that since Nature does all things, even the most amazing things must be done by her that we shall be able to explain them all someday, when science has got a little farther. And the theologian says that some things are so evidently out of the reach of Nature that they must be done by a supernatural power. Well, where's the point of reconciliation?"

Father Jervis was silent for a while.

The two were sitting on the upper deck of an air-ship towards evening, traveling straight towards the setting sun.

He had grown almost accustomed to such views by now; and yet the sight that had been unrolling itself gradually during the last half-hour had held him fascinated for minute after minute. They had taken ship in Rome after a day or two more of sight-seeing, and had moved up the peninsula by stages, changing boats soon after crossing the frontier, for one of the high-flying, more leisurely and more luxurious vessels on which the more wealthy classes traveled. They were due in Lourdes that evening; and, ever since the higher peaks of the Pyrenees had come into sight, had moved over a vision of bewildering beauty. To their left rose the mountains, forming, it seemed to them at the

    h they traveled, an enormous jagged and gigantic pile,
    teel, yet irradiated with long rays, patches, and pools of
    ight alternated by amazing depths of the shadow whose
    peacock to indigo. Then from the foot of the tumbled

pile there ran out what appeared a loosely flung carpet vivid and yet a soft green, patched here and there with white towns, embroideries of woodland, lines of silver water. Yet this, too, was changing as they watched the shadows grow longer with almost visible movement. New and strange colors, varying about a fixed note of blue according to the nature of that with which the earth was covered, slowly came into being. Here, in front, now and again a patch of water glowed suddenly, three thousand feet beneath, as it met the shifting angle between the eye and the sun; and beyond, far out across the darkening plain, shone the remote line of the sea, itself ablaze with gold, and above and about in every quarter burned the enormous luminous dome of sky.

"I can't put it all accurately," said Father Jervis at last. "I mean I can't tell you off-hand all the tests that are exactly applied to every case. But it's something like this."

He paused.

"Yes, tell me," said the other, still staring out at the softly rolling landscape.

"Well, first," began the old priest slowly, "in the last fifty years we've classified almost exhaustively everything that nature can do. We know, for instance, for certain that in certain kinds of temperaments body and mind are in far greater sympathy than in others; and that if, in such a temperament as this, the mind can be fully persuaded that such and such a thing is going to happen—a thing within the range of natural possibility, of course—it will happen, merely through the action of the mind upon the body."

"Give me an instance."

"Well," (he hesitated again). "Well, I'm not a physician, and cannot define accurately; but there are certain nervous diseases—hysterical simulation, nervous affections such as St. Vitus' dance—as well, of course, as purely mental diseases, such as certain kinds of insanity—"

"Oh, those," said the other contemptuously.

"Wait a minute. These, I say, given the right temperament and receptiveness to suggestion, can be cured *instantaneously*."

"Instantaneously?"

"Certainly—given those conditions. Then there are certain other diseases, very closely related to the nervous system, in which there have been changes of tissue, not only in the brain, but in the organs or the limbs. And these, too, can be cured by mere natural suggestion; but—and this is the point—not instantaneously. In cases of this kind, cured in this way, there is always needed a period, I won't say as long as, but proportionate to, the period during which the disease has been developing and advancing. I forget the exact proportions now, but I think, so far as I remember, that at least two-thirds of the time is required for recovery by suggestion as was occupied by the growth of the disease. Take lupus. That certainly belongs to the class I'm speaking of. Well, lupus has been cured in mental laboratories, but never instantaneously, or anything like instantaneously."

"Go on, Father."

"Finally, there are those physical states that have practically nothing to do directly with the nervous system at all. Take a broken leg. Of course the cure of a broken leg is affected by the state of the nervous system, since it depends upon the amount of vital energy, the state of the blood, and so on. But there are distinct processes of change of tissue that are bound to take a certain fixed period. You may—as has been proved over and over again in the mental laboratories—hasten and direct the action of the nervous energy, so that a man under hypnotic suggestion will improve more rapidly than a man who is not. But no amount of suggestion can possibly effect a cure instantaneously. Tuberculosis is another such thing; certain diseases of the heart—"

"I see. Go on."

"Well, then, science has fixed certain periods in all these various matters which simply cannot be lessened beyond a certain point. And miracle does not begin—authorized miracle, I mean—unless these periods are markedly shortened. Mere mental cures, therefore, do not come under the range of authorized miracle at all—though, of course, in many cases where there has been little or no suggestion, or where the temperament is not receptive, practically speaking, the

miraculous element is most probably present. In the second class—
organic nervous diseases—no miracle is proclaimed unless the cure is
instantaneous, or very nearly so. In the third class, again, no miracle
is proclaimed unless the cure is either instantaneous, or the period of
it very considerably shortened beyond all known examples of natural
cure by suggestion."

"And you mean to say that such cures are frequent?"

The old priest smiled.

"Why, of course. There is an accumulation of evidence from the
past hundred years which—"

"Broken limbs?"

"Oh, yes; there's the case of Pierre de Rudder, at Oostacker, in the
nineteenth century. That's the first of the series—the first, I mean, that
has been scientifically examined. It's in all the old books."

"What was the matter with him?"

"Leg broken behind the knee for eight years."

"And how long did the cure take?"

"Instantaneous."

There was silence again.

Monsignor was staring out and downwards at the flitting meadowland far below. A flock of white birds moved across the darkening
gray, like flying specks seen in the eye, yet it seemed with extraordinary slowness and deliberation, so great was the distance at which
they flew. He sighed.

"You can examine the records," said the priest presently, "and, better than that, you can examine some of the cases for yourself, and the
certificates. They follow still the old system which Dr. Boissaire began
nearly a century ago."

"What about Zola?" demanded Monsignor abruptly.

"I beg your pardon?"

"Zola, the great French writer. I thought he had had advanced
some very sharp criticisms of Lourdes."

"Er—when did he live?"

"Why, not long ago; nineteenth century, at the end."

Father Jervis shook his head, smiling.

"I've never heard of him," he said, "and I thought I knew Lourdes literature pretty well. I'll inquire."

"Look," said the prelate suddenly, "what's that place we're coming to?"

He nodded forward with his head to where vast white lines and patches began to be visible on the lower slopes and at the foot of long spurs that had suddenly come into sight against the sunset.

"Why, that's Lourdes."

II

As the two priests came out next morning from the west doors of the tall church where they had said their masses, Monsignor stopped.

"Let me try to take it in a moment," he said.

They were standing on the highest platform of the pile of three churches that had been raised over a hundred years ago, now in the very center of the enormous city that had grown, little by little, around the sacred place. Beneath them, straight in front, approached from where they stood by two vast sweeps of balustraded steps, lay the place, perhaps sixty feet beneath, of the shape of an elongated oval, bounded on this side and that by the old buildings where the doctors used to have their examination rooms, now used for a hundred minor purposes connected with the churches and the grotto. At the farther end of the place, behind the old bronze statue of Mary, rose up the comparatively new *Bureau de Constatations*—a great hall (as the two had seen last night), communicating with countless consulting and examination rooms, where the army of State-paid doctors carried on their work. The whole of the open place between these buildings crawled with humanity—not yet packed as it would be by evening—yet already sufficiently filled by the two ever-flowing streams—the one passing downwards to where the grotto lies out of sight on the left, the other passing up towards the lower entrance of the great hall. It resembled an amphitheater, and the more so, since the roofs of the buildings on every side, as well as the slope up which the steps rose to the churches, adapted now as they were to accommodate at least three hundred thousand spectators, were already beginning to show groups and strings of onlookers who came up here to survey the city.

On the right, beyond the place, lay the old town, sloping up now, up even to the medieval castle, which fifty years ago had stood in lonely detachment, but now was faced on hill-top after hill-top, at its own level, by the enormous nursing homes and hostels, which under the direction of the Religious Orders had gradually grown up about this shrine of healing, until now, up to a height of at least five hundred feet, the city of Mary stood on bastion after bastion of the lower slopes of the hills, like some huge auditorium of white stone, facing down towards the river and the holy place.

Finally, on the left, immediately to the left of the two priests who stood silently looking, fifty feet below, ran the sweep of the Gave, crossed by innumerable bridges which gave access to the crowding town beyond the water, where once had been nothing but meadowland and the beginning of the great southern plain of France.

There was an air of extraordinary peace and purity about this place, thought Monsignor. Whiteness was the predominating color—whiteness beneath, and whiteness running up high on the right onto the hills—and above the amazing blue of the southern sky. It was high and glorious summer about them, with a breeze as intoxicating as wine and as fresh as water. From across the place they could hear the quick flapping of the huge Mary banner that flew above the hall, for there were no wheels or motors here to crush out the acuteness of the ear. The transference of the sick from the hostels above the town was carried out by aeroplanes—great winged decks, with awnings above and at the sides, that slid down as if on invisible lines, to the entrance of the other side of the hall, whence after a daily examination by the doctors they were taken on by hand-litters to the grotto or the bathing-pools.

Monsignor heard a step behind him as he stood and looked, still pathetically bewildered by all that he saw, and still struggling, in spite of himself, with a new up-break of scepticism; and turning, saw Father Jervis in the act of greeting a young monk in the Benedictine habit.

"I knew we should meet. I heard you were here," the old man was exclaiming. "You remember Monsignor Masterman?"

They shook hands, and Monsignor was not disappointed in his friend's tact.

"Father Adrian absolutely haunts Lourdes nowadays," went on Father Jervis. "I wonder his superiors allow him. And how's the book getting on?"

The monk smiled. He was an exceedingly pleasant person to look upon, with a thin, refined face and large, startlingly blue eyes. He shook his head as he smiled.

"I'm getting frightened," he said. "I cannot see with the theologians in all points. Well, the least said, the soonest mended."

Father Jervis' face had fallen a little. There was distinct anxiety in his eyes.

"When will the book be out?" he asked quickly.

"I'm revising it for the last time," said the other shortly. "And you, Monsignor? I had heard of your illness."

"Oh, Monsignor's nearly himself again. And will you take us into the Bureau?" asked the old priest.

The young monk nodded.

"I shall be there all day," he said. "Ask for me at any time."

"Monsignor wants to see for himself. He wants to see a case straight through. Is there anything—"

"Why, there's the very thing," interrupted the monk. (He fumbled in his pocket a moment.) "Yes, here's the leaflet that was issued last night." (He held out a printed piece of paper to Monsignor.) "Read that through."

The prelate took it.

"What's the case?" he asked.

The leaflet will give you the details. It's decay of the optic nerve—a Russian from St. Petersburg. Both eyes completely blind, the nerves destroyed, and he saw light yesterday for the first time. He'll be down from the Russian hospice about eleven. We expect a cure today or tomorrow."

"Well," said Father Jervis, "we mustn't detain you. Then, if we look in about eleven?"

The monk nodded and smiled as he moved off. "Certainly," he said. "At eleven then."

Monsignor turned to his friend.

"Well?"

Father Jervis shook his head. "It's a sad business," he said. "That's Dom Adrian Bennett. He's very daring. He's had one warning from Rome; but he's so extraordinarily clever that it's very hard to silence him. He's not exactly heretical; but he will work along lines that have already been decided."

"Dear me! He seems very charming."

"Certainly. He is most charming, and utterly sincere. He's got the entrée everywhere here. He is a first-rate scientist, by the way. But, Monsignor, I'd sooner not talk about him. Do you mind?"

"But what's his subject? Tell me that."

"It's the miraculous element in religion," said the priest shortly. "Come, we must go to our coffee."

III

THE hall was already crowded in every part as the two priests looked in at the lower end a few minutes before eleven o'clock. It was arranged more or less like a theater, with a broad gangway running straight up from the doors at one end to the foot of the stage at the other. The stage itself, with a statue of Mary towering at the back, communicated with the examination-rooms behind the two doors, one on either side of the image.

"What's going on?" whispered Monsignor, as he glanced up first on this side and that at the array of heads that listened, and then at the two figures that occupied the stage.

"It's a doctor lecturing on a cure. This goes on nearly all day. We must get around to the back somehow."

As they passed in at last from the outside through the private door through which the doctors and privileged persons had access behind the stage, they heard a storm of clapping and voices from the direction of the public hall on their right.

"That's finished then. Follow me, Monsignor."

They went through a passage or two, after their guide—a young man in uniform—seeing as they went, through half-open doors here and there, quiet white rooms, glimpses of men in white, and once at least a litter being set down; and came at last into what looked like some kind of committee-room, lighted by tall windows on the left, with a wide horseshoe table behind which sat perhaps a dozen men, each wearing on his left breast the red and white cross which marked them as experts. Opposite the examiners, but half hidden from the two priests by the back of his tall chair, sat the figure of a man.

Their guide went up to the end of the table, and almost immediately they saw Father Adrian stand up and beckon to them.

"I've kept you two chairs," he whispered when they came up. "And you'd better wear these crosses. They'll admit you anywhere." (He pointed to the two red and white badges that hung over the backs of their chairs.)

"Are we in time?"

"You're a little late," whispered the monk. Then he turned again towards the patient, a typical fair-haired, bearded Russian with closed eyes, who at that moment was answering some question put to him by the presiding doctor in the center.

The monk turned again.

"Can you understand Russian?"

Monsignor shook his head.

"Well, I'll tell you afterwards," said the other.

It seemed very strange to be sitting here, in this quiet room, after the rush and push of the enormous crowds through which they had made their way this morning. The air of the room was exceedingly business-like, and not in the least even suggestive of religion, except in the matter of a single statue of Our Lady of Lourdes on a bracket on the wall above the President's head. And these dozen men who sat here seemed quietly business-like, too. They sat here, men of various ages and nationalities, all in the thin white doctor's dress, with papers spread before them, and a few strange instruments scattered here and there, leaning forward or leaning back, but all intently listening to and watching the Russian, who, still with closed eyes, answered the short questions put to him continuously by the President. There seemed no religious excitement even in the air; the atmosphere was one, rather, of simple science.

There seemed something faintly familiar in all this to the man who had lost his memory.

Certainly he had known of Lourdes as soon as it was mentioned to him, and he seemed now to remember that some such claim to be perfectly scientific had always been made by the authorities of the place. But he had supposed, somehow, that the claim was a false one.

The Russian suddenly rose.

"Well!" whispered Monsignor sharply, as the doctors began to talk.

The monk smiled.

"He's just said an interesting thing. The President asked him just now whether he had seen anything of the crowds as he came down this morning."

"Yes?"

"He said that people looked like trees moving about… Oh, no! He didn't know he was making a quotation. Look! he's going off down to the grotto. He'll be back in half an hour to report."

Monsignor leaned back in his chair.

"And you tell me that the optic nerves were destroyed?"

The monk looked at him in wide-eyed wonder. "Certainly. He was examined on Tuesday, when he came. Today's Friday."

"And you believe he'll be cured?"

"I shall be very much surprised if he's not." There was a stir by the door as the Russian disappeared. A young, bright-eyed doctor looked in and nodded, and the next instant a brancardier appeared, followed by a litter.

"But how have you time to examine all these thousands of cases?" asked the prelate, watching the litter advance.

"Oh, not one in a hundred comes through to us here. Besides, this is only one of a dozen committee-rooms. It's only the most sensational cases—where there's real organic injury of a really serious kind—that ever come at all before the highest courts. Cases, I mean, where, if there's a cure, the publication of the miracle follows as a matter of course. What's this case, I wonder?" he ended sharply, glancing down at the printed paper before him, and then up again at the litter that was being arranged.

Monsignor looked, too, at the paper that lay before him. Some thirty paragraphs, carefully numbered, dated, and signed, gave, as it seemed, a list of the cases to be examined.

"Number fourteen," murmured the monk. Number fourteen, it appeared, was a case of fractured spine—a young girl, aged sixteen; a German. The accident had happened four months before. The notes, signed by half a dozen names, described the complete paralysis below the waist, with a few other medical details. Monsignor looked again at the girl on the other side of the table, guarded by the brancardiers and a couple of doctors, while the monk talked to him rapidly in Latin. He saw her closed eyes and colorless lips.

"This case has attracted a good deal of attention," whispered the monk. "The Emperor's said to be interested in it, through one of the ladies of the court, whose servant the girl was. It's interesting for two or three reasons. First, the fracture is complete, and it's marvelous she hasn't died. Then it's been taken up as a kind of test case by a group of materialists in Berlin. They've taken it up, because the girl has declared again and again that she is perfectly certain she will be cured at Lourdes. She claims to have had a vision of Our Lady, who told her so. Her father's a freethinker, by the way, and has only finally allowed her to come so that he can use her as an argument afterwards."

"Who has examined her?" asked Monsignor sharply.

"She was examined last night on her arrival, and again this morning. Dr. Meurot, the President here"—he indicated with his head the doctor who sat three places off, who was putting his questions rapidly to the two attending physicians—"Dr. Meurot examined her himself early this morning. This is just the formal process before she goes to the grotto. The fracture is complete. It's between the eleventh and twelfth vertebra."

"And you think she'll be cured?"

The monk smiled.

"Who can tell?" he said. "We've only had one case before, and the papers on that are not quite in order, though it's commonly believed to be genuine."

"But it's possible?"

"Oh, certainly. And her own conviction is absolute. It'll be interesting."

"You seem to take it pretty easily," murmured the prelate.

"Oh, the facts are established a hundred times over—the facts, I mean, that cures take place here which are not even approached in mental laboratories. But—"

He was interrupted by a sudden movement of the brancardiers.

"See, they're removing her," he said. "Now, what'll you do, Monsignor? Will you go down to the grotto, or would you sooner watch a few more cases?"

"I think I'd sooner stay here," said the other, "at least for an hour or two."

IV

IT was the hour of the evening procession and of the Benediction of the Sick.

All day long the man who had lost his memory had gone to and fro with his companions, each wearing the little badge that gave them entrance everywhere; they had lunched with Dr. Meurot himself.

If Monsignor Masterman had been impressed by the social power of Catholicism at Versailles, and by its religious reality in Rome, he was ten thousand times more impressed by its scientific courage here in Lourdes. For here religion seemed to have stepped down into an arena hitherto (as he fancied) restricted to the play of physical forces. She had laid aside her oracular claims, her comparatively unsupported assertions of her own divinity; had flung off her robes of state and authority; and was competing here on equal terms with the masters of natural law—more, she was accepted by them as their mistress. For there seemed nothing from which she shrank. She accepted all who came to her desiring her help; she made no arbitrary distinctions to cover her own incapacities. Her one practical desire was to heal the sick; her one theoretical interest to fix more and more precisely, little by little, the exact line at which nature ended and supernature began. And, if human evidence went for anything, if the volumes of radiophotography and sworn testimony went for anything, she had established a thousand times over during the preceding half-century that under her aegis, and hers alone, healing and reconstituting forces were at work to which no merely natural mental science could furnish any parallels. All the old quarrels of a century ago seemed at an end. There was no longer any dispute as to the larger facts. All that now remained to be done by this huge organization of international experts was to define more and more closely precisely where the line lay between the two worlds. All cures that could be even remotely paralleled in the mental laboratories were dismissed as not evidently supernatural; all those which could not be so paralleled were recorded, with the most minute detail, under the sworn testimonies of doctors who had examined the patients immediately before and immediately after the cure itself. In a series of libraries that abutted on the *place*, Monsignor Masterman, under the guidance of Dom Adrian Bennett, had spent a couple of hours this afternoon in examining the most striking of the records and photographs preserved there. He was amazed to find that even by the end of the nineteenth century cures had taken place for which the most modern scientists could find no natural explanation.

Ten minutes ago he had taken his place in the procession of the Blessed Sacrament, with the monk's last words still in his head.

"It is during the procession itself," he had said, "that the work is done. We lay aside all deliberate knowledge as the Angelus rings, and give ourselves up to faith."

And now the procession had started, and already, it seemed to him, he had begun to understand. It was as he himself emerged, a few paces in front of the Blessed Sacrament itself, walking with the prelates, that that understanding reached its climax. He paused at the head of the steps, to wait for the canopy to come through, and his heart rose within him so mightily that it was all he could do not to cry out.

Beneath him, seen now from the opposite end from which he had looked this morning, lay the *place*, under a wholly different appearance. The center of the great oval was cleared, with the exception of a huge pulpit, surmounted by a circular sounding-board, that stood in the middle. But around this empty space rose, in tier after tier, masses of humanity beyond all reckoning, up and up, as on the sides of an enormous amphitheater, as far as the highest roofs of the highest buildings that looked onto the space. Before him rose the pile of churches, and here, too, on every platform, roof, and stair, swarmed the spectators. The doors of the three churches were flung wide, and far within, in the lighted interiors, lay the heads of countless crowds, as cobblestones, seen in perspective. The whole *place* was in shadow now, as the sun had just gone down, but the sky was still alight overhead, a vast tender-colored vault, as sweet as a benediction. Here and there, in the illimitable blue, like crumbs of diamond dust, gleamed the first stars of evening.

And from this vast multitude, swayed by a white figure beneath the pulpit, articulate now as the listener emerged, rose up a song to Mary, as from one soft and gigantic voice, appealing to Her Presence who for over a century and a half, it seemed, had chosen to dwell here by virtue and influence, the Great Mother of the redeemed and the Consoler of the afflicted, whose divine Son was even now on His way, as at Cana itself, to turn the water of sorrow into the wine of joy. Then, as the canopy came out, at an imperious gesture from the tiny swaying figure, the music ceased; great trumpets sounded a phrase; there was a rustle and a movement as of a breaking wave as the crowds knelt; and the *Pange Lingua* rose up in solemn adoration.

THE DAWN OF ALL

103

As he came down the steps, his eyes quick with tears, he saw for the first time the lines of the sick in the place to which he had been told to look. There they lay, some four thousand in number, placed side by side in two great circling rows around the whole arena, a fringe of pain to the exultant crowds, in litters laid so close together that they seemed but two great continuous beds, and between them the broad flower-strewn platform along which Jesus of Nazareth should pass by. There they lay, all of them bathed today in the strange water that had sprung up a hundred and fifty years ago under the fingers of a peasant child, waiting for the sacramental advent of Him who had made both that water and those for whose healing it was designed.

And yet not all were cured, not perhaps one in ten of all who came in confidence. That surely was wonderful. Was it then that that same Sovereign Power who had permitted the pain elected to retain His own sovereignty, and to show that the Lawgiver was fettered by no law? One thing at least was certain, if those records which the priest had examined this morning were to be believed, that no receptiveness of temperament, no subjective expectancy of cure, guaranteed that the cure would take place. Natures that had responded marvelously in the mental laboratories seemed ineffective here; natures that were inert and immovable under the influence of sympathetic science leapt up here to meet the call of some voice whose very existence a hundred years ago had been in doubt.

The front of the long procession, Monsignor saw, had reached now the doors of the basilica, and would presently, after making the complete around, pour down into the arena to allow the Blessed Sacrament to move more quickly. It was an exquisite sight, even from here, as the prelate set foot on the platform and began to move to the left. The long lines of tapers, four deep, went like some great serpent, rippling with light, above the heads of the sick; and here and there in the slopes of the crowded spectators shone out other lights, steady as stars in the motionless half-lit evening air. Then, as he went, slowly, pace by pace, he remembered the sick and glanced down, as the music on a sudden ceased.

Ah! There they lay, those living crucifixes shrouded in white, their faces on either side turned inwards that they might see their Lord.

There lay a woman, her face shriveled with some internal horror—some appalling disease which even the science of these days dared not handle, or at least had not; her large eyes staring with an almost terrible intensity, fixed, it seemed, in her head, yet waiting for the vision that even now might make her whole. There a child tossed and moaned and turned away his head. There an old man crouched forward upon his litter, held up on either side by two men in the uniform of the brancardiers. And so, in endless lines, they lay; from every nation under heaven; the very air in which he walked seemed alight with pain and longing.

A great voice broke in suddenly on his musings; and, before he could fix his attention as to what it said, the words were taken up by the hundreds of thousands of throats—a short, fervent sentence that rent the air like a thunder-peal. Ah! He remembered now. These were the old French prayers, consecrated by a century of use; and as he passed on, slowly, step by step, watching now with a backward glance the blessing of the sick that had just begun—the sign of the cross made with the light golden monstrance by the bishop who carried it—now the agonized eyes of expectation that waited for their turn, he, too, began to hear, and to take up with his own voice those piteous cries for help.

"*Jesu! heal our sick… Jesu! grant that we may see—may hear—may walk. Thou art the Resurrection and the Life. Lord! I believe; help Thou mine unbelief.*"

Then with an overwhelming triumph: "*Hosanna to the Son of David! Hosanna, Hosanna!*"

Then again, soft and rumbling: "*O Mary, conceived without sin, hear us who have recourse to thee.*"

The sense of a great circumambient power grew upon him at each instant, sacramentalized, it seemed, by the solemn evening light, and evoked by this tense ardor of half a million souls, and focused behind him in one looming point.

Ah! There was the first miracle! A cry behind him, an eddy in the circle of the sick and the waiting attendants, a figure with shrouding linen fallen from breast and outstretched arms, and then a roar, mighty beyond reckoning, as the whole amphitheater swayed and cried out in exultation. He saw as in a vision the rush of doctors to the place, and the gesticulating figures that held back the crowd behind the barrier. Then a great moan of relief; and a profound silence as the *miraculé* kneeled again beside the litter which had borne him. Then again the canopy moved on; and the passionate voice cried, followed in an instant by the roar of response:

"*Hosanna to the Son of David!*"

* * *

IT was half-way around, at the foot of the church steps, that the German girl was laid; and as the prelates drew near Monsignor looked rapidly to this side and that to identify her.

Ah! There she lay, still with closed patient eyes and colorless face, in the outer circle facing inwards towards the pulpit. A doctor knelt on either side of her—one of them the young man who had announced her coming into the hall this morning, with a rosary between his fingers. It was known to the crowd generally, Monsignor had learnt, that her case was exceptional; but it had been kept from them as to where she would lie, for fear that the excitement might be too much concentrated.

He looked at her again, intently and carefully—at that waxen, fallen face, her helpless hands clasped across her breast with a string of beads interwoven within them; and even as he looked distrust once more surged within him. It was impossible, he told himself—in spite of what he had seen that day, in spite of that score of leaping figures and the infectious roar that more than twenty times in that short journey had set his pulses a-beat. He passed her, quickening his steps a little; then faced about and watched.

Slowly came the canopy. Its four bearers sweated visibly with the effort; and the face of the bishop who bore the monstrance was pale and streaked with moisture from the countless movements he had made. Behind him came row after row of downcast faces, men and women of every religious order on earth, and the tapers seen in perspective appeared as four almost continuous waving lines of soft light.

There had been a longer pause than usual since the last exulting cry of a sick man healed; and the silence between the cries from the pulpit grew continually more acute. And yet nothing happened.

The bishop was signing now outwards over a man who lay next the German, with his face altogether hidden in a white and loathsomely suggestive mask; but there was no stir in answer. The bishop turned inwards and signed over a woman, and again there was no movement.

"Thou art the Resurrection and the Life," cried the voice from the pulpit.

"*Thou art the Resurrection and the Life*," answered the amphitheater, as the bishop turned again outwards.

Monsignor heard him sigh with the effort, and with the consciousness too, perhaps, of whom it was that lay here; he lifted the monstrance; the eyes of the girl opened. As he signed to left and right she smiled. As he brought the monstrance back she unclasped her hands and sat up.

V

THE three priests stood together that evening on the high roof of a Carmelite priory, on the other side of the river, half a mile away, yet opposite the grotto, as the German girl came down to make her thanksgiving.

From where they stood it was impossible to make out a single detail of that at which they looked. The priory stood on high ground, itself towering above the crowded roofs that lay between them and the river; and opposite rose up the masses of the hill at the foot of which was the sacred place itself. It resembled tonight a picture all of fire. The churches on the left were outlined all in light, up to the last high line of roof against the dark starlight sky; and upon the spaces in between lay the soft glow from the tens of thousands of torches that the crowds carried beneath. Above the grotto the precipitous face of the cliff showed black and somber, except where the zigzag paths shone out in liquid wondering lines, where the folks stood packed together, unseeing, yet content to be present. In front, at the foot, over the lake of fire where the main body of worshipers stood, glowed softly the cavern where Mary's feet had once rested, and where her power had lived now far beyond the memory of the oldest man present.

From this distance few sounds could be heard except the steady murmur of voices of those countless thousands. It was as the steady roll of far off wheels or of the tide coming in over a rocky beach; and even the sudden roar of welcome and triumph that announced that the little procession had left the place was soft and harmonious. There followed a long pause.

Then, on a sudden, trumpets rang out, clear as silver, sharpened and reverberated by the rocks from which they sounded, and like the voice of a dreaming giant, came the great words, articulate and distinct:

"*Magnificat: anima mea Dominum.*"

* * *

"AND you, Monsignor," asked Dom Adrian, as they stood half an hour later, still watching the lines of light writhe this way and that as the crowds went home, "you have asked Our Lady to give you back your memory?"

"I was at the grotto this afternoon," he said. "It is not for me."

"Then there will be something better instead," smiled the young monk.

CHAPTER VIII

I

"Do you go back to England tomorrow?" said Father Adrian, as they sat a night or two later in the guest-room of the French Benedictines, where the monk was staying.

"We start tomorrow night," said the old priest. "Monsignor is infinitely better, and we must both get back to work. And you?"

"I stay here to finish the revising of my book," said the monk quietly.

The man who had lost his memory had piled impression on impression during the last forty-eight hours. There was first the case of the German girl. She had been examined by the same doctors as those who had certified to her state half an hour before the cure, and the result had been telegraphed over the entire civilized world. The fracture was completely repaired; and although she was still weak from her long illness, she gained strength every hour. Then there was the case of the Russian. He, too, had received back his sight, although not instantaneously; it had come to him step by step. An hour ago he had been pronounced healed, and had passed the usual tests in the examination-rooms. But these cases, and others like them which the priests had investigated, were only a part of the total weight of impressions which Monsignor Masterman had received. He had seen here for himself a relation between science and faith—a cooperation between them with the exigencies of each duly weighed and observed by them both—which set nature and supernature before him in a completely new light. As Mr. Manners had said at Westminster a week or two before, the two seemed to have met at last, each working from different quarters, on a platform on which they could work side by side. The facts were no longer denied by either party. Science allowed for the mysteries of faith; faith recognized the achievements of science. Each granted that the other possessed a perfectly legitimate sphere of action in which the methods proper to that sphere were imperative and final. The scientist accepted the fact that religion had a right to speak in matters that lay beyond scientific data; the theologian no longer denounced as fraudulent or disingenuous the claims of the scientist to exercise powers that were at last found to be natural. Neither needed to establish his own position by attacking that of his partner, and the two accordingly, without prejudice or passion, worked together to define yet further that ever-narrowing range of ground between the two worlds which up to the present remained unmapped. Suggestion, for example, acting upon the mutual relations of body and mind, was recognized by the theologian as a force sufficient to produce phenomena which in earlier days he had claimed as evidently supernatural. And, on the other side, the scientist no longer made wild acts of faith in nature, in attributing to her achievements which he could not for an instant parallel by any deliberate experiment. In a word, the scientist repeated, "I believe in God"; and the theologian, "I recognize Nature."

Monsignor sat apart in silence, while the others talked.

He had thought in Rome that he had reached interior conviction; he understood now in Lourdes that his conviction had not gone so deep as he had fancied. He had learned in Versailles that the Church could reorganize society, in Rome that she could reconcile nations; he had seen finally in Lourdes that she could resolve philosophies.

And this very discovery made him the more timid. For he began to wonder whether there were not yet further discoveries which he would have to make—workings out and illustrations of the principles he had begun to perceive. How, for example, he began to ask himself, would the Church deal with those who did not recognize her claims—those solitary individuals or groups here and there who, he knew, still clung pathetically to the old dreams of the beginning of the century to the phantom of independent thought and the intoxicating nightmare of democratic government? It was certain now that

these things were dreams—that it was ludicrously absurd to imagine
that a man could profitably detach himself from Revelation and the
stream of tradition and development that flowed from it; that it was
ridiculous to turn creation upside-down and to attempt to govern the
educated few by the uneducated many. Yet people did occasionally
hold impossible and absurd theories.

How, then, would these be treated by the Church when once her
power had been finally consolidated? How was she to reconcile the
gentleness of the Christian spirit with the dogmatism of the Christian
claim? He recalled one or two hints that Father Jervis had let drop,
and he was conscious of a touch of fear.

He woke up to externals again at the sound of a sentence or two
from the monk.

"I beg your pardon," he said. "What was that?"

"I was saying that the news from Germany is disquieting."

"Why?"

"Oh, nothing definite. They expect trouble. They say that the
Emperor is extraordinarily interested in this girl's case, and that the
Socialists of Berlin are watching him. Berlin is their last stronghold,
you know."

"By the way," interrupted Father Jervis suddenly, "I've inquired
about that man with the curious name—Zola. I find he had quite a
vogue at one time. And now I come to think of it, I believe Manners
mentioned him."

"Zola?" mused the monk. "Yes, I'm nearly sure I've heard of him.
Wasn't he an Elizabethan?"

"No, no. He died at the end of the last century. I find he did write
a little romance about Lourdes. There was even a copy in the library
here. I hadn't time to look at it; but M. Meurot told me it was one of
those odd little attacks on religion that were popular once. That's all I
could find out."

Monsignor compressed his lips. Somewhere out of his abysmal
memory there lurked a consciousness that Zola had once been of
some importance; but he could add nothing to the discussion.

Dom Adrian stood up and stretched himself. "It's time for bed," he said. "Look," (he nodded towards the window), "the devotions are just ending."

From out of the luminous gulf beneath, beyond the tiers of roofs that lay, step-like, between this hostel and the river, rose up that undying song of Lourdes—that strange, haunting old melody of the story of Bernadette, that for a hundred and fifty years had been sung in this place—a ballad-like song, without grace of music or art, which yet has so wonderful an affinity with the old carols of Christendom, which yet is so unforgettable and so affecting. As the three stood side by side looking out of the window they saw the serpent of fire, that rope-coil of tapers that, stretching around the entire *place,* humped over the flights of steps and the platforms set amongst the churches, writhes incessantly on itself. But, even as they watched, the serpent grew dim and patchy, and the lights began to go out, as group after group broke away homewards. They had wished their Mother good night, there in that great French town which has so wonderful an aroma of little Nazareth; they had sung their thanksgivings; they had offered their prayers. Now it was time to sleep under Her protection, who was the Mother both of God and man.

"Well, good night," said Monsignor. "We shall meet in London."

"I hope so," said the young monk gravely.

"I am afraid that young man will be in trouble," said Father Jervis softly, as they came down the steps. "His book, you know."

"Eh?"

"Well, it's best not to talk of it. We shall soon know. He's as brave as a lion."

✣ PART TWO ✣

CHAPTER I

I

MONSIGNOR Masterman sat in his room at Westminster, busy at his correspondence. A week had passed since his return, and he had made extraordinary progress. Even his face showed it. The piteous, bewildered look that he had worn, as he first realized little by little how completely out of touch he was with the world in which he had found himself after his lapse of memory, had wholly disappeared; and in its place was the keen, bright-eyed intelligence of a typical ecclesiastic. It was not that his memory had returned. Still, behind his sudden awakening in Hyde Park, all was a misty blank, from which faces and places and even phrases started out, for the most part unverifiable. Yet it seemed both to him and to those about him that he had an amazing facility in gathering up the broken threads. He had spent three or four days, after his return from Lourdes, closeted in private with Father Jervis or the Cardinal, and had found himself at last capable of readmitting his secretaries and of taking up his work again. The world in general had been informed of his nervous breakdown, so that on the few occasions when he seemed to suffer small lapses of memory no great surprise was felt.

He found, of course, a state of affairs that astonished him enormously. For example, he discovered that as the Cardinal's secretary

he was an extremely important person in the country. He had not
yet ventured much on private interviews—these were for the present chiefly conducted by the Cardinal, with himself present; but his
correspondence showed him that his good word was worth having,
even by men who were foremost in the government of the day. There
was, for instance, an immense amount of work to be done on the
subject of the relations of Church and State; for the Church, it must
be remembered, while not actually established, stood for the whole
religious sentiment of the country, and must be consulted on every
measure of importance. There was, further, the matter of the restoration of Church property not yet finally concluded in all its details,
with endless adjustments and compensations still under discussion.
This morning it was on the University question that he was chiefly
engaged, and particularly the question as to the relative numbers of
the lay and clerical Fellows on the old Catholic foundations.

A bell struck a single soft note; and one of his secretaries, sitting
at the broad table near the window, lifted the receiver to his ear. Then
he turned.

"His Eminence wishes to have a word with you, Monsignor, on
two matters."

Monsignor stood up.

"I'll come now, if it's convenient," he said. "I have to be at Westminster at twelve."

The secretary spoke again through the telephone. "His Eminence
is ready," he said.

The Cardinal looked up as the priest came in a minute later.

"Ah, good morning, Monsignor. Yes, sit down there. There are just
two matters I want to have a word with you on. The first is as regards
a heresy-trial of a priest."

Monsignor bowed. It was his first experience of the kind, so far
as he could remember; and he did not yet fully understand all that it
meant.

"I wish you to select the judges. You'll look up the procedure,
if you forget? A Dominican must be on it, of course; so you must

communicate with the Provincial. The other two must be seculars, as the accused is a Religioso. He has elected to be tried in England."

"Yes, your Eminence."

"He has behaved very reasonably, and refuses to take advantage of the *Nenivitus* clause."

"I forget at this moment," began Monsignor, vaguely conscious that he had heard of this before.

"Oh, that gives him the right to suppress the book before publication. It's part of the new legislation. He has sent the thesis of his book, privately printed, to Rome, and it has been condemned. He refuses to withdraw, as he is perfectly confident of his orthodoxy. I understand that the book is not yet completely finished, but he has his thesis clear enough. It is on the subject of the miraculous element in religion."

"I beg your Eminence's pardon, but is the author a Benedictine by any chance?"

The Cardinal smiled.

"Yes. I was coming to that. His name is Dom Adrian Bennett. He is—or rather ought to be—a Westminster monk, but his return has been deferred for the present."

"I met him at Lourdes, your Eminence."

"Ah! He is a very clever young man, and at the same time perfectly courageous…. Well, you'll look up the procedure, if you're not perfectly clear? And I should wish to have the names of the judges by tomorrow night. The Canon Theologian of the diocese may not be well enough to act. But you will make arrangements."

"Yes, your Eminence."

"The second matter is exceedingly important." (The Cardinal began to play with the pen that lay on his desk.) "And no rumor of it must get out from this house. It may be made public at any moment, and I wish you to know beforehand in order that you may not be taken by surprise. Well, it is this. I have had information that the Emperor of Germany will be received into the Catholic Church tonight. I needn't tell you what that means. He is quite fearless and quite conscientious; and there is not the slightest doubt that he will, sooner or later, make it impossible for the Socialists to congregate any longer in Berlin. That will mean either civil war in Germany—(I hear the Socialists have been in readiness for this for some time past)—or it will mean their dispersal everywhere. Europe, at any rate, will have to deal with them. However, that's in the future. The important thing at the present is that we should be able to show our full strength when the time comes. There will be thanksgivings throughout England, of course, as soon as the news is published, and I wish you to be in readiness to make what arrangements are necessary. It was the Lourdes miracle, which you witnessed, that has finished the affair. As you know, the Emperor has been on the edge of this for months past."

The Cardinal spoke quietly and diplomatically enough; but the other could see how deeply moved he was by this tremendous development. The Emperor's position had been the one flaw in the Catholic organization of Europe—and indeed of the world. Now the last stone was laid, and the arch was complete. The single drawback was that no statesman or prophet could conjecture with certainty what the effect on the Socialists would be.

"And how are you, Monsignor?" asked the Cardinal suddenly, smiling at him.

"I am getting on very well, your Eminence!"

"I should like to say that, for myself, I am more than satisfied," went on the other. "You seem to me to have regained all your old grip on things—and in some points to have more than regained it. I have written to Rome—" (he broke off).

"It's the details that still trouble me, your Eminence. For instance, in this heresy-trial, I cannot remember the procedure, or the penalties, or anything else."

"That'll all come back," smiled the Cardinal. "After all, the principles are the point. Well, I mustn't detain you. You're to be at Westminster at twelve."

"Yes, your Eminence. We've nearly finished now. The monks are very well satisfied. But the main body of them do not come to

Westminster until they formally re-enter. Cardinal Campello has
written to say that he will be with us on the 20th for certain."

"That is very good. Then good morning, Monsignor."

II

IT was nearly midnight before Monsignor Masterman pushed away
the book that lay before him and leaned back in his chair. He felt sick
and dazed at what he had read.

First, he had studied with extreme care the constitution of the
Heresy-Court, and had sent off a couple of hours ago the formal letters to the Dominican Provincial and two other priests whom he had
selected. Then he had studied the procedure of the court, and the penalties assigned.

At first he could not believe what he read. He had turned more
than once to the title-page of the great quarto, thinking that he must
find it to be a reprint of some medical work. But the title was unmistakable. The book was printed in Rome in the spring of the present
year, and contained an English supplement, dealing with the actual
relations of the Church laws with those of the country. There were
minor penalties for minor offenses; there was at every turn an escape
for the accused. He might, even in the last event, escape all penalties
by a formal renouncement of Christianity; but if not, if he persisted
simultaneously in claiming a place in the Church of Christ and in
holding to a theological opinion declared erroneous by the Court of
Appeal ratified by the Pope, he was to be handed over to the secular
arm; and by the laws of England—as well as of every other European
country except Germany—the penalty inflicted by the secular arm
was, in the instance of a tonsured clerk, death.

It was this that staggered the priest.

Somewhere within him there rose up a protest so overwhelmingly
strong as to evade even an attempt at deliberate analysis—a protest
that rested on the axiom that spiritual crimes deserved only spiritual
punishment. This he could understand. He perceived clearly enough
that no society can preserve its identity without limitations; that no

association can cohere without definite rules that must be obeyed. He
was sufficiently educated then to understand that a man who chooses
to disregard the demands of a spiritual society, however arbitrary these
demands may seem to be, can no longer claim the privileges of the
body to which he has hitherto adhered. But that death—brutal physical death could by any civilized society—still less any modern Christian
society—be even an alternative penalty for heresy, shocked him beyond
description. A ray of hope had shone on him when he first read the
facts. It might be, perhaps, that this was merely a formal sentence, as
were the old penalties for high treason abandoned long before they
were repealed. He turned to the index; and after a search leaned back
again in despair. He had seen half a dozen cases quoted, within the last
ten years, in England alone, in which the penalty had been inflicted.

It was half an hour before he stood up, with one determination
at least formed in his mind—that he would consult no one. He had
learnt in the last few weeks sufficient distrust of himself to refrain
from formulating conclusions too soon, and he learnt enough of the
world in which he found himself to understand that positions accepted
as self-evident by society in general, which yet seemed impossible to
himself, after all occasionally turned out to be at least not ridiculous.

But to think that it was the young monk with whom he had
talked at Lourdes who was to be the center of the process he himself had to prepare! He understood now some of the hints that Dom
Adrian Bennett had let fall.

III

A card was brought up to him a couple of evenings later as he sat at
his desk; and as he turned it over Father Jervis himself hurried in.

"May I speak to you alone an instant?" he said, and glanced at the
secretaries, who rose and went out without a word.

"You look unwell," said the old priest keenly, as he sat down.

Monsignor waved a deprecatory hand.

"Well—I'm glad I caught you in time," went on the other. "I saw
the man come in; and wondered whether you knew about him."

"Mr. Hardy."

"Yes—James Hardy."

"Well—I just know he's not a Catholic; and something of a politician."

"Well, he's quite the shrewdest man the secularists have got. He's a complete materialist. And I've not the slightest doubt he's heard of your illness and has come to see whether he can fish anything out of you. He's exceedingly plausible; and very dangerous. I don't know what he's come about, but you may be certain it's something important. It may be to do with the Religious Houses; or the Bill for the re-establishment of the Church. But you may depend upon it, it's something vital. I thought I'd better remind you who he is."

The priest stood up.

"Thank you very much, Father. Is there anything else? Have you any news for me?"

Father Jervis smiled.

"No, Monsignor. You know more than I do, now.... Well, I'll tell Mr. Hardy you'll see him. Number one parlor?"

"That'll do very well. Thanks."

It was growing towards dusk as Monsignor Masterman passed down the corridor a few minutes later; and he paused a moment to glance out upon the London street through the tall window at the end. Not that there was anything particular to be seen there; indeed the street, at the moment he looked, was entirely empty. But he looked up for an instant at the great electric news-sheet where the headlines were displayed, above the corner shop on the way to Victoria Street where the papers were sold. But there was no news. There was the usual announcement of the weather conditions, a reference to one or two land-cases, and a political statement.

Then he went on.

The parlor with the glass doors was lighted as he came in, and a man in a black lawyer's dress stood up to greet him. He was rosy-faced and genial, clean-shaven, above the middle-height, and his manner was very deferential and attractive.

The first minute or two was taken up by Mr. Hardy's congratulations on the other's appearance, and on his complete recovery. There was not a trace of anxiety or nervousness in his manner; and the priest almost insensibly found himself beginning to discount his friend's warning. Then, quite suddenly, the other turned to business.

"Well, I suppose I must come to the point. What I want to ask is this, Monsignor. Can you tell me in confidence (I assure you I will be discreet) whether the ecclesiastical authorities here realize the rush of Socialists that is bound to come, so soon as the Emperor's conversion is publicly announced?"

"I—" began the priest.

"One moment, please, Monsignor. I do not in the least want to force any confidences. But you know we infidels"—(he smiled charmingly and modestly)—"we infidels regard you as our best friends. The State seems to know nothing of mercy. But the Church is always reasonable. And we poor Socialists must live somewhere. So I wished—"

"But my dear sir," began Monsignor. "I think you're assuming too much. Has the Emperor shown any signs—?"

Across the other's face he suddenly saw pass a look of complete vacancy, as if he were no longer attending; and, simultaneously, he heard a sudden sound which he could not at first identify, through the open windows looking onto Ambrosden Avenue.

"What is that?" exclaimed the lawyer sharply, and stood up.

Again from the street there rose the roar of voices, cheering, followed by a sharp punctuating cry.

"Come this way," said the priest. "We can see from the corridor."

When they reached the window the whole aspect of the street had changed. Halfway from where they stood, to the end where the sheet placard was erected, was a gathering, surging mob, increasing as they looked. From the left, from behind the west end of the cathedral clock a continual stream poured in, met by two others, the one down the avenue of figures that ran and gesticulated, the other from the direction of Victoria Street. And from the whole arose gusts of cheering, marking the pauses in the speech of some tiny figure

THE DAWN OF ALL

which, mounted beside the news-sheet, appeared to be delivering a speech.

Monsignor glanced at the news-sheet, and there, in gigantic letters, over the space where the weather had been discussed just now, was the announcement made public at the very instant when the leader of the English Socialists was attempting to discover the truth of the rumor that had reached him:

THE EMPEROR OF GERMANY WAS RECEIVED INTO
THE CATHOLIC CHURCH
ON THURSDAY EVENING

And beneath it:

PROCLAMATION TO THE SOCIALISTS
ANNOUNCED FOR TONIGHT

Monsignor read it, unconscious of all else except the astounding fact. Then he turned to speak, but found himself alone.

IV

LONDON went soberly mad with enthusiasm that night, and Monsignor Masterman, standing on the cathedral roofs with half a dozen priests, watched what could be seen of the excitement for half an hour, before going downstairs for the *Te Deum* in the great church.

The cathedral was, indeed, largely, the center around which the enthusiasm concentrated itself. Two other whirlpools eddied in Parliament Square, and around St. Paul's, where the Archbishop of London preached a sermon from the steps. Even these facts, although in a sense he knew they must be so, drove home into the priest's mind the realization of how the Church was, once again, as five hundred years ago, the center and not merely a department of the national life.

In every direction, as he leaned over Ambrosden Avenue, as he looked down Francis Street to right and left, everywhere nothing of the streets was visible under the steadily moving pavement of heads. Every space between the tall houses resembled the flow of an intricate stream, with its currents, its eddies, its back-waters, beneath the clear radiance of the artificial light. Here and there actors were seen gesticulating in dumb show, for all sounds were drowned in the steady subdued roar of voices. There was no delirium, no horse-play; the citizens were too well disciplined. Occasionally from this point or that a storm of cheering broke out as some great man was recognized.

About half-past nine mounted policemen began to make their appearance from Victoria Street, and an open way was gradually formed leading to a cleared space in front of the Cathedral. Ten minutes later cars began to follow, as the great folks began to arrive for the *Te Deum,* and almost simultaneously the bells broke out, led by the solemn crash of the great "St. Edward" from the campanile.

V

THEY read in the morning the full text of the proclamation to the Socialists.

As Monsignor Masterman came up from breakfast, he felt his arm taken, and there was Father Jervis, his clever old face lit up by excitement. He, too, carried a morning paper under his arm.

"I would have a talk with you about this," he said. "Have you seen the Cardinal yet?"

"I'm to see him at ten. I feel perfectly helpless. I don't understand in the least."

"Have you read it through yet?"

"No, I glanced at it only, I wish you'd help me through, Father."

The old priest nodded.

"Well, well, read every word of it first."

As they passed into the sitting-room, the prelate slipped forward the little door-plate that announced that he was within, but engaged. Then, without a word, they sat down, and there was dead silence for twenty minutes, broken only by the rustle of turning pages, and an occasional murmur or raised voices from the groups that still wandered around the Cathedral—pools of that vast river that had filled every channel last night. Father Jervis uttered a small exclamation once or twice.

Monsignor laid down the sheets at last and sighed.

"Finished, Father?"

"Oh, yes! I've been re-reading. Now let us talk." Father Jervis turned back to the front page, settled the paper on his knee, and leaned back.

"The main point is this," he said. "Repressive measures will be passed in Germany, as soon as the act can be got through. That will mean that Germany will be brought up into line with the rest of Europe, America, Australia, and half Asia, throughout her whole empire. That will mean again that our own repressive measures will really and truly be put into force. At present they are largely inoperative."

"How do you mean?"

"Well, we've got laws against things like blasphemy and heresy, and particularly the dissemination of heresy, and all the rest; but they're practically never put into force except in very flagrant cases. For instance, Socialist and infidel speeches can be delivered freely in what are called private houses, which are really clubs. Well, that sort of thing cannot possibly go on. The infidels have complained of tyranny, of course—that's part of the game. As a matter of fact they've been perfectly free, unless they gave actually public offense. They've distributed their pamphlets and done what they liked. Well, of course it was impossible to be really strict so long as Germany was lax. They could always meet in Berlin, and have their pamphlets printed there; and we could do nothing. But, you see, the whole situation's changed with the Emperor's conversion. He's one of those heavy, consistent men—quite stupid, of course—who act their principles right out to the furthest detail. So long as he was agnostic he allowed almost anything to go on. And now he's a Christian he'll understand that that must stop. He's responsible before God, you see, as the ruler—"

"But the people. What of the people?"

Father Jervis stared.

"The people? Why, they're the ruled, aren't they?"

"But—er—democracy—"

"Democracy? Why, no one believes in that, of course. How could they?"

"Go on, Father."

"But, Monsignor, you must get that clear. You must remember we're really educated people, not half-educated."

Monsignor twitched with irritation. He could not understand even yet.

"Father, do you mean that the people won't resent this sudden change of front on the part of the Emperor? Certainly, if they're really liberally minded they'll tolerate his following his own conscience. But how can they justify his suddenly dictating to them?"

The priest leaned forward a little. His old manner came back, and once more he spoke to Monsignor as to a child.

"Monsignor, listen carefully, please. I assure you you're completely out of date. What the German people will say now is this: 'Up to now the Emperor has been agnostic, and therefore he has not allowed any laws against heresy. Now he is a Catholic, and therefore he will cause laws to be passed against heresy.'"

"And they won't resent that?" snapped the prelate, now thoroughly irritated.

Father Jervis lifted a pacific hand.

"My dear friend, the Germans—like all other educated nations—believe that their ruler is meant by God to rule them. And they also believe that Catholicism is the true religion. Very well, then. When a ruler is Catholic they obey him implicitly, because they know that he will be kept straight in all matters of right and wrong by the Pope, who is the representative of God. In non-vital matters they will obey him because he is their ruler, and therefore they are bound in conscience to do so."

"And when the ruler is not Catholic?"

"Again, in non-vital matters they will obey him. And in vital matters—supposing, that is, he passed a law against Christianity (which, of course, nowadays no man could certainly do)—then they would appeal to the Pope, and, if the law was enforced, destroy it and take the penalties."

"Then the Pope is the real ruler—the final court of appeal?"

"Certainly. Who else should be? Isn't he the Vicar of Christ?"

There was a pause. "There," said the priest more easily. "And now we really must get back to the point. I said just now that the conversion of the Emperor will mean a tightening up of repressive measures against the infidels everywhere. They won't be allowed to congregate, or disseminate their views any longer."

"Yes?"

"Well, the point is, what will happen? There must be an explosion or a safety-valve. And even if there is an explosion there must be a safety-valve afterwards, or there will be another explosion."

"What you told me about America—"

"That was on the tip of my tongue," said Father Jervis. "And I expect there'll be the solution."

"Let's see," said Monsignor reflectively; "you told me there were certain cities in America where infidels were tacitly allowed to have things their own way—I think you mentioned Boston?"

"I did."

"And you think that that will be officially authorized now—I mean that there will be definite colonies where the infidels will be allowed complete liberty?"

"Under restrictions—yes."

"What sort of restrictions?"

"Well, they won't be allowed to have an army or an aery—"

"Eh?"

"An aery," repeated Father Jervis. "An airfleet, I mean. That wouldn't do: they might make war."

"I see."

"I don't see what better safety-valve could be suggested. They could work out their own ideas there as much as they liked. Of course, details would come later."

"And the rest of the Proclamation?" asked the other, lifting the sheet.

"I think we've got at the essentials," said the priest, glancing again at his own copy, "and at the immediate results. Of course, all his other measures don't come into force till the Houses pass them. In fact, nothing of the Proclamation has force until that happens. I expect the Bill for the Establishment of Catholicism will take some time. We shall get ours through before that. They'll pass a few small measures immediately, no doubt as to the Court chaplains and so on."

There was a pause.

"I really think we've got at the principles," said the priest again, meditatively. "Are they clear to you?"

Monsignor rose.

"I think so," he said. "I'm very much obliged, Father. I'm sorry I was stupid just now; but you know it's extraordinarily bewildering to me. I still don't seem to be able to grasp all you said about Democracy."

The old priest smiled reassuringly.

"Well, you see, the universal franchise reduced Democracy *ad abundum* fifty years ago. Even the uneducated saw that. And then there came the reaction to the old king-idea again."

Monsignor shook his head.

"I don't see how the people ever consented to give up the power when once they'd got it."

"Why, in the same way that kings used to lose it in the old days— by revolution."

"Revolution? Who revolted?"

"The many who were tyrannized over by the few. For that's what democracy really means."

Monsignor smiled at what he conceived to be a paradox.

"Well, I must go to the Cardinal," he said. "It's just on ten o'clock."

CHAPTER II

I

IT was three weeks later that the Benedictines took formal possession of Westminster Abbey, and simultaneously that Pontifical High Mass was sung in the University churches of Oxford, Cambridge, and Durham, to mark the inauguration of their new life.

Monsignor Masterman was appointed to attend upon the Cardinals in the Abbey; and as he awoke that morning, it seemed to him once more as if he were living in a dream of strange and intoxicating unreality. Everywhere in the house, as he passed along the corridors, as he gave and received last instructions before starting, there seemed the same tension of expectancy. Finally, as he went up to the Cardinals' rooms to announce the start, he found the two prelates, both in their scarlet, sitting in silence, looking out over the crowded silent streets.

He bowed at the door without speaking, and then, turning, led the way.

As they came down to the door where the horsed State carriages were waiting, for a moment the wall and the avenue of faces, in front and to right and left, struck him almost with a sense of hostility. A murmur that was almost a roar greeted the gleam of scarlet as the cardinals came out; then silence again, and a surge of downbent heads as the two raised their hands in blessing.

Monsignor himself sat facing the Cardinals in the glass coach, as at a foot-pace the six white horses, with grooms and postilions, drew them slowly past the long length of the Cathedral, around to the right, and into Victoria Street. There he drew a long breath, for he had never seen or dreamed of such a sight as that which met him. From end to end of the side street, and in the direction of Old

Victoria Station, across the roadway as well, from every window and
from every roof, looked a silent sea of faces, that broke into sound and
rippling motion as the last carriage came in sight. He had not realized
till this moment the tremendous appeal to the imagination which this
formal restoration of the old Abbey to the sons of its original founders
and occupants made to the popular mind. Here again there had been
working in his mind an undefined sense that the Church had her
interests, and the nation hers. He had not understood that the two
were identified once more; and identified, too, to a degree which had
perhaps never before been reached. Even in medieval days there had
been crises and even periods during which the secular power stood
on one side and the sacred on another; as when Henry had faced St.
Thomas, with the nation torn in factions behind the two champions.
But the lesson, it seemed, had been learned at last; Caesar had learned
that God was his ultimate sanction; and Church and nation, now perhaps for the first time, stood together as soul and body united in one
personality.

If Victoria Street suggested such a thought as this, Parliament
Square drove it home. As the coach drew up at the west door of the
Abbey, and Monsignor stepped out with his robes about him, like a
ground-bass to the ecstatic pealing of the bells overhead, he heard the
great roar of welcome roll out over the wide space, reverberate back
from Westminster Hall and the Government buildings opposite, and
die down into heart-shaking silence again, as the scarlet flash was
seen at the Abbey doors. The great space was filled in every foot with
a crowd that was of one heart and soul in its welcome of this formal
act of restitution.

Within, the monks waited, headed by their abbot, in a wide circle
of some hundred persons, in the extreme end of the nave about the
door. The proper formalities were carried out; and the seculars, led by
the cardinals, passed up the enormous church between the tapestries
that hung from every pillar to the music of the *Ecce Sacerdos magnus.*

The old monuments were gone, of course—removed to St.
Paul's—and for the first time for nearly three hundred years it was

possible to see the monastic character of the church as its builders had designed it. Over the screen hung now again the Great Rood with Mary and John; and the altars of the Holy Cross and St. Benedict stood on either side of the choir-gates.

And so they waited, the Cardinals in their thrones beside the high-altar, and the man who had lost his memory beside them; while the organ pealed out continuously overhead and endless footsteps went to and fro over the carpeted ways and the open stone spaces of the transepts. Once more upon this man, so bewildered by this new world in which he found himself, descended a flood of memories and half-perceived images. He looked up to the far-off vaulted roof and the lantern beneath the central tower; he looked down the long row of untenanted stalls; across the transepts, clean and white again now as at the beginning, filled from end to end across the floor with the white of surplices and the dusky colors of half the religious habits of the world; he caught here and there the gleam of candle-flames and gold and carving from the new altars, set back again, so far as might be, in their old stations; and again it seemed to him that he had lived in some world of the imagination, as if he saw things which kings and prophets had desired to see and had not seen unless in visions of faith and hope that never found fulfillment.

He whispered softly to himself sometimes; old forgotten names and scenes and fragments came back. It seemed to him as if in some other life he had once stood here—surely there in that transept a stranger and an outcast—watching a liturgy which was strange to him, listening to music, lovely indeed to the ear, yet wholly foreign in this home of monks and prayer. Surely great statues had stood before them—statesmen in perukes who silently declaimed secular rhetoric in the house of God, swooning women, impossible pagan personifications of grief, medallions, heathen wreaths, and broken columns. Yet here as he looked there was nothing but the decent furniture of a monastic church—tall stalls, altars, images of the great ones of heaven, wide eloquent spaces that gave room to the soul to breathe. He had dreamed the other perhaps; he had read histories; he had seen pictures.

He again broke off in full blast; and under the high roofs came pealing the cry of a trumpet. He awoke with a start; the Cardinals were already on their feet at a gesture from a master of ceremonies. Then he stepped into his place and went down with them to the choir-gates to meet the King.

II

IT was in the Jerusalem chamber when the King was gone, a couple of hours later, that the new abbot of Westminster came up to him. He was a small, rosy man with very clear, beautiful eyes.

"Can you speak to me for five minutes, Monsignor?" he said.

The other glanced across at the Cardinals.

"Certainly, Father Abbot."

The two went out, down a little passage, and into a parlor. They sat down.

"It's about Dom Adrian," said the abbot abruptly.

Monsignor checked the sudden shock that ran through him. He knew he must show no emotion.

"It's terribly on my conscience," went on the other, with distress visibly growing as he spoke. "I feel I ought to have seen which way he was going. He was one of my novices, you know, before we were transferred. He would have been here today if all had been well. He was to have been one of my monks. I suggested his name."

Monsignor Masterman began to deprecate the self-accusation of the other.

"Yes, yes," said the abbot sharply. "But the point is whether anything can be done. The trial begins on Monday, you see."

"Will he submit?"

The abbot shook his head.

"I don't think so. He's extraordinarily determined. But I wanted to know if you could give me any hope on the other side. Could you do anything for him with the Cardinal, or at Rome?"

"I—I will speak to the Cardinal, certainly, if you wish. But—"

"Yes, I know. But you know a great deal depends on the temper of the court. Facts depend for their interpretation upon the point of view."

"But I understand that it's definite heresy—that he denies that there is any distinction between the miracles of the Church and—"

The abbot interrupted.

"Yes, yes, Monsignor. But for all that there's a great deal in the way these things are approached. You see there's so much neutral ground on which the Church has defined nothing."

"I am afraid, from what I've seen of the papers, that Dom Adrian will insist on a clear issue."

"I'm afraid so; I'm afraid so. We'll do our best here to persuade him to be reasonable. And I thought that if you perhaps would do your best on the other side—would tell the Cardinal, as from yourself, what you think of Dom Adrian—"

Monsignor nodded.

"If we could but postpone the trial for a while," went on the abbot almost distractedly. "That poor boy! His face has been with me all today."

For an instant Monsignor almost gave way. He felt himself on the point of breaking out into a burst of protest against the whole affair—of denouncing the horror and loathing that during these last days had steadily grown within him—a horror that so far he had succeeded in keeping to himself. Then once more he crushed it down, and stood up for fear his resolution should give way.

"I will do what I can, my lord," he said coldly.

III

A great restlessness seized upon the man who had lost his memory that night.

He had thought after his return from abroad that things were well with him again—that he had learned the principles of this world that was so strange to him; and his busy days—all that had to be done and recovered, and his success in doing it—these things at once distracted and soothed him. And now once more he was back in his bewilderment. One great principle it was which confused his whole outlook—the employment of force upon the side of Christianity. Here, on the large scale, was the forcible repression of the Socialists; on a small scale, the punishment of a heretic. What kind of religion was this that preached gentleness and practiced violence?

Between eleven and twelve o'clock he could bear it no longer. The house was quiet, and the lights for the most part gone out. He took his hat and thin cloak, throwing this around him so as to hide the purple at his throat, went softly down the corridors and stairs, and let himself out noiselessly into Ambrosden Avenue. He felt he must have air and space; he was beginning almost to hate this silent, well-ordered ecclesiastical house, where wheels ran so smoothly, so inexorably, and so effectively.

He came out presently into Victoria Street and turned westwards.

He did not notice much as he went. Only his most superficial faculties paid attention to the great, quiet, lighted thoroughfare, to the few figures that moved along, to the scattered sentinels of the City of Westminster police in their blue and silver, who here and there stood at the corners of the cross-streets, who saluted him as he went by; to the little lighted shrines that here and there hung at the angles. Certainly it was a Catholic city, he perceived in his bitterness, drilled and disciplined by its religion; there was no noise, no glare, no apparent evil. And the marvel was that the people seemed to love to have it so! He remembered questioning a friend or two soon after his return to England as to the revival of these curfew laws, and the extraordinary vigilance over morals; and the answer he had received to the effect that those things were taken now as a matter of course. One priest had told him that civilization in the modern sense would be inconceivable without them. How else could the few rule the many?

He came down, across Parliament Square, to the river at last, walking swiftly and purposelessly. A high gateway, with a guard-room on either side, spanned the entrance to the wide bridge that sprang across to Southwark, and an officer stepped out as he approached, saluted, and waited.

He drove down his impatience with an effort, remembering the *espionage* (as he called it) practiced after nightfall.

"I want to breathe and look at the river," he said sharply.

The officer paused an instant.

"Very good, Father," he said.

Ah, this was better! The bridge, empty from end to end, so far as he could see, ran straight over to the south side, where, once again, there rose up the guard-house. He turned sharply when he saw it, and leaned on the parapet looking eastwards.

The eternal river flowed beneath him, clean and steady and strong, between the high embankments. (He knew by now all about the loch-system that counteracted the ebb and flow of the tides.) Scarcely a hundred yards away curved out another bridge, and behind that another and another, down into the distance, all outlined in half-lights that shone like stars and flashed back like heaven itself from the smooth-running water beneath. An extraordinary silence lay over all—the silence of a sleeping city—though it was scarcely yet midnight, and though the city itself on either side of the river lay white and glowing in the lights that burned everywhere till dawn.

At first it quieted him—this vision of earthly peace, this perfection to which order and civilization had come; and then, as he regarded it, it enraged him.

For was not this very vision an embodiment of the force that he hated? It was this very thing that oppressed and confined his spirit—this inexorable application of eternal principles to temporal affairs. Here was a city of living men, each an individual personality, of individual tastes, thoughts, and passions, each a world to himself and monarch of that world. Yet by some abominable trick, it seemed, these individuals were not merely in external matters forced to conform to the society which they helped to compose, but interiorly, too; they actually had been tyrannized over in their consciences and judgments, and loved their chains. If he had known that the fires of revolt lay there sleeping beneath this smooth exterior he would have hated it far less; but he had seen with his own eyes that it was not so. The crowds that had swarmed a while ago around the Cathedral, poured in and filling it for the *Te Deum* of thanksgiving that one more country had been brought under the yoke; the sea of faces that had softly applauded and bowed beneath the blessing of those two Cardinals in scarlet; the enthusiasm, the more amazing in its silent orderliness, which had greeted the restoration of the old national Abbey to its Benedictine founders—even the very interviews he had had with quiet, deferential men, who, he understood, stood at the very head of the secular powers; the memory of the young King kissing the ring of the abbot at the steps into the choir—all these things proved plainly enough that by some supernatural alchemy the very minds of men had been transformed, that they were no longer free to rebel and resent and assert inalienable rights—in short, that a revolution had passed over the world such as history had never before known, that men no longer lived free and independent lives of their own, but had been persuaded to contribute all that made them men to the society which they composed.

He perceived now clearly that it was this forced contribution that he hated—this merging of the individual in the body, and the body one of principles that were at once precise and immutable. It was the extinction of self.

Then, almost without perceiving the connection, he turned in his mind to Christianity as he conceived it to be—to his ideal figure of Christ; and in an instant he saw the contrast, and why it was that the moral instinct within him loathed and resented this modern Christian State.

For it was a gentle figure that stood to him for Christ—God? Yes, in some profound and mysterious way, but, for all earthly purposes of love and imitation, a meek and persuasive man whose kingdom was not of this world, who repudiated violence and inculcated love; One who went through the world with simple tasks and soft words, who suffered without striking, who obeyed with no desire to rule. And what had this tranquil, tolerant figure in common with the strong discipline of this Church that bore His name—a Church that had waited so long, preaching His precepts, until she grew mighty and could afford to let them drop; this Church which, after centuries of blood and tears, at last had laid her hands upon the scepter, and ruled the world with whom she had pleaded in vain so long; this Church who, after two thousand years of pain, had at last put her enemies under her feet—"repressed" the infidel and killed the heretic?

And so the interior conflict went on within this man, who found within him a Christianity with which the Christian world in which he lived had no share or part. He still stared out in the soft autumn night at the huge quiet city, his chin on his hands and his elbows on the parapet, half perceiving the parable at which he looked. Once it was this river beneath him that had made the city; now the city set the river within bars and ordered its goings. Once it was Christianity—the meek and gentle spirit of Christ—that had made civilization; now civilization had fettered Christianity in unbreakable chains. Yet even as he resented and rebelled he felt he dared not speak. There were great forces about him, forces he had experienced for himself—science tamed at last, self-control, organization, and a peace which he could not understand. Every man with whom he had to do seemed kind and tender; there was the patient old priest who taught him and bore with him as with a child, the fatherly Cardinal, the quiet, serene ecclesiastics of the house in which he lived, the controlled crowds, the deferential great men with whom he talked. But it was their very strength, he saw, that made them tender; the appalling power of the machine, which even now he felt that he but half understood, was the very thing that made it run so smoothly. It had the horror of a perfectly controlled steel piston that moves as delicately as a feather fan.

For he saw how inexorable was that strength which controlled the world; how ruthless, in spite of smooth and compassionate words, towards those who resisted it. The Socialists were to be "repressed"; the heretic was to be tried for his life; and in all that wide world in which he lived it seemed that there was not one Christian who recoiled, not one breath of public opinion that could express itself.

And he—he who hated it—must take his part. A fate utterly beyond his understanding had set him there as a wheel in that mighty machine; and he must revolve in his place motionlessly and unresist-ingly in whatever task was set before him.

Once only, as he stared out at the great prospective view, did his heart sicken and fail him. He dropped his face upon his hands and cried to the only Christ whom he knew in silence.

CHAPTER III

I

IT was not until the afternoon of the third day, as the trial of Dom Adrian Bennett drew to its close, that the man who had lost his memory could no longer resist the horrible fascination of the affair, and presented himself at the door of the courtroom. He had learned that morning that the end of the trial was in sight.

It was outside a block of buildings somewhere to the north of St. Paul's Cathedral that the car set him down. He learned at the porter's lodge the number of the court, and then passed in, following his directions, through a quadrangle that was all alight with scarlet creepers, where three or four ecclesiastics saluted him, up a staircase or two, and found himself at last at a tall door bearing the number he wanted. As he hesitated to knock, the door opened, and a janitor came out.

"Can I go in?" asked the priest. "I am from the Archbishop's House."

"I can take you into the gallery at the back, Monsignor," said the man. "The body of the court is full."

"That will do."

They went around a corner together and came to a door up three or four stairs. The janitor unlocked this and threw it back. Further steps rose within the doorway, and Monsignor, as he set foot on the first, had a vivid impression that the court he was approaching was crowded with people. There was no sound at first, but an atmosphere of intense and expectant force.

It was a little curtained gallery in which the priest found himself, not unlike a box at a theater, looking out upon the court from the corner immediately adjacent to the wall against which the raised seats of the judges were placed. He looked around the court, himself sitting a little back in a kind of shame, first identifying the actors in this dreadful drama. He was glad that the gallery had no other occupant than himself.

First there were the judges—three men sitting beneath a canopied roof, beneath which, over their heads, hung a large black and white crucifix. He knew them, all three. There was the Dominican in the center—one of that Order which has had charge of heresy courts since the beginning—a large-faced, kindly-featured, rosy man, with a crown of white hair, leaning back now with closed eyes, listening, and obviously alert; on his right, farther from the spectator, sat the Canon-Theologian of Westminster, a small, brown-faced man with black eyes, looking considerably younger than his years; and on this side the third judge, pale and bald and colorless—a priest who held the degree of Doctor in Physical Science as well as in Theology—he at this instant was drumming gently with a large white hand on the edge of his desk.

Beneath the judges' dais was the well of the court, very much, somehow, as Monsignor had expected (for this was his first experience in a Church court), with the clerks' table immediately beneath the desks, and half a dozen ecclesiastics ranged at it. Some strange-looking instruments stood within reach of the presiding clerk, but he recognized these as the mechanical recorders, of which he had had some experience himself. They were of the nature of phonographs, and by an exceedingly ingenious and yet very simple system could be made to repeat aloud any part of the speeches or answers that had been uttered in the course of the trial. At either end of the clerks' table rose up a structure like a witness-box, slightly below the level of the judges' desks. Opposite the desks was the lightly railed dock for the prisoner. The rest of the court was seated for the public, and as the spectator saw, was completely filled, chiefly with ecclesiastics. Even the gangways were thronged with standing figures. And over all hung that air of intense expectancy and attention.

He glanced once more around the court, once more at the judges.

Then he allowed himself to look full at the prisoner, whom he had not seen since his departure from Lourdes.

Dom Adrian was just as he remembered him, perhaps a shade paler from the fierce attention of the last three days, but he had the same serene, confident air; his eyes were bright and luminous, and his voice (for he was speaking at this moment) perfectly natural and controlled.

It was hard at first to pick up the thread of what he was saying. He had a sheet or two of paper before him, to which he referred as he spoke, and he seemed to be summing up, in a very allusive manner, some earlier speeches of his. Technical terms made their appearance from time to time, and decrees were quoted by their initial Latin words—decrees which conveyed nothing to the listener in the gallery. It was difficult, too, at this distance, to understand the very swift Latin which he spoke in a conversational voice that was almost casual. His whole air was of one who is interested, but not overwhelmingly concerned, in the subject under debate.

He ended at last, and bowed.

Obviously they were not at a very critical part of the trial, thought Monsignor. He felt extraordinarily reassured. He had expected more of a scene.

The Dominican opened his eyes and took up a pen. He glanced at his companions, but they made no sign or movement.

"You have made it perfectly clear," he said. "Nothing could be clearer. I see" (he turned slightly to right and left, and his fellow-judges nodded gently in acquiescence)—"I see no reason to modify what I said just now, and the judgment of the court must stand. Nothing can be clearer to my mind—and I must say that my assessors wholly concur, as you heard just now—nothing can be clearer than that you have contradicted in the most express terms the decrees in question, and that you have refused to modify or to withdraw any of the theses under dispute. Further, you have refused to avail yourself of any of the releases which are perfectly open to you by law. You declined all those openings which I indicated to you, and you appear determined to push the matter to extremes. I must tell you then plainly that I see nothing for it but the forwarding of our opinions to Rome, and I cannot hold out to you the smallest prospect that you will meet with a different judgment from the highest court."

He paused a moment.

There was a profound silence in the court. As Monsignor Masterman glanced around, unable to understand what it was that caused this sense of tremendous tension, he noticed a head or two in that array of faces drop suddenly as if in overwhelming emotion. He looked at the prisoner; but there was no movement there. The young monk had put his papers neatly together, and was standing, upright and motionless, with his hands clasped upon them. The Dominican's voice went on abruptly.

"Have you anything further to say before the court dissolves?"

"I should like to express my sense of the extreme fairness and considerateness of my judges," said the monk, "to say again, as at the beginning, that I commit my cause unreservedly into the hands of God."

The three judges rose together; a door opened behind and they disappeared. Instantly a buzz of tongues began and the sound of shifting feet. As Monsignor glanced back again at the dock, amazed at the sudden change of scene, he saw the monk's head disappearing down the staircase that led below from the dock. He still did not understand what had happened. He still thought that it was some minor stage of the process that was finished, probably on some technical point.

II

He still sat there wondering, thinking that he would let the corridors clear a little before he went out again, and asking himself what it was that had caused that obvious sensation during the judge's last words. To all outward appearance, nothing could be less critical than what he had seen and heard. Plainly the trial was going against the prisoner, but there had been no decision, no sentence. The inquisitors and the prisoner had talked together almost like friends discussing a not very vital matter. And yet the sensation had been overwhelming.

As he rose at last, still watching the emptying court, he heard a tap on the door, and before he could speak, the Abbot of Westminster rustled up the steps, in his habit and cross and gold chain. His face looked ominously strained and pale.

"I—I saw you from the court, Monsignor. For God's sake sit down again an instant. Let me speak with you."

Monsignor said nothing. He could not even now understand.

"I must thank you for your kind offices, Monsignor. I know you did what you could. His Eminence sent for me after he had seen you. And—and I must ask you to help us again at Rome."

"Certainly—anything. But—"

"I fear it's hopeless," went on the abbot, staring out into the empty court, where an usher was moving quickly about from table to table setting papers straight. "But any chance that there is must be taken. Will you write for us, Monsignor? Or better still, urge the Cardinal? There is no time to lose."

"I don't understand, my lord," said the prelate abruptly, suddenly convinced that more had happened than he knew. "I was only here just at the end, and what is it I can do?"

The abbot looked at him.

"That was the end," he said quietly. "Did you not hear the sentence?"

Monsignor shook his head. A kind of sickness seemed to rise from his heart and envelope him.

"I heard nothing," he said. "I came in during Dom Adrian's last speech."

The abbot licked his dry lips; there was a wondering sort of apprehensiveness in his eyes.

"That was the last formality," he said. "Sentence was given twenty minutes ago."

"And—"

The abbot bowed his head, plucking nervously at his cross.

"It has to go to Rome to be ratified," he said hurriedly. "There will be a week or two of delay. Dom Adrian refused any release. But...but he knows there is no hope."

Monsignor Masterman leaned back and drew a long breath. He understood now. But he perceived he must give no sign. The abbot talked on rapidly; the other caught sentences and names here and there: he grasped that there was no real possibility of a reversal of the judgment, but that yet every effort must be made. But it was only with one part of his mind, and that the most superficial, that he attended to all this. Interiorly he was occupied wholly with facing the appalling horror that, with the last veil dropped at last, now looked him in the eyes.

He stood up at last, promising he would see the Cardinal that night; and then his resolve leapt to the birth.

"I should like to see Dom Adrian alone," he said quietly, "and I had better see him at once. Can you arrange that?"

The abbot stopped at the door of the gallery.

"Yes," he said, "I think so. Will you wait here, Monsignor?"

III

MONSIGNOR Masterman lifted his eyes as the door closed, and saw the young monk standing beside the little table.

He had sat down again in the gallery while the abbot was gone, watching mechanically the ushers come into the court and remove the recording-boxes one by one; and meantime in his soul he watched also, rather than tried to arrange, the thoughts that fled past in ceaseless repetition. He could plan nothing, formulate nothing. He just perceived, as a man himself sentenced to death might perceive, that the supreme horror was a reality at last. The very ordinariness of the scene he had witnessed, the familiarity of some of the faces (he had sat next at dinner, not a week ago, the brown-faced Canon-Theologian), the conversational manner of the speakers, the complete absence of any dramatic solemnity—these things increased the terror and repugnance he felt. Were the preliminaries of death for heresy so simple as all that? Was the point of view that made it possible so utterly accepted by everyone as to allow the actual consummation to come about so quietly?

The thing seemed impossible and dreamlike. He strove to hold himself quiet till he could understand. But at the sight of the young monk, pale and tired-looking, yet perfectly serene, his self-control broke down. A spasm shook his face; he stretched out his hands blindly and helplessly, and some sound broke from his mouth.

He felt himself taken by the arm and led forward. Then he slipped into a chair, and dropped his face in his hands upon the table.

It was a few moments before he recovered and looked up.

"There, there, Monsignor," said the monk. "I...I didn't expect this. There's nothing to—"

"But...but—"

"It's a shock to you, I see. It's very kind. But I knew you must have known all along—"

"Surely I never dreamt of it. I never thought it conceivable. It's abominable; it's—"

"Monsignor, this isn't kind to me," rang out the young voice sternly; and the elder man recovered himself sharply. "Please talk to me quietly. Father Abbot tells me you will see the Cardinal."

"I'll do anything—anything in my power. Tell me what I can do."

He had recovered himself, as under a douche of water, at the sharpness of the monk's tone just now. He felt but one thing at this instant, that he would strain every force he had to hinder this crime. He remained motionless, conscious of that sensation of intense tightness of nerve and sinew in which an overpressed mind expresses itself.

The monk sat down, on the further side of the table.

"That's better, Monsignor," he said, smiling. "Well, there's really not much to do. Insanity seems the only possible plea." He smiled again, brilliantly.

"Tell me the whole thing," said the prelate suddenly and hoarsely. "Just the outline. I don't understand; and I can do nothing unless I do."

"You haven't followed the case?"

Monsignor shook his head.

The monk considered again.

"Well," he said. "This is the outline. I'll leave out technical details. I have written a book (which will never see the light now) and I sent an abstract of it to Rome, giving my main thesis. It's on the miraculous element in religion. I'm a Doctor in Physical Science, you know, as well as in Theology. Now there's a certain class of cure (I won't bother you with details, but a certain class of cure) that has always been claimed by theologians as evidently supernatural. And I'll acknowledge at once that one or two of the decrees of the Council of 1960 certainly seem to support them. But my thesis is, first, that these cures are perfectly explicable by natural means, and secondly, that therefore these decrees must be interpreted in a sense not usually received by theologians, and that they do not cover the cases in dispute. I'm not a willful heretic, and I accept absolutely, therefore, that these decrees, as emanating from an ecumenical council, are infallibly true. But I repudiate entirely—since I am forced to do so by scientific fact (or, we will say, by what I am persuaded is scientific fact)—the usual theological interpretation of the wording of the decrees. Well, my judges take the other view. They tell me that I am wrong in my second point, and therefore wrong also in my first. They tell me that the decrees do categorically cover the class of cure I have dealt with; that such cures have been pronounced by the Church, therefore, to be evidently supernatural; and that therefore I am heretical in both my points. On my side, I refuse to submit, maintaining that I am differing, not from the Catholic Church as she really is (which would be heretical), but from the Catholic Church as interpreted by these theologians. I know it's rash of me to set myself against a practically universal and received interpretation; but I feel myself bound in conscience to do so. Very well; that is the point we have now reached. I could not dream of separating myself from Catholic Unity, and therefore that way of escape is barred. There was nothing for it, then, but for my judges to pronounce sentence; and that they did, ten minutes before you came in. (I saw you come in, Monsignor.) I am sentenced, that is to say, as an obstinate heretic, as refusing to submit to the plain meaning of an ecumenical decree. There remains Rome. The whole trial must go there *verbatim*. Three things may happen. Either I am summoned to explain any statements that may seem obscure. (That certainly will not happen. I have been absolutely open and clear.) Or the sentence may be quashed or modified. And that I do not think will happen, since I have, as I know, all the theologians against me."

There was a pause.

The prelate heard the words, and indeed followed their sense with his intellect; but it appeared to him as if this concise analysis had no more vital connection with the real facts than a doctor's diagnosis with the misery of a mourner. He did not want analysis; he wanted reassurance. Then he braced himself up to meet the unfinished sentence. "Or—" he murmured.

"Or the sentence will be ratified," said the monk quietly. And again there was silence. It was the monk again who broke it. "Where Father Abbot seems to think you can help me, perhaps, Monsignor, is in persuading the Cardinal to write to Rome. I do not quite know what he can do for me; but I suppose the idea is that he may succeed in urging that the point is a disputed one, and that the case had better wait for further scientific as well as theological investigation."

Monsignor flung out his hands suddenly. The strain had reached breaking-point. "What's the good!" he cried. "It's the system—the whole system that's so hateful…hateful and impossible."

"What?"

"It's the system," he cried again. "From beginning to end it's the system that's wrong. I hate it more every day. It's brutal, utterly brutal and unchristian." He stared miserably at the young monk, astonished at the cold look in his eyes.

The monk looked at him questioningly without a touch of answering sympathy, it seemed—merely with an academic interest.

"I don't understand, Monsignor. What is it that you—"

"You don't understand! You tell me you don't understand! You who are suffering under it! Why—"

"You think I'm being unjustly treated? Is that it? Of course I, too, don't think that—"

"No, no, no," cried the elder man. "It's not you in particular. I don't know about that—I don't understand. But it's that any living being can live under such tyranny—such oppression of free thought and judgment! What becomes of science and discovery under a system like this? What becomes of freedom—of the right to think for oneself? Why—"

The young monk leaned a little over the table. "Monsignor, you don't know what you are saying. Tell me quietly what it is that's troubling you. Quietly, if you please. I can't bear much more strain."

The man who had lost his memory mastered himself with an effort. His horror had surged up just now and overwhelmed him altogether, but the extraordinary quiet of the other man and his apparently frank inability to understand what was the matter brought him down again to reality. Subconsciously, too, he perceived that it would be a relief to himself to put his developing feeling into words to another.

"You wish me to say? Very well—" He hesitated again for words.

"You are sure you'd better? I know you've been ill. I don't want to—"

Monsignor waved it away with a little gesture. "That's all right," he said. "I'm not ill now. I wish to God I were!"

"Quietly, please," said the young man.

He swallowed in his throat and rearranged himself in his chair. He felt himself alone and abandoned, even where he had been certain of an emotional sympathy.

"I know I'm clean against public opinion in what I think. I've learnt that at last. I thought at first that it was the other way, as... as I think it must have been a hundred years ago. But I see now that all the world is against me—all except, perhaps, the people who are called infidels."

"You mean the Socialists?"

"Yes, I suppose so. Well, it seems to me that the Church is..." (he hesitated, to pick his words) "is assuming an impossible attitude. Take your own case; though that's only one: it's the same everywhere. There are the sumptuary and domestic laws; there's the 'repression,' as they call it, of the Socialists. But take your own case. You are perfectly satisfied that your conclusions are scientific, aren't you?"

"Yes."

"You're a Christian and a Catholic. And yet, because these conclusions of yours are condemned—not answered, mind you, or refuted by other scientists—but just condemned—condemned by ecclesiastics as contrary to what they assume to be true—you...you are—"

He broke off, struggling again with fierce emotion.

He felt a hand on his arm.

"Monsignor, you're too excited. May I ask you some questions instead?"

Monsignor nodded.

"Well, don't take my case only. Take the system, as you said just now. I really want to know. You think that the Socialists ought not to be repressed—that every man ought to be free to utter his opinions, whatever they may be. Is that it?"

"Yes."

"However revolutionary they may be?"

Monsignor hesitated. He had considered this point before. He felt his answer was not wholly satisfactory. But the monk went on.

"Suppose these opinions were subversive of all law and order. Suppose there were men who preached murder and adultery—doctrines that meant the destruction of society. Would you allow these, too, to publish their opinions broadcast?"

"Of course, you must draw the line somewhere," began Monsignor. "Of course—"

"Where?"

"I beg your pardon?"

"You said that we must draw the line somewhere. I ask you where?"

"Well, that, of course, must be a matter of degree."

"Surely it must be one of principle. Can't you give me any principle you would allow?"

The passion of just now seemed wholly gone. Monsignor had an uncomfortable sense that he had behaved like a child and that this young monk was on firmer ground than himself. But again he hesitated.

"Well, would you accept this principle?" asked Dom Adrian. "Would you say that every society has a right to suppress opinions which are directly subversive to the actual foundations on which itself stands? Let me give an instance. Suppose you had a country that was a republic, but that allowed that other forms of government might be equally good. (Suppose, for instance, that while all acquiesced more or less in the republic, yet that many of the citizens personally preferred a monarchy.) Well, I suppose you would say it was tyranny for the republic to punish the monarchists with death?"

"Certainly."

"So should I. But if a few of the citizens repudiated all forms of government and preached Anarchy, well, I suppose you would allow that the government would have a perfect right to silence them?"

"I suppose so."

"Of course," said Dom Adrian quietly. "It was what you allowed just now. Society may, and must, protect itself."

"What's that got to do with it? These Socialists are not Anarchists. You're not an atheist. And even if you were, what right would the Church have to put you to death?"

"I beg your pardon, but the Church wouldn't put me to death then."

Monsignor made an impatient movement.

"I don't understand in the least," he said. "It seems to me—"

"Well, shall I give you my answer?"

Monsignor nodded.

The monk drew a breath and leaned back once more. To the elder man the situation seemed even more unreal and impossible than at the beginning. He had come, full of fierce and emotional sympathy, to tell a condemned man how wholly his heart was on his side, to repudiate with all his power the abominable system that had made such things possible. And now, in five minutes, the scene had become one of almost scholastic disputation; and the heretic, it seemed—the condemned heretic—was defending the system that condemned him to a man who represented it as an official! He waited, almost resentfully.

"Monsignor," said the young man, "forgive me for saying so; but it seems to me you haven't thought this thing out—that you're simply carried away by feeling. No doubt it's your illness.... Well, let me put it as well as I can." He paused again, compressing his lips. He was pale, and evidently holding himself hard in hand; but his eyes were bright and intelligent. Then he abruptly began again.

"What's wrong with you, Monsignor," he said, "is that you. don't realize—again, no doubt, owing to your loss of memory—that you don't realize that the only foundation of society at the present day is Catholicism. You see we *know* now that Catholicism is true. It has reasserted itself finally. Every other scheme has been tried and has failed; and Catholicism, though it has never died, has once more been universally accepted. Even heathen countries accept it *de facto* as the scheme on which the life of the human race is built. Very well, then, the man who strikes at Catholicism strikes at society. If he had his way society would crumble down again. Then what can Catholic society do except defend itself, even by the death penalty? Remember, the Church does not kill. It never has; it never will. It is society that puts to death. And it is certainly true to say that theologians, as a whole, would undoubtedly abolish the death penalty tomorrow if they could. It's an open secret that the Holy Father would do away with it tomorrow if he could."

"Then why doesn't he? Isn't he supreme?" snapped the other bitterly.

"Indeed not. Countries rule themselves. He only has a veto if an actually unchristian law is passed. And this is not actually unchristian. It's based on universal principles."

"But—"

"Wait an instant. Yes, the Church sanctions it. So did the Church approve of the death penalty in the case of murder—another sin against society. Well, Christian society a hundred years ago inflicted death for the murder of the body; Christian society today inflicts death for a far greater crime against herself—that is, murderous attacks against her own life-principle."

"Then the old Protestants were right after all," burst in Monsignor indignantly; "they said that Rome would persecute again if she could."

"If she could?" said the monk questioningly.

"If she was strong enough."

"No, no, no!" cried the other, beating his hand on the table in gentle impatience. "It would be hopelessly immoral for the Church to persecute simply because she was strong enough—simply because she had a majority. She never persecutes for mere opinions. She has no right to use force. But, as soon as a country is convincedly Catholic—as soon, that is to say, as her civilization rests upon Catholicism *and nothing else,* that country has a perfect right to protect herself by the death penalty against those who menace her very existence as a civilized community. And that is what heretics do; and that is what Socialists do. Whether the authorities are right or wrong in any given instance is quite another question. Innocent men have been hanged. Orthodox Catholics have suffered unjustly. Personally I believe that I myself am innocent; but I am quite clear that *if I am a heretic*" (he leaned forward again and spoke slowly), "*if I am a heretic,* I must be put to death by society."

Monsignor was dumb with sheer amazement, and a consciousness that he had been baffled. He felt he had been intellectually tricked; and he felt it an additional outrage that he had been tricked by this young monk with whom he had come to sympathize.

"But the death penalty!" he cried. "Death! That is the horror. I understand a spiritual penalty for a spiritual crime—but a physical one."

Dom Adrian smiled a little wearily.

"My dear Monsignor," he said, "I thought I had explained that it was for a crime against society. I am not put to death for my opinions; but because, holding those opinions, which are declared heretical, and refusing to submit to an authoritative decision, I am an enemy of the *civil state* which is upheld solely by the sanctions of Catholicism. Remember it is *not* the Church that puts me to death. That is not her affair. She is a spiritual society."

"But death! Death, anyhow!"

The man's face grew grave and tender.

"Is that so dreadful," he said, "to a convinced Catholic?"

Monsignor rose to his feet. It seemed to him that his whole moral sense was in danger. He made his last appeal.

"But Christ!" he cried. "Jesus Christ! Can you conceive that gentle Lord of ours tolerating all this for one instant! I cannot answer you now; though I am convinced there is an answer. But is it conceivable that He who said, 'Resist not evil,' that He who Himself was dumb before his murderers—"

Dom Adrian rose, too. An extraordinary intensity came into his eyes, and his face grew paler still. He began in a low voice, but as he ended his voice rang aloud in the little room.

"It is you who are dishonoring our Lord," he said. "Certainly He suffered, as we Catholics, too, can suffer, as you shall see one day—as you have seen a thousand times already, if you know anything of the past. But is that all that He is? Is He just the Prince of Martyrs, the supreme Pain-bearer, the silent Lamb of God? Have you never heard of the wrath of the Lamb? Of the eyes that are as a flame of fire? Of the rod of iron with which He breaks in pieces the kings of the earth? The Christ you appeal to is nothing. It is but the failure of a man with the divinity left out…the Prince of sentimentalists, and of that evil old religion that once dared to call itself Christianity. But the Christ we worship is more than that—the Eternal Word of God, the Rider on the White Horse, conquering and to conquer.

"Monsignor, you forget of what Church you are a priest! It is the Church of Him who refused the kingdoms of this world from Satan, that He might win them for Himself. He has done so! *Christ reigns!* Monsignor, that is what you have forgotten! Christ is no longer an opinion or a theory. He is a Fact. *Christ reigns!* He actually rules this world. And the world knows it."

He paused for one second, shaking with his own passion. Then he flung out his hands.

"Wake up, Monsignor! Wake up! You are dreaming. Christ is the King of men again, now—not of just religiously minded devotees. He

rules, because He has a right to rule. And the civil power stands for
Him in secular matters, and the Church in spiritual. I am to be put
to death! Well, I protest that I am innocent, but not that the crime
charged against me does not deserve death. I protest, but I do not
resent it. Do you think I fear death? Is that not in His hands, too?
Christ reigns, and we all know it. And you must know it, too!"

All sensation seemed to have ebbed from the man who listened.
He was conscious of a white ecstatic face with burning eyes looking
at him. He could no longer actively resist or rebel. It was only by
the utmost effort that he could still keep from yielding altogether.
Some great pressure seemed to enfold and encircle him, threatening
his very existence as an individual. So tremendous was the force with
which the words were spoken, that for an instant it seemed as if he
saw in mental vision that which they described—a supreme dominant figure, wounded indeed, yet overmastering and compelling in
His strength—no longer the Christ of gentleness and meekness, but a
Christ who had taken His power at last and reigned, a Lamb that was
a Lion, a Servant that was Lord of all; One that pleaded no longer,
but commanded.

And yet he clung still desperately and blindly to his old ideal. He
pushed off from Him this dominating presence; his whole self and
individuality would not yield to Him who demanded the sacrifice of
both. He saw this Christ at last, and by a flash of intuition perceived
that this was the key to this changed world he found so incomprehensible; and yet he would not have it—he would not have this man
to rule over him.

He made one last effort; the vision passed and he stood up, feeling once more sensation come back, understanding that he had saved
himself from an extinction more utter than that of death.

"Well," he said quietly—so quietly that he almost deceived himself, too—"well, I will remember what you say, Dom Adrian, and I will
do what I can with the Cardinal."

CHAPTER IV

I

"I'm afraid it's been a great shock," said Father Jervis soothingly. "And I'm not surprised, after your illness. Yes, I quite see your point. Of course it must seem very strange.... Now what about coming over to Ireland for a week? The Cardinal will be delighted, I'm sure."

The blow had fallen this morning—a fortnight after the trial had ended.

First, the answer had come back from Rome that the sentence was ratified—a sentence simply to the effect that the Church could no longer protect this tonsured and consecrated son of hers. Then the formalities of handing over the monk to the secular authorities had taken place, in accordance with the Clergy Discipline Amendment Act of 1964—an Act by which the secular houses of Representatives had passed a code of penalties for clerks condemned by the ecclesiastical courts—clerks, that is to say, who had availed themselves of Benefit of Clergy and had submitted themselves to ecclesiastical jurisdiction. Under that Act Dom Adrian had been removed to a secular prison, his case had been re-examined and the secular sentence passed. And this morning Monsignor had read that the sentence had been carried out. He neither knew nor dared to ask in what form. It was enough that it was death.

There had been a scene with the startled secretaries. Fortunately Monsignor had been incoherent. One of them had remained with him while the other ran for Father Jervis. Then the two laymen had left the room, and the priests alone together.

Things were quieter now. Monsignor had recovered himself, and was sitting white and breathless with his friend beside him.

"Come to Ireland for a week," said the old man again, watching
him with those large, steady, bright eyes of his. "It is perfectly natural,
under the circumstances, that the thing should be a shock. To us, of
course—"

He broke off as Monsignor looked up with a strange white glare
in his eyes.

"Well, well," said the old man. "You must give yourself a chance.
You've been working magnificently; I think perhaps a little too hard.
And we don't want another breakdown. Then I take it you'll come to
Ireland? We'll spend a perfectly quiet week, and be back in time for
the meeting of Parliament."

Monsignor made a small movement of assent with his head. (He
had had Ireland explained to him before.)

"Then I'll leave you quietly here for a little. Call me up if you
want me. I'll tell the secretaries to work in the next room. I'll see the
Cardinal at once, and we'll go by the five o'clock boat. I'll arrange
everything. You needn't give it a thought."

A curious process seemed to have been at work upon the mind
of the man who had lost his memory, since his interview with the
monk immediately after the trial. At first a kind of numbness had
descended upon him. He had gone back to his business, his correspondence, his interviews, his daily consultation with the Cardinal,
and had conducted all these things efficiently enough. Yet, underneath, the situation arranged itself steadily and irresistibly. It had
become impressed upon him that, whether for good or evil, the world
was as it was; that Christian civilization had taken the form which
he perceived around him, and that to struggle against it was as futile,
from a mental point of view, as to resent the physical laws of the
universe. Nothing followed upon such resistance except intense discomfort to oneself. It might be insupportably unjust that one could
not fly without wings, yet the fact remained. It might be intolerably
unchristian that a tonsured clerk should be put to death for heresy, yet
he was put to death, and not a soul, it seemed (not even the victim
himself) resented it. Dom Adrian's protest had been not against the

execution of heretics, but against the statement that he was a heretic. But he had refused to submit to a decision which he acknowledged as authoritative, and found no fault, therefore, with the consequence of such refusal. The condemnation, he granted, was perfectly legal and therefore extrinsically just; and it was the penalty he had to pay for an individualism which the responsible authorities of the State regarded as dangerous to the conditions on which society rested. And the rest was the business of the State, not of the Church.

The scheme then was beginning to grow clear to this man's indignant eyes. Even the "repression" of the Socialists fitted in, logically and inexorably. And he began to understand a little more what Dom Adrian had meant. There stood, indeed, imminent over the world (whether ideally or actually was another question) a tremendous figure that was already even more Judge than Savior—a personality that already had the power and reigned; one to whose feet all the world crept in silence, who spoke ordinarily and normally through His Vicar on earth, who was represented on this or that plane by that court or the other; one who was literally a King of kings; to whose model all must be conformed; to whose final judgment every creature might appeal if he would but face that death through which alone that appeal might be conveyed. Such was the scheme which this priest began to discern; and he saw how the explanation of all that bewildered him lay within it. Yet nonetheless he resented it; nonetheless he failed to recognize in it that Christianity he seemed once to have known, long ago. Outwardly he conformed and submitted. Inwardly he was a rebel.

He sat on silent for a few minutes when his friend had left him, gradually recovering balance. He knew his own peril well enough, but he was not yet certain enough of his own standpoint—and perhaps not courageous enough—to risk all by declaring it. He felt helpless and powerless—like a child in a new school—before the tremendous forces in whose presence he found himself. For the present, at least, he knew that he must obey.

II

"You will be astonished at Ireland," said Father Jervis a few hours later, as they sat together in the little lighted cabin on their way across England. "You know, of course, the general outlines?"

Monsignor roused himself.

"I know it's the Contemplative Monastery of Europe," he said.

"Just so. It's also the mental hospital of Europe. You see it's very favorably placed. None of the great lines of volors pass over it now. It's entirely secluded from the world. Of course there are the secular business centers of the country, as they always were, in north and south—Dublin and Belfast; they're like any other towns, only rather quieter. But outside there you might say that the whole island is one monastic enclosure. I've brought a little book on it I thought you might like to look at."

He handed a little volume out of his bag. (It was printed on the usual nickel-sheets, invented by Edison fifty years before.)

"And tonight?" asked Monsignor heavily.

"Tonight we're staying at Thurles. I made all arrangements this afternoon."

"And our program?"

Father Jervis smiled.

"That'll depend on the guest-master," he said. "We put ourselves entirely under his orders, as I told you. He'll see us tonight or tomorrow morning; and the rest is in his hands."

"What's the system?" asked Monsignor suddenly and abruptly looking at him.

"The system?"

"Yes."

Father Jervis considered.

"It's hard to put it into words," he said. "I suppose you might say that they used atmosphere and personality. They're the strongest forces we know of—far stronger, of course, than argument. It's very odd how they used to be neglected—"

"Eh?"

"Yes; until quite recently there was hardly any deliberate use of them at all. Well, now we know that they effect more than any persuasion or diet. And of course enclosed Religious naturally become experts in interior self-command, and therefore can apply these things better than anyone else."

He waved his hands vaguely and explanatorily. "It's impossible to put it into words," he said. "The very essence of it is that it can't be."

Monsignor sighed and looked drearily out of the window.

As the hours of the day had gone by it had been this dreariness that had deepened on him, after the violent emotions of the morning. It was as if he already saw himself beaten down and crushed by those forces he had begun to recognize. And even this reminder that he was passing for a few days under a tyranny that was yet more severe failed to reawaken any resentment. Inwardly the fire smoldered still red and angry; outwardly he was passive and obedient, and scarcely wished to be otherwise.

There was nothing of interest to be seen out of the window. The autumn evening was drawing in, and the far-off horizon of hills, with the rim of the sea already visible beyond it, was dark and lead-colored under the darkening sky. He thought vaguely of Dom Adrian, in that melancholy and ineffective mood that evening suggests. He had been alive at this hour last night...and now.... Well, he had passed to the secret which this world interpreted now so confidently.

They halted above Dublin, and he watched, as weeks ago at Brighton, the lighted stage swing outside the windows. He noted a couple of white-frocked monks or friars, hooded in black, standing among the rest. Then he watched the stage drop out of sight, and the lights of Dublin spin eastwards and vanish. Then he turned listlessly to the book his friend had given him, and began to read.

As he stood himself on the platform at Thurles, bag in hand (they brought no servants to Ireland), it seemed to him that already there was a certain sense of quietness about him. He told himself it was probably the result of self-suggestion. But, for all that, it seemed curiously still. Beneath he saw great buildings, flattened under the height at which he stood—court after court, it appeared, each lighted invisibly and as clear as day. Yet no figures moved across them; and in the roadways that ran here and there was no crawling stream of ant-like beings such as he had seen elsewhere. Even the officials seemed to speak in undertones; and Father Jervis said no word at all. Then, as he felt the swift dropping movement beneath his feet, he saw the great lighted ship he had just left whirl off westwards, resembling a gigantic luminous moth, yet without bell or horn to announce its journey.

He followed his friend out through the doorway of the ground-platform to which the stage descended, and into the interior of a great white car that waited—still with a strange sense of irresponsibility and heaviness. He supposed that all was well—as well as could be in a world such as this. Then he leaned back and closed his eyes. There were three or four others in the great car, he noticed; but all were silent.

He opened them again as the car stopped. But the priest beside him made no movement. He looked out and saw that the car was halted between two high walls and in front of a great arched gateway. Even as he looked the gates rolled back noiselessly and the car moved through. (The others had got out, he noticed.) It seemed, as they sped on, as if they were going through the streets of some strange dead city. All through which they passed was perfectly visible in the white artificial light. Now they ran between high walls; now along the side of a vast courtyard; now a structure resembling the side of a cloister slid by them swiftly and steadily—gone again in an instant. It was not until afterwards that he realized that there had hardly been one window to be seen; and not one living being.

And then at last the car stopped, and a monk in brown opened the door of the car.

III

Monsignor woke next morning, already conscious of a certain sense of well-being, and looked around the little white room in which he lay, agreeably expectant.

Last night had helped to soothe him a little. He had supped with his friend in a small parlor downstairs, after having been warned not to speak, except in case of absolute necessity, to the lay brother who waited on them; and after supper had had explained to him more at length what the object of the expedition really was. It was the custom, he heard, for persons suffering from overstrain or depression, whether physical, mental, or spiritual, to come across to Ireland to one of those Religious Houses with which the whole country was covered. The only thing demanded of these retreatants was that they should obey, absolutely and implicitly, the directions given to them during their stay, and that their stay should not be less than for three full days.

"We shall not meet after tonight," said Father Jervis, smiling. "I shall be under as strict orders as you."

After they had parted for the night, the man who had lost his memory had studied the little book given to him, and had learned more or less the system under which Ireland lay. The whole island, he learned, was the absolute and inalienable possession, held under European guarantees, of the enclosed Religious Orders, with whose dominion no interference was allowed. All the business offices of the country and the ports of the enormous agricultural industries were concentrated in Dublin and Belfast; the rest of the island was cultivated, ruled, and cared for by the monks themselves. (He read drearily through the pages of statistics showing how once again, as in medieval days, under the labor of monks the land had blossomed out into material prosperity; and how this prosperity still increased, year by year, beyond all reckoning.) Of men, there were the Carthusians, the Carmelites, the Trappists, and certain sections of Benedictines; of women, there were the Carmelites, the Poor Clares, the Augustinian canonesses, and certain other Benedictines. Special arrangements between these regulated the division of the land and of the responsibilities; and the Central Council consisted of the Procurators and other representatives of the various bodies.

In return for the possession of the land, and for the protection guaranteed by the European governments, one, and one only demand was made—namely, that a certain accommodation should be offered—the amount determined by agreement year by year—both for these Retreat-houses in general, and for what were called "Hospitals of God" in particular. These hospitals were nothing else in reality than enormous establishments for the treatment of the mentally unbalanced; for it had been found by recent experience that the atmosphere supremely successful in such cases—especially those of certain well-marked types—was the atmosphere of the strongest and most intense religion. Statistics had shown without a doubt that, even apart from cases of actual possession (a phenomenon perfectly recognized now by all scientists), minds that were merely weak or subject to neutral delusions recovered incalculably more quickly and surely in the atmosphere of a Religious House than in any other. These cases, too, were isolated with the greatest care, owing to the extraordinary discoveries recently made, and verified over and over again, in the realm of "mental infection."

So Monsignor had learned last night; and as he lay in his little white room this morning, waiting for the instructions that he had been informed would arrive before he need get up, it seemed that even to his own tortured brain some breath of relief had already come. The world seemed perfectly still. Once from far away he heard the note of a single deep-toned bell; but, for the rest, there was silence. There was no footstep in the house, no footstep outside. From where he lay he could see out through his low window into a tiny windowless court, white like his own room, except where the level lawn ran to the foot of the wall and a row of tawny autumn flowers rose against it. Above the white carved parapet opposite ran skeins of delicate cloud against the soft blue sky. It was strange, he thought, to be conscious in this utter solitude and silence of an incomparable peace.

When he opened his eyes again, he saw that the hooded lay brother had come in while he dozed, and had begun to set the room to rights. A door, white like the wall, which he had not noticed last night, stood open opposite his bed, and he caught sight of a tiny bathroom beyond. A little fire of wood was leaping in the white-tiled chimney;

and before it stood a table. The window, too, was set open, and the pleasant autumn air streamed in.

Then the brother came up to the bedside, his face invisible under the peaked hood that hung over it. He uttered a sentence or two in Latin, bidding him get up and dress. He was not to say Mass this morning. "Father" would come in as soon as he had breakfasted and give him his instructions for the day. That was all.

Monsignor got out of bed and went into the bathroom, where his clothes were already arrayed.

When he came back a quarter of an hour later, he found a tray set out with simple food and milk on the table beside the fire. As he finished and said grace the door opened noiselessly, and a priest in the Carthusian habit came in, closing the door behind him.

IV

As the two faced one another for an instant, the Englishman perceived in a glance that this monk was one of the most impressive-looking men he had ever set eyes on. He was well over six feet in height, and, in his rough, clumsy white dress he seemed enormously muscular and powerful. He carried himself loosely, with an air of strength, almost swinging in his gait. But it was his face that above all was remarkable. His hood lay back on his shoulders, and from its folds rose his strong throat and head, all as hairless as a statue's; and as the priest glanced at him he saw that strange suggestion as of a bird's head that some types convey. His nose was long, thin, and curved; his lips colorless and compressed; his cheeks modeled in folds and hollows over the bones beneath; and his eyes, of an extraordinarily light gray, looked out under straight upper lids, as of an eagle.

So much for the physical side.

But, stranger than all this, was the unmistakable atmosphere that seemed to enter with him—an atmosphere that from one side produced a sense of great fear and helplessness, and on the other of a kind of security. In an instant Monsignor felt as a wounded child might feel in the presence of a surgeon. And, throughout the interview that followed, this sensation deepened incalculably.

The man said nothing—not even a word of greeting—as he came across the room. He just inclined his head a little, with a grave and businesslike courtesy, and waved the other back into his chair. Then, still standing himself, he began to speak in a deep but quite quiet voice, and very slowly and distinctly.

"You understand, Monsignor, the terms on which you are here? Yes. Very well. I do not wish you to say Mass until your last morning. I have spoken to Father Jervis about you.

"Meanwhile, for today you are at liberty to walk in the court outside as much as you wish, to read as you wish—in fact, to occupy yourself as you like in this room, the ambulatory downstairs, the roof overhead, and the garden. You are to write no letters, and to speak to no one. You will have your meals in the next room alone, where you will also find a few books. I wish you to get as quiet and controlled as you can. Tomorrow morning I will come in again at the same time and give you further directions. You will find a tribune opening out at the end of this corridor, looking into a chapel where the Blessed Sacrament is reserved. But I do not wish you to spend there more than one hour in the course of the day."

The monk was silent again, and did not even raise his eyes. Monsignor said nothing. There was really nothing to say. He felt entirely powerless, and not even desirous to speak. He understood that to obey was simply inevitable, and that silence was what was wished.

"I do not wish you to rehearse at all what you intend to say to me tomorrow," went on the monk suddenly. "You are here to show me yourself and your wounds, and there must be no false shame. You will say what you feel tomorrow, and I shall say what I think. I wish you a happy retreat."

Then, again without a word, but with that same inclination of his head, he went swiftly across the room and was gone.

It was all completely unexpected, and Monsignor sat a few minutes astonished, without moving. He had not uttered a syllable; and yet, in a sense, that seemed quite natural. He had seen the monk look at him keenly as he came in, and was aware that that had been the inspection by some new kind of expert. Probably the monk had heard the outlines of the case from Father Jervis, and had just looked in this morning, not only to give his instructions, but to ratify by some peculiar kind of intuition the account he had heard. Yet the ignominy of it all did not touch him in the least. He felt more than ever like a child in the hands of an expert, and, like a child, content to be so. Conventions and the mutual little flatteries of the world outside appeared meaningless here.

He said a little office presently, and then set out to explore his ground.

The room he was in communicated with a lobby outside, from which a staircase descended to a little cloistered and glazed ambulatory opening onto the garden. Another staircase rose to a door obviously leading to the roof. Besides the bedroom door there were two others; the one which he entered first took him into a little sitting-room also looking onto the garden, and furnished simply with a table, an easy chair, and a few books; the other opened directly onto a tiny gallery looking out sideways upon a perfectly plain sanctuary, with a stone altar, a lamp, and a curtained tabernacle, which seemed to be a chapel of some church whose roof only was visible beyond a high closed screen. He knelt here a minute or two, then he passed back again to the lobby and ascended the staircase leading to the roof. He thought that from here he might form some idea as to the place in which he was.

The flat roof, tiled across, and guttered so as to allow the rain-water to escape, at first seemed closed in on all sides with walls over six feet high. Then he perceived that each wall was pierced with a tiny double window, so contrived that it was possible to see out easily and comfortably without being seen. He went straight to one of these and looked through. As far as he could see stretched what looked like the roofs of a great town, for the most part flattish, but broken here and there, and especially towards the horizon, by tall buildings pierced with windows, and in three or four cases by church towers. Immediately beneath him lay a vast courtyard like that of a college, with a cluster of elms, ruddy with autumn colors, in the midst of the central lawn. There was no human being in sight on this side; the roofs, many of them parapeted like his own, stretched out into the distance, their ranks here and there broken by lines which appeared to indicate roadways running beneath. He saw a couple of cats on the grass below.

On all sides, as he went from window to window of the little roofless room, there was the same kind of prospect. In one direction he thought he recognized the way he must have come last night; and, looking more carefully, noticed that the town seemed to be less extended. Half a mile away the roofs ceased, standing up against a mass of foliage that blotted out all beyond. It was here that he caught sight of a man—a white figure that crossed a patch of road that curved into sight and out again. It was extraordinarily still in this religious town.

Certainly there were a few sounds; a noise of far off hammering came from somewhere and presently ceased. Once he heard a door close and footsteps on stone that faded into silence; once he heard the cry of a cat, three or four times repeated; and once, all together, from every direction at once, sounded bells, each striking one stroke.

He began to walk up and down after a while, marveling, trying to reconstruct his ideas once more, and to take in the astonishing system and organization whose signs were so evident about him. Certainly it was thorough and efficient. There must be countless institutions—hospitals, retreat-houses, cloisters, besides all the offices and business centers necessary for carrying on this tremendous work; and yet practically no indication of any movement or bustle made itself apparent. So far as solitude was concerned, he might be imprisoned in a dead city. And all this deepened his impressions of peace and recuperation. The silence, through his knowledge, was alive to him. There must be, almost within sound of a shout, hundreds of living persons like himself yet all intent, in some form or another, upon that same overwhelming silence in which facts could be received and relations readjusted.

Yet even this, as he reflected upon it, had certain elements of terror. Here again, under another disguise, was the force that he had feared in London, the force that had sent Dom Adrian noiselessly out of life, that proposed to deal with refractory instincts in human nature—such as manifested themselves in Socialism—as a householder might deal with a plague of mice, drastically and irresistibly; the force that moved the wheels and drove the soundless engines of that tremendous social-religious machine of which he, too, was a part. It was here, too, then; it was this that had closed him in here for three days in his tiny domicile in this great dumb city; it was this that held the whole under an invisible discipline; it was this that had looked at him out of the hawk's eyes and spoken to him through the colorless lips of the monk who had given him his instructions this morning.

Once more then his individuality began to reassert itself, and to attempt to cast off the spell even of this peace that promised relief. He became aware of an extraordinary loneliness of soul, an isolation in the deepest regions of his soul from all others. The rest of the world, it seemed, had an understanding about these matters. Father Jervis and the Carthusian, no doubt, had talked him over; they accepted as an established and self-evident philosophy this universal unity and authority; they regarded himself, who could not yet so accept it, as a spiritual, if not an actual mental invalid.

He had been brought here to be treated. Well, he would hold his own.

And then another mood comes on him—a temptation, as it seemed to him then, to fling personal responsibility overboard; to accept this tremendous claim of authority to control even the thoughts of the heart. Surely peace lay this way. To submit to this crowned and sceptered Christ; to reject forever the other—this meant relief and sanity.

He walked more and more quickly and abruptly up and down the little tiled space. He was conscious of a conflict all confused with dust and smoke. He began to hesitate as to which was the higher, even which was the tolerable course—to sink his individuality, to throw up his hands and drown, or to assert that individuality openly and defiantly, and to take the consequences.

V

HE awoke the next morning after a troubled night, conscious instantly of a sense of crisis. In one way or another, it seemed, he would have to come to a decision. The monk would be with him in less than an hour.

He dressed as before and breakfasted. Then, as the monk did not come, he went out to the tribune to pray and to prepare himself.

Ten minutes later the door opened quietly, and the lay-brother who had attended on him bowed to him as he turned, in sign that he was to come.

The monk was standing by the fireplace as he came in; he bowed very slightly. Then the two sat down.

"Tell me why you have come here, Monsignor."

The prelate moistened his lips. He was aware again of an emotion that was partly terror and partly confidence. And there was mixed with it, too, an extraordinary sense of simplicity. Conventionalities were useless here, he saw; he was expected to say what was in his heart, but at first he dared not.

"I—I was recommended to come," he said. "My friends thought I needed a little rest."

The other nodded gently. He was no longer looking straight at him, the secular priest was relieved to see.

"Yes? And what form does it take?"

Still the patient hesitated. He began a sentence or two, and stopped again.

Then the monk lifted his great head and looked straight at him.

"Be quite simple, Monsignor," he said, "you need fear nothing. You are here to be helped, are you not? Then tell me plainly."

Monsignor got up suddenly. It seemed to him that he must move about. He felt restless, as a man who has lived in twilight might feel upon coming out into sudden brilliant and healthful sunlight. He began to walk to and fro. The other said nothing, but the restless man felt that the eyes were watching and following every movement. He reflected that it was unfair to be stared at by eyes that were gray, outlined in black, and crossed by straight lids. Then he summoned his resolution.

"Father," he said, "I am unhappy altogether."

"Yes? (Sit down, please, Monsignor.)"

He sat down, and leaned his forehead on his hands.

"You are unhappy altogether," repeated the monk. "And what form does that unhappiness take?"

Monsignor lifted his face.

"Father," he said, "you know about me? You know about my history? My memory?"

"Yes, I know all that. But it is not that which makes you unhappy?"

"No," cried the priest suddenly and impulsively, "it is not that. I wish to God it were! I wish to God my memory could leave me again!"

"Quietly, please."

But the other paid no attention.

"It is…it is the world I am living in—this brutal world. Father, help me!"

The monk drew a breath and leaned back, and his movement had the effect of a call for silence. Neither spoke for a moment.

Then…

"Just tell me quite simply, from the beginning," said the monk.

VI

It was nearly half an hour later that Monsignor ended, and leaned back, at once exhausted and excited. He had said it all—he had said even more than he had previously formulated to himself. Now and then, as he paused, the monk with a word or two, or a strangely compelling look, had soothed or encouraged him. And he had told the whole thing—the sense that there was no longer any escape from Christianity, that it had dominated the world, and that it was hateful and tyrannical in its very essence. He confessed that logic was against him, that a wholly Christian society must protect itself, that he saw no way of evading the consequences that he had witnessed; and yet that his entire moral sense revolted against the arguments of his head. It seemed to him, he said in effect, as if he were held in a grip which controlled his whole sentiment; as if the universe itself were in a conspiracy against him. For there was wanting, he said, exactly that which was most characteristic of Christianity, exactly that which made it divine—a heavenly patience and readiness to suffer. The cross had been dropped by the Church, he said, and shouldered by the world.

The monk sat silent a moment or two, as motionless as he had been at the beginning. Monsignor perceived by now, even through his fierce agitation, that this man never moved except for a purpose; he made no gestures when he spoke; he turned his head or lifted his eyes only when it was necessary. Then the monk's voice began again, level and unemotional.

"A great deal of what you say, Monsignor, is merely the effect of a nervous strain. A nervous strain means that the emotional or the receptive faculties gain an undue influence over the reasonable intelligence. You admit that the logic is flawless, yet that fact does not reassure you, as it would if you were in a normal condition."

"But—"

"Wait, please, till I have done. I know what you wish to say. It is that your sense of protest is not merely sentimental, but rather moral. Is it not so?"

Monsignor nodded. It was precisely what he had wished to say.

"That is not true, however. It is true that your moral sense seems outraged, but the reason is that you have not yet all the data (the moral sense is a department of the reason, remember). You admit the logic of society's defending itself; but it seems to you that that which is, as you very properly said, the divine characteristic of Christianity—I mean, readiness to suffer rather than to inflict suffering—is absent from the world; that the cross, as you said again, has been dropped by the Church. Now, if you will reflect a moment, you will see that it is very natural that that should appear so, in a world that is Christian. It is very natural that there should not be persecution of Christians, for example, since there is no one to persecute them, and therefore that

you should see only the rights of the Church to rule and not its divine
prerogative of pain. But I suppose that if you saw the opposite, if you
were to watch the other process, and see that the Church is still able to
suffer, and to accept suffering, in a manner in which the world is never
capable of suffering, I imagine you would be reassured."

Monsignor drew a long breath.

"I thought so. Well, does not the Contemplative Life reassure
you? And are you aware that in Ireland alone there are four millions of
persons wholly devoted to the Contemplative Life? And that, so great
is the rush of vocations, the continent of Europe—"

"No," cried the priest harshly. "Voluntary suffering is not the same
thing. I…I long to see Christians suffering at the hands of the world."

"You mean that you are doubtful as to how they would bear it?"

"Yes."

The monk smiled, slowly and brilliantly, and there was a look of
such serene confidence in his face that the other was amazed.

"Well," he paused again. "Well, I take it that we have laid our
finger upon what it is that troubles you. You admit that the Church is
right to be active—"

"No—I—"

"By your *reason*, I mean, Monsignor."

"Yes," said Monsignor slowly. "By my *reason*."

"But that you are not satisfied that the Church can still suffer;
that it seems to you she has lost that which is of her very essence. If
you saw that, you would be content."

"I suppose so," said the other hesitatingly. The monk rose abruptly.

"We have talked enough for today," he said. "You will kindly
spend the rest of the day as yesterday. Do not say Mass in the morning. I will be with you at the same time."

VII

It was on the last morning of their stay at Thurles that Monsignor
had an opportunity of seeing something of the real character of the
place.

The lay monk came to him again, as he was finishing breakfast, and abruptly suggested it.

"I shall be very happy," said Monsignor.

Certainly his stay had done him good in some indefinable manner he could not altogether understand. Each morning he had talked; but there was no particular argument which he could recall that had convinced him. Indeed, the monk had told him more than once that bare intellectual arguments could do nothing except clear the ground of actual fallacies. Certainly the points had been put to him clearly and logically. He perceived now that, so far as reason was concerned, Christian society could not do otherwise than silence those who attacked the very foundations of its existence; and he also understood that this was completely another matter from the charge that men had been accustomed to bring against the Church, that she "would persecute if she had the power." For it was not the Church in any sense that used repression; it was the State that did so; and as Dom Adrian had pointed out, this "was of the very essence of all civil government." But this was not new to him. Rather his stay in Thurles had, by quieting his nervous system, made it possible for him to elect to follow his reason rather than his feelings. His feelings were as before. Still in the bottom of his consciousness he felt that the Christ which he had known was other than the Christ who now reigned on earth. But now he had been enabled to make the decision over which he had previously hesitated; he had sufficiently recovered at least so far as to go back to his work and to do what seemed to be the duty to which his reason pointed, and in action at least to ignore his feelings. This much had been done. He did not yet understand by what means.

A car waited in the little court to which the two came down. The monk beckoned him to enter, and they moved off.

"This quarter of the monastery," began the monk abruptly, "is entirely of the nature you have seen. It is composed of flats and apartments throughout, for the simple retreats such as your own. Each father who is employed in this kind of work has his round of visits to make each day."

"How many monks are there altogether, Father, in Thurles?"

"About nine thousand."

"I beg your pardon?"

"About nine thousand. Of these about six thousand live a purely Contemplative life. No monk undertakes any work of this kind until he has been professed at least fifteen years. But the regulations are too intricate to explain just now."

"Where are we going first—"

"Stay, Monsignor" (the monk interrupted him by a hand on his arm). "We are just entering the northern quarter. It is the serious cases that are dealt with here."

"Serious?"

"Yes, where there is a complete breakdown of mental powers. That building there is the first of the block of the gravest cases of all—real mania."

Monsignor leaned forward to look.

They were passing noiselessly along the side of a great square; but there was nothing to distinguish the building indicated from the rest. It just stood there, a tall pile of white stone; and the top of a campanile rose above it.

"You have worked there, Father?"

"I worked there for two years," said the monk tranquilly. "It is distressing work at first. Would you care to look in?"

Monsignor shook his head.

"Yes, it is distressing work, but there are great consolations. Two out of every three cases at least are cured, and we have a certain number of vocations from the patients."

"Vocations!"

"Certainly. Mania in the majority of cases is nothing else than possession. In fact some authorities are inclined to say that it is exceptional to find it otherwise. And in the other cases it is generally the force of an exceptionally strong will that has lost its balance, and is powerful enough to disregard all ordinary checks of reason and common sense and human emotion. Well, a character like that is capable of a good deal. Each case is, of course, completely isolated in this department as in all others. It is incredible to think that less than a hundred years ago such patients were herded together. The system now, of course, is to surround them with completely healthy conditions and completely self-restrained attendants. That gradually rebuilds the physical and nervous conditions, and exorcism is not administered until there is sufficient reserve force for the patient partly, at any rate, to cooperate."

Monsignor was silent. Again he felt bewilderment at the amazing simplicity and common sense of it all.

"I am taking you," said the monk presently, "to the central quarter—to the monastery proper. It is there that the main body of the monks lives. The church is remarkable. It is the third largest monastic church in the world. We are just entering the quarter now," he added.

Monsignor leaned forward as the air darkened, and was in time to see great gates swinging slowly together again as if to meet after the car had passed. It was still twilight as they sped on, and he perceived that they were passing with that extreme and noiseless swiftness with which they had come up some kind of tunnel lit by artificial light. Then again there was a rush of daylight and the car stopped.

"We must go on foot here," said the monk, and opened the door.

The priest, still marveling, stepped out after him, and followed through a postern door; and then, as he emerged, understood more or less the arrangement of the buildings.

He stood on the edge of an enormous courtyard, perhaps five hundred yards across. This was laid down with a lawn, crossed in every direction with paved paths. But that at which he chiefly stared was at a church whose like he had never set eyes on before. It was the sanctuary end, obviously, that faced him; the farther end ran back into the high walls, pierced here and there by low doors, with which the court was surrounded. The church itself rose perhaps two hundred feet from floor to roof. It was straight from end to end, the line broken only by a tall, severe tower at the point where it joined the wall of the court; and running around it, jutting out in a continuous block, like a platform, was a low building, plainly containing chapels. The whole was of white stone, unrelieved by carving of any kind. Enormous narrow lancet windows showed above the line of chapels, springing perhaps forty feet from the ground, and rising to a line immediately below the roof. The whole gave an impression of astounding severity and equally astounding beauty. It had the kind of beauty of a perfectly bare mountain or of an iceberg. It was graceful, and yet as strong as iron; it was cold, and yet obviously alive.

"Yes," said the monk, as they went across the court, "it is impressive, is it not? It is the monastic church proper. It can hold, if necessary, ten thousand monks. But you will see when we look in.

"The court we are now in is surrounded by cloisters. There are just nine thousand cells; there are, perhaps, fifty unoccupied now. Each cell, as you know, is a little house in itself, with three or four rooms and a garden; so we need space. The cemeteries are beyond the cloisters. We bury, as you know, in the bare earth without a coffin."

It was like the creation of a dream, thought the priest, as he walked with his guide, listening to the quiet talk. He had seen some of these facts in the book that Father Jervis had lent him; but they had meant little to him. Now he began to understand, and once more a kind of inexplicable terror began to affect him.

But as, five minutes later, he stood in the high western gallery of the church, and saw that enormous place stretching beyond calculation to where thin, clear, glass, sanctuary windows rose in a group, like snow-blades, above the white pavement before the altar; as he saw the ranks of stalls running up, tier above tier, and understood that, all told, they numbered ten thousand, one-third of them on this side of the screen, in the lay brothers' choir, and two-thirds beyond; as he imagined what it must be to watch this congregation of elect souls stream in, each with his lantern in his hand, through the countless doors that ended each little narrow gangway that disappeared among the stalls; as he pictured the thunder of the unemotional Carthusian plainsong—as he saw all this with his bodily eyes, standing silent beside the silent monk, and began little by little to take in what it all meant, and what this world must be in which such a condition of things was accepted—a world where Contemplatives at last were honored as the kings of the earth, and themselves controlled and soothed the lives of whom the world despaired; as his imagination ran out still farther, and he remembered that this was but one of innumerable houses of the kind—as he began to be aware of all this, and of what it signified as regards the civilization in which he found himself—his terror began to pass, and to give place to an awe, and to a kind of exaltation, such as neither Rome nor Lourdes nor London had been able even to suggest.

VIII

"Well?" said Father Jervis, smiling as the two met on the platform that evening, to wait for the English-bound air-ship.

Monsignor looked at him.

"I am glad I came," he said. "No, it is not all well with me, even yet. But I will try again."

The other nodded, still smiling.

"Who was the father who looked after me?" added the prelate. "He said he had talked with you."

"He is considered one of the best they have," said the other. "I asked for him specially. He hardly ever fails. You are impressed by him?"

"Oh, yes, but he did nothing particular."

"That is just it," smiled the old priest. He added after a pause, as the bell rang. "You feel ready for work again? You know what lies before you?"

Monsignor nodded slowly.

"You mean the Establishment of the Church? Yes, I am ready."

CHAPTER V

THE scheme had been in the air for nearly two years, as Monsignor learned from his papers; and for the last month or two had come more to the front than ever. But he had not realized how close it was.

It was at the end of October that the Cardinal sent for him and revealed two more facts. The first was that it was the intention of His Majesty's Government to appoint a Commission to consider once more the Establishment of Catholicism as the State religion of England; and the second was that secret negotiations had been proceeding now for the last eight months between China, Japan, the Persian Empire, and Russia, as to the formal recognition of the Pope as Arbitrator of the East.

"Both points," said the Cardinal, "are absolutely *sub sigillo* until you hear of them from other sources. And I need not tell you, Monsignor, that they have the very strongest mutual effects."

"I beg your pardon?"

"Think it over," said the Cardinal, and waved him pleasantly away.

From that time forward, as week followed week, the work became enormous. He was present at interviews of which he understood not more than one-half of the allusions; yet with that extraordinary skill of which he was made aware by the compliments of the Cardinal and of his own friends, he showed never a sign of his ignorance. Papers constantly passed under his hands, disclosing to him the elaborate preparations that had already been made on the part of the State authorities; and questions on various points of discipline were continually submitted to him, at the bearing of which he could only guess.

It seemed to him remarkable that so much fuss should be made upon what was by now almost entirely a matter of form, since by the restoration of Catholic property, recognition of Church courts, and a hundred other details, as well as by the affection of the people, the Church already enjoyed supreme power.

He put this once, lightly, to Father Jervis.

"The public is affected by forms much more than by principles," said that priest, smiling. "They have already accepted the principles; but even at the eleventh hour they might take fright at the forms."

"Do you mean it is possible that a Bill, if it was brought forward, might not pass?"

"Certainly it's possible. Otherwise, why haven't we had a Commission appointed? The Socialists aren't beaten yet. But it's not likely; or the Bill wouldn't be brought forward at all."

The prelate said nothing.

It was not until a few days before Christmas that the Cardinal was sent for.

At the beginning of the month the Commission had been appointed by an overwhelming majority in the House. The proposal had been brought forward suddenly by the Government, and with a speed and an employment of business-like methods that seemed very strange to the man who had lost his memory, and who still had hanging about him a curious atmosphere of earlier days, the Commission had dispatched an immense amount of work within three weeks.

It was impossible to know how far negotiations had got; but even the Cardinal himself was taken by surprise when he received an invitation to attend the sitting of the Commission. He sent for Monsignor Masterman at once.

"You will attend me, Monsignor, please. I shall have to appear alone, but I should like you to be at hand."

It was with very much confused emotions that Monsignor found himself, a day or two later, walking up and down a corridor in the House of Representatives. He had arrived with the Cardinal, had gone up the broad staircase behind him, and had followed him even into the committee room. A long table faced him as he entered, and he noticed with an odd little thrill how every man sitting there, from the white-faced, white-haired man at the head, down to the clean-shaven, clever-looking young man nearest the door, had risen as the two ecclesiastics came in. The table, he noticed, was strewed with papers. An empty chair stood at the lower end of the table—a red chair, he saw, with gilded wood.

The Cardinal sat down. The rest sat down, all in silence. Monsignor placed the dispatch-box in front of his chief, opened it, laid a few books in order, and went out.

Even now, in spite of all the knowledge that he had, and the constant contemplation of the cold facts of the case, it seemed to him, as on a dozen occasions before since his lapse of memory, as if life was not as real as it seemed. Somewhere, down in the very fiber of him, was an assumption that England and Catholicism were irreconcilable things—that the domination of the one meant the suppression of the other. Certainly history was against him. For more than a thousand years Church and State in England had been partners. It was but for three hundred years—and those years of confusion and of the gradual elimination of the supernatural—that the two had been at cross-purposes.

Was it not historically certain, therefore, that, should the supernatural ever be reaccepted in all its force, a partnership should again spring up between a State that needed a divine authority behind its own and the sole institution which was not afraid to stand out for the supernatural with all its consequences? Theology was against him; for if there was anything that theology thought explicitly, it was that the soul was naturally Christian, and therefore imperfect without the full Christian Revelation.

And yet, as he walked, he was annoyed. The proposed Establishment of the Church by the State appeared to him uncharacteristic of both—of the Church, since he still tended to think that she must in her essence be at war with the world; of the State, since he still tended to think that that, too, in its essence, must be at war with religion. In spite of what he had seen, he had not yet grasped with his imagination that which both experience and intellect justified as true—namely, that it is the function of the Church to guide the world, and the highest wisdom of the world to organize itself on a supernatural basis.

He walked up and down, saying nothing. At one end of the long corridor a couple of secretaries whispered together on a settee; at the other he saw passing and repassing hurrying figures that went about their business. Doors opened occasionally, and a man came out; once or twice he saluted an acquaintance. But all the while his attention remained fixed upon the door numbered "XI," behind which this quietly significant affair proceeded. The whole place seemed a very temple of stillness. The thick carpet underfoot, the noiseless doors, the admirable system of the place—all contributed to make a great solemnity.

He tried to remind himself that he was present at the making of history, but it was useless. Again and again as, with an effort, he forced the principles before his mind, his attention whirled off to a detail, to a contemplation of his chief taking his seat in the House of Lords and to the fabric of the carpet on which he walked; to the silent whisper of one of the two conversational secretaries; to a wonder as to the form of prayer with which the first professedly Catholic Parliament in England for more than four hundred years would open.

Then he checked himself, reminded himself of certain old proverbs about cups and hares, reflected that Socialism was not beaten yet (in Father Jervis's phrase), as recent events in Germany had shown.

Once as he turned at the end of the corridor furthest from the secretaries, an interesting little incident happened. A door opened abruptly, and a man coming out quickly almost ran against him. Then the man took off his hat and smiled.

"I beg your pardon, Monsignor. I can guess your business here."

Monsignor smiled, too, a little guiltily. He recognized the Socialist leader who had called on him a few months before.

"Yes, and I'm afraid you don't approve," he said.

Mr. Hardy made a little deprecatory gesture, still holding his hat in his hand.

"Oh! I'm a believer in majorities," he said. "And there's no doubt you have the majority. But—"

"Yes."

"I hope you will be merciful. That is your Gospel, you know."

"You think we have the majority?"

"Oh, certainly. The enfranchisement of women settled all that. They are always clerical, you know."

Monsignor felt the point prick him. He riposted gently.

"Well, you will have to take refuge in Germany," he said.

The face of the other changed a little; his eyelids came down just a fraction.

"That's exactly what I'm going to do, Monsignor."

"But I think there's somebody wanting you." Monsignor turned.

There was a hand beckoning him from behind a face, as if in agitation, from the entrance to door numbered "XI."

"If you'll excuse me," he said, and hurried off.

"I thought you'd like to be present at the end, Monsignor," whispered the member who had beckoned him. "The Cardinal is just speaking."

Committee room number "XI" seemed strangely quiet, as the prelate slipped in behind his friend and stood motionless. One voice was speaking; and, as he tried to catch the sense, he looked around the faces, that were all turned in his direction. He saw Mr. Manners on the extreme left.

Every man sat without moving, simply listening, it seemed, with an extraordinary attention; some leaning forward, some back, with the papers disregarded on the table. A couple of recording machines stood now in the center. Then he began to catch the words.

"I think, gentlemen," said the voice from behind the high-backed chair, "that I need say no more. We have discussed at length, and I hope to your satisfaction, the particular points on which you desired information: and my answers have brought out, I think, the essence of all the conditions on which alone the Church can accept the terms proposed.

"I wish it to be brought before the House, perfectly clearly, that in her own province the Church must be supreme. She must have an entire and undisputed right over her own doctrine and discipline; for that is at the root of her only claim to be heard. In respect to any legislation which, in her opinion, touches the eternal principles of morality—in all such things, for example, as the marriage law—her supreme authority must be respected; as well as in all those other matters of the same nature upon which you have questioned me.

"But on the other side the Church recognizes, and always will recognize, the right of a free people to govern themselves; and, not only recognizes that right, but will support it with all the power at her command. I have acknowledged that in a few instances in history ecclesiastics have interfered unduly with what did not concern them—interfered, that is, not as citizens (for that is their right, in common with all other citizens)—but in the name of religion. Now that, gentlemen, is simply a thing of the past. If secular rulers have learned by experience, so have ecclesiastical rulers. I have invited investigation into the history of the last hundred years; and I have answered those few charges that have been brought—I hope to your satisfaction." (There was a murmur of applause.) "In secular matters, therefore, the Church will be wholly on the side of liberty. Ecclesiastical authorities, for example, would be the first to welcome a repeal of legislation as regards heresy; but, on the other hand, we fully recognize the right of a secular State to protect itself, even by the death penalty, against those who threaten the existence of the sanctions at which a secular State takes its stand. We recognize her right, I say; but I do not mean by that that you will not find ecclesiastics who hold that it is, to put it mildly, a deplorable policy.

"However, I have said all this before, both in public, and now again in answer to your questions; and I think that, at any rate, so far as I am concerned, I shall not be to blame if the nation accepts the proposed change under a misapprehension.

"You see, gentlemen, the attempt that ended fifty years ago—the attempt that was called in its day Protestantism—to establish a religion which was to be secondary in any sense to the State, failed and failed lamentably, in spite of the noble lives that were spent in laboring for such a compromise. For it is the whole essence of a supernatural religion to be supreme in its own province—the very adjective asserts it; and any endeavor to compromise on this entirely vital point is in itself a denial of the principle. For a while this was not perceived. Men regarded the Christian Church—or rather, that which they took to be the Christian Church—merely, on its earthly side, as an organization comparable to a State. They did not seem to see that religion must always have a wider basis than any secular body, since it deals with eternity as well as with time, while the State, professedly, treats only of temporal things. The consequence was either conflict, whenever supernatural elements clashed with natural, or else the subservience of religion, and its consequent loss of prestige, as well as of its supernatural character. A National Church, therefore, is a contradiction in terms, since it asserts that that which is in its very nature larger than this world must yet be confined within the limits not only of this world, but even of a part of it.

"Well, I need not labor that point. You grasped it, gentlemen, even before you were good enough to ask me to give evidence before this Commission. I felt it, however, only right that such conditions should be reiterated and recorded before matters went any further.

"The Church, therefore, is perfectly content to remain as she has always remained in this country for the last four centuries—a free society governing the consciences of her children. Or she is content to take outwardly and officially that position which she has always, at least tacitly, claimed, and to reassume her civil dignity and her civil responsibilities. But she is not content to waive any of those divine rights with which her Founder endowed her, even in return for the greatest privileges; still less is she content to receive those privileges under false pretenses."

Again the low murmur of applause broke out, and three or four men shifted their positions slightly.

Monsignor was conscious again, suddenly and vividly, of that double sense of unreality and of intense drama which he had felt so often before at critical moments. It seemed to him amazing, and yet more amazingly simple, that such claims should be put in such words under such circumstances. It was astounding that such things should be said, and yet more astounding that they needed to be said, for were they not, after all, the very elements of civil and religious relations?

There was something, too, in the voice of the invisible speaker that thrilled his very heart. The tones were completely tranquil, there were no gestures, and the very force that spoke was unseen. Yet in the quiet fluency, the note of absolute assurance, there was a dominating appeal that was almost hypnotic in its effect. He had perceived this characteristic of the Cardinal often before; he had noticed it first on that occasion on which, for the first time in his knowledge, he had come into his presence, still staggered by the shock of his mental failure and recovery. But he had never appreciated the strength of the personality so clearly. The Cardinal was no orator in the ordinary sense; there was no thunder or pathos or drama in his manner. But his complete assurance and the long, gentle, incisive sentences, moving like rollers in a calm sea, were more affecting than any passion could be.

It seemed to him now the very incarnation of that spirit of the Church that at once attracted and repelled him—of its serenity, its gentleness, its reasonableness, and its irresistible force.

Then, in a slightly higher note, and with a perceptible increase of deliberation, the voice went on.

"I must add one word, gentlemen.

"I said just now that the Church was content to be as she has recently been in this country—content, that is, so long as she continues to enjoy the liberty with which England endows her. And perhaps, as her chief minister in this country, I ought to say no more. But, gentlemen, I am an Englishman as well as a Catholic, and I love England only less than I love the Church. I say frankly that I do love her less. No man who has any emotion that can be called religious can say otherwise. I tell you plainly that should it come to be a choice between Caesar and God—between the King and the Pope—I should throw myself at once on the side of Christ and His Vicar."

(Monsignor drew a breath. It seemed to him that this was appallingly plain speaking. He expected a murmur of remonstrance. He glanced at the faces, but there was no movement or change, except that a young member suddenly smiled, as with pleasure.)

"But I love England," went on the voice, "passionately and devotedly. And in spite of what I said just now I must add that, as an Englishman, there is but one more thing that I desire for my country, and that is that she may carry out that project on whose account you, gentlemen, have met today."

(Again a murmur of applause rose, and sank again instantly.)

"You have kindly asked me to make this little speech, and I do not wish to turn it into a sermon, but I must conclude by saying that, splendid as is the history of England in many points, there is one black blot upon the page, and that, the act of hers by which she renounced Christ's Vicar, by whom kings reign. You have done justice at last in returning to us those possessions which our forefathers dedicated to God's service. But there remains one more thing to do, formally and deliberately as one kingdom, to return to Him who is King of kings. I know it will come someday. As individuals, Englishmen have already returned to Him. But a corporate crime must be expiated by corporate reparation, and it is that reparation which has already waited too long. I am an old man, gentlemen. That, no doubt, is why I have been so verbose, but my one prayer for the last thirty years has been that the corporate reparation may be made within my own lifetime."

The voice suddenly trembled.

Then the watcher saw the chair pushed back, and the little scarlet cap covering the white hair rise above it. Simultaneously every man rose to his feet.

"That is all, gentlemen."

There was a moment's silence.

Then the applause broke out. It was not loud or noisy, as there were scarcely two dozen men in the room, yet it was astonishingly affecting, just the tapping of hands on the table and a murmur of voices.

The Cardinal silenced it by a gesture.

"One word, gentlemen. I have said nothing of any opposition. Perhaps it would have been better if I had. But I will only say this, and it is something of a warning, too. I do not believe that this Bill that is spoken of will necessarily mean peace. I am aware of the dangers that are threatening; perhaps I am even more aware of them than any other person present. And yet, for all that, I am not in favor of delay."

He turned suddenly, and with his long smooth step was at the door almost before Monsignor had time to open it and step aside. There was no time for any other man to speak.

The car had hardly moved off from the door before Monsignor turned to his chief.

"Your Eminence," he said, "what was that about danger? I did not understand."

The thin face was a little pale with the exertions of the speech, as it turned to him in answer.

"I will tell you that," he said, "as soon as the Bill becomes law."

CHAPTER VI

I

IT was an astounding scene in which Monsignor found himself, six weeks later—extraordinary from the extreme quietness of it, and the enormous importance of the issue for which they waited.

The Cardinal and he had gone down to Lord Southminster's house on the coast of Kent for three or four days to wait for the final news, as it was wished to avoid the possibility of any dangerous excitement on the night of the division; and it was thought that the Cardinal's absence might be of service in preventing any formidable demonstration at Westminster. He was to return to London, in the event of the Bill passing, on the following morning.

The situation was as follows:

A completely unexpected opposition had showed itself as soon as the Bill was announced. It was perfectly well known that this opposition was almost entirely artificial; but it was so well engineered that there was grave doubt whether it might not affect the voting in the Lower House. The Upper House, it was notorious, was practically unanimous in favor of the Bill; and there had been one or two unpleasant demonstrations outside the entrance to the Second Chamber.

The opposition was artificial—that is to say, its activities were managed after the manner of a stage-army, and the protesters were largely German; but the crowds were so great, and the genuineness of their opposition, such as it was, so obvious, that very clear signs of wavering had become apparent, even on the part of some of the more prominent Ministers of the Crown. Twice, also, during public appearances of the King, who was well known as a strong advocate of the Bill, there had been considerable disturbances amongst the crowds.

All this had come, of course, to the ears of the ecclesiastical authorities far more forcibly than the world outside suspected. There had been threatening letters; twice the Cardinal's carriage had been mobbed; a dozen well-known priests had been molested in the public streets. There had been meetings and consultations of all kinds; there had even been a moment when it seemed as if the Cardinal and the Prime Minister stood almost alone in their complete resolution. It was not that any really responsible persons contemplated the abandonment of the Bill; but a party had almost been formed for its postponement, in the hope that when once the opposition had been dissolved it would be difficult to reorganize it again. On the other hand, the resolutes stood for the assertion that just because things were really critical in Germany (in the state of affairs that followed the Emperor's conversion)—it was now the time for England to advance, that any hesitation shown now would be taken as a sign of weakness, and that the Socialists' cause would be thereby enormously advanced.

Three or four results therefore were possible, from the determination of the Government to push the Bill forward and to present it for its second reading this evening. First, it might pass triumphantly, if the leaders could succeed in inspiring their followers with confidence. Secondly, it might be rejected, if the panic spread; for, under the new parliamentary system that had succeeded fifty years ago to the old Party Government, it was impossible to reckon accurately on how members would ultimately vote. Thirdly, it might pass with a narrow majority; and in this event, it was certain that a very long delay would follow before the Upper House would have an opportunity of handing it in for the royal assent. Fourthly…well, almost anything else might happen, if the crowd, assembled in Parliament Square, and swelled every hour by new arrivals, showed itself predominantly hostile.

Lord Southminster's house needs no description. It is probably, even today, as well-known as any place in England: there is no guide book which does not give at least three or four pages to the castle, as well as a few lines to the tiny historical seaside village beneath from which the marquisate derives its name. And it was in the little dining-room that adjoined the hall that the man who had lost his memory found himself on this evening with half a dozen other men and a couple of ladies.

It was a small octagonal room, designed in one of the towers that looked out over the sea; paneled in painted wood and furnished with extreme plainness. On one side a door opened upon the three little parlors that were used when the party was small; at the back a lobby led into the old hall itself; on the third side was the door used by the servants. Lord Southminster himself was still a young man, who had not yet married. His grandfather had become a Catholic in the reign of Edward VII; and the whole house had reverted to the old religion under which it had been originally built, with the greatest ease and grace. The present owner was one of the rising politicians who were most determined to carry the Bill through; and he had already made for himself something of a reputation by his speeches in the Upper House. Monsignor had met him half a dozen times already, and thoroughly liked this fair-haired, clean-shaven young man who was such a devoted adherent of the Catholic cause.

A little silence had fallen after old Lady Southminster and her sister had gone out, and it had been curious to notice how little had been said during dinner of the event that was proceeding in London.

Half a dozen times already since they had sat down a silent man in the black gown of a secretary had slipped in with a printed slip of paper and laid it before the Marquis and then disappeared again, and it was astonishing how the conversation had ceased on the instant, as the paper was read and passed round.

Those messages had not been altogether reassuring.

The first was timed at 8:14, London, and had been read before the clock chimed the quarter-past. It ran:

MEMBERS ARE ARRIVING AFTER DINNER.
HAZELTON MOBBED IN THE SQUARE.

The second, ten minutes later, ran:

FOUR TITANIC-LINE BOATS FROM GERMANY REPORTED
IN SIGHT. CORDON OF POLICE-VOLORS COMPLETED.

The third:

MOB REPORTED DIRECTION OF HAMPSTEAD. THE PRIME
MINISTER HAS BEGUN HIS SPEECH. HOUSE FULL.

The fourth, fifth, and sixth contained abstracts from the speech
and added that it was becoming increasingly difficult to hear, owing
to the noise from outside.

Twenty minutes had now elapsed and no further message had
been received.

Monsignor looked up at the Victorian clock over the carved man-
telpiece and glanced at his host. The young man's eyes met his own.

"It's twenty-five past nine," said Lord Southminster.

The Cardinal looked up. He had not spoken for three or four
minutes, but otherwise had shown no signs of discomposure.

"And the last message was just after nine?" he said.

The other nodded.

"What time is the division expected?"

"Not before midnight. Three guns will be fired, as I said, your
Eminence, as soon as the division has taken place. We shall know
before my secretary will have time to cross the hall."

Again there was silence.

Outside the night was quiet. The village itself lay, spread out above
the beach, a hundred feet below the windows, and the only sound was
the steady lap and plash of the rollers upon the shingle. The place was
completely protected by the Southminster estate from any encroach-
ment of houses, and even the station itself lay half a mile away inland.

Monsignor looked again at the faces of those who sat with him.
Opposite was Lord Southminster himself in the ordinary quiet evening dress of his class, his guild-badge worn, as the custom was, like
a star on his left breast. His face showed nothing except an air of

attention; there was no excitement in it, nor even suspense. On his right sat the Cardinal in his scarlet. He was smiling gravely to himself, and his lips moved slightly now and then. At this moment he was playing gently with a walnut-shell that lay on his plate. The three others showed more signs of excitement. Old General Hartington, who could remember being taken to London to see the festivities at the coronation of George V, was leaning back in his chair frowning. (He had been reminiscent this evening in a rather voluble manner, but had not uttered a word now for five minutes.) The chaplain had shifted around in his chair, watching the door, and the sixth man, a cousin of the host, who, Monsignor understood, held some responsible post in the Government volor service, was sitting just now with his head in his hands.

Still no one spoke.

The cousin pushed back his chair suddenly and went to the window.

"Well, Jack?" said the host.

"Nothing…just going to have a look at the weather."

He stood there, having pulled back the curtain a little and unlatched the shutter, looking out through the glass.

Then Lord Southminster's reserve broke down.

"If it's not done tonight," he said abruptly, "God only knows— Well, well."

"It will be done tonight," said the Cardinal, still without lifting his eyes.

"Certainly, your Eminence, if nothing interferes; but how can we be sure of that? I know the Cabinet means business."

"It's half an hour since the last message," observed the General.

Lord Southminster got up suddenly and went to the lobby-door. As he went the door into the parlors opened and his mother looked in.

"Any more news, my son?"

"No, mother. I was just going to ask."

The old lady came forward as her son went out—a splendid old creature in her lace and jewels—active still and upright in spite of her years. She made a little gesture as the men offered to move, and went and leaned by the old-fashioned open fireplace, such as her husband had put in at the restoration throughout the house.

"Your Eminence, can you reassure us?" she said, smiling.

The Cardinal, too, smiled as he turned in his chair.

"I am confident the Bill will pass," he said. "But I do not know yet what the price will be."

"Your Eminence means in England? Or elsewhere?" asked the chaplain abruptly.

"In England and elsewhere, Father."

Old Lady Jane Morpeth appeared at this moment, and the two ladies sat down on the high oak sette that screened the fire from the window. They showed no signs of anxiety; but Monsignor perceived that their return at all to this room just now was significant. Simultaneously the young man came in again, closing the door behind him.

"Our inquiries are not answered," he said sharply. "We are trying to get into touch with another office."

No one spoke for a minute. Even to Monsignor, who still found it hard always to understand the communication system of the time, it was obvious that something must have happened. He knew that Southminster Castle had been put into wireless touch with the great Marconi office in Parliament Square, and that a failure to be answered meant that something unexpected had happened. But it was entirely impossible to conjecture for certain what this something might be.

"That is serious," remarked Lady Southminster, without moving a muscle.

"I suppose so," said her son, and sat down again. Then the man who was looking out of the window turned and came back into the room, latching the shutters and putting the curtains into place.

"Well, Jack?" asked the General.

"I have counted eight or nine volors," he said, "usually there are only two at this time. I went to look for them."

"Which way?"

"Three this way and five the other."

Monsignor did not dare to ask for an interpretation. But he was aware that the air of tenseness in the room tightened up still further.

The General got up.

"Southminster," he said, "I think I'll take a stroll outside if I may. One might see something, you know."

"Go up to the keep, if you like. There's a covered path most of the way up. There's a look-out there, you know. I had one set in case the wireless failed. At any rate, they may see the rockets farther along the coast."

Monsignor, too, stood up. His restlessness increased every moment, although he scarcely knew why.

"May I come with you, too?" he said. "Will your Eminence excuse me?"

II

THE two said nothing as they went out through the dimly lighted hall. Overhead hung the old banners in the high wooden roof; a great fire blazed on the hearth; and under the musician's gallery at the farther end they saw the bright little window behind which sat the secretary.

They stopped here and peered in.

He was seated with his back to them before an instrument not altogether unlike an old-fashioned organ. A long row of black keys was in front of him; and half a dozen stops protruded on either side. Before him, in the front, a glass panel protected some kind of white sheet; and as the priest looked in he could see a movement as of small bluish sparks playing upon this. He had long ago made up his mind not to attempt to understand modern machinery; and he had no kind of idea what all this meant, beyond a guess that the keys were for sending messages, and the white sheet for receiving them.

"Any news?" said the General suddenly.

The secretary did not move or answer. His hands were before him, hidden, and he appeared entirely absorbed.

It must have been a minute before he turned around, drawing out as he did so, from before him, a slip of paper like those he had already brought in. "This is from Rye, sir," he said shortly. "They, too, have lost communication with Parliament Square. That is all, sir. I must take this in at once."

The two passed on, still without speaking; and it was not until they were going slowly up the long covered staircase that ran inside the skirting wall that connected the keep with the more modern part of the castle that Monsignor began.

"I'm very ignorant," he said. "Can you tell me the possibilities?"

The General paused before answering.

"Well," he said, "the worst possibility is a riot, engineered by the Socialists. If that is successful, it means a certain delay of at least several years; and, at the worst, it means that the Socialists will increase enormously throughout Europe. And then anything may happen."

"But I thought that all real danger was past, and that the Socialists were discredited."

"Certainly, in one sense. In every country, that is to say, they are in a negligible minority. But if all these minorities are added together, they are not negligible at all. The Cabinet has produced this Bill suddenly, as of course you know, in order to prevent any large Continental demonstration, as this would certainly have a tremendous effect upon England. But it seems that they've been organizing for months. They must have known this was coming."

"And if the Socialists fail?"

"Well, then they'll make their last stand in Germany. But you know this better than I do, Monsignor?"

"I know a good deal here and there," confessed the other; "but I find it hard sometimes to combine it all. I had an illness, you know—"

"Ah, yes, yes."

They paused for breath in an embrasure in the wall, where a section of a half-tower supported the wall, itself running down onto the cliff-side. A couple of windows gave a view of the sea, now a dark gulf under the cloudy sky, sprinkled with a few moving lights, here and there, of vessels going up or down the channel.

"And suppose the Bill passes?" began the priest.

"If the Bill passes, we need fear nothing in England, if it passes with a good majority. You know Government is an extraordinarily delicate machine nowadays; and if the Bill goes through really well, it'll be an infallible sign that the country refuses to take alarm. And if it fails, or only narrowly passes—well, it'll be the other way. The whole work will have to be done again, or at least begun—"

He faced around suddenly.

"Monsignor," he said, "I wouldn't say this to everyone. But I tell you we're at a very critical moment. These Socialists are stronger than anyone dreamed. Their organization is simply perfect. Do you know any of them?"

"I have met Hardy."

"That's a brilliant man, you know."

They talked no more during the rest of the ascent, until they emerged at last onto the top of the round keep, where the old bonfires used to burn, and where the old iron cradle, used even now at coronations and great national events, still thrust up its skeleton silhouette against the pale sky. To the priest's surprise the silhouette was largely filled in. A figure came towards them, saluted, and stood waiting.

"Eh? Who's this?" snapped the soldier.

"The look-out, sir. We've orders to watch Rye."

"Why?"

"The wireless is out of communication, sir. His lordship arranged a week ago that there should be supplementary rockets."

"Where are the guns?" asked Monsignor, who was looking about him, at the empty leads, the battlemented parapet against the sky, and then back at the servant's figure.

"Down below, Father. They're to be fired from here if three white rockets go up."

While the two others still talked, the priest went to the side and looked over, again suddenly overwhelmed by the strangeness of the whole position. Once again there came on him the sense of irresponsible unreality. He stared out, hardly seeing that on which he looked: the gray mass of the lower castle beneath with lighted windows, at the blankness beyond; again with the scattered lights the nearer ones, within what seemed a stone's throw, along the village street—the farther ones, infinitely remote, out upon the invisible sea. There again, too, far off across the land, shone another cluster of lights, seen rather as a luminous patch, that marked Rye. There, too, eyes were watching; there, too, it was felt that interests were at stake, so vast and so unknown, that heaven or hell might be within their limits. He looked inland, and there, too, was darkness, but darkness unrelieved. Near at hand, immediately below the bounding walls, rose up the dark swelling outlines that he knew to be the woods of the park, crowding up against the very castle walls themselves; and beyond dimness after dimness, to meet the sky.

It seemed to him incredible, as he looked, that things of such moment should be under way, somewhere beyond that sleeping country; and yet, as his eyes grew accustomed to the night, he could make out at last a faint glow in the sky to the north that marked the outskirts of that enormous city of which he was a citizen, where such matters even now were approaching a decision.

For it was only little by little that he had become aware that a real crisis was at hand. The Cardinal had told him the facts, indeed, in the dispassionate, tolerant manner that was characteristic of him; but the point of view necessary to take them in as a coherent whole, to see them, not as isolated events, but with the effect of the past upon them and their hidden implications and probabilities for the future, this needed that the observer should be of the temper and atmosphere of the time. For prophecy just now was little better than feeling at outlines in the dark. Facts could be discerned and apprehended by all—and the priest was well aware of his own capacities in this—but their interpretation was another matter altogether. He felt helpless and muzzled.

The General came towards him.

"Well," he said, "anything to be seen?"

"Nothing."

"We may as well make our way down again. There's nothing to be gained by stopping here."

As they made their way down again through the covered passage, the General once more began to talk about the crisis.

Monsignor had heard it before; but he listened for all that. It seemed to him worthwhile to collect opinions; and this soldier's very outspoken remarks cast a sharp clarity upon the situation that the priest found useful. The establishment of the Church in England was being regarded on the continent as a kind of test case; and even more by the Anglo-Saxon countries throughout the world. In itself it was not so vast a step forward as might be thought. It would make no very radical changes in actual affairs, since the Church already enjoyed enormous influence and complete liberty. But the point was that it was being taken as a kind of symbol by both sides; and this explained on the one hand the tactics of the Government in bringing it suddenly forward, and the extraordinary zeal with which the Socialists were demonstrating against it.

"The more I think of it," said the General, "the more—"

Monsignor stepped suddenly aside into the embrasure at which they had halted on the way up.

"What's the matter?"

"I thought I saw—"

The General uttered a sharp exclamation, pressing his head over the priest's shoulder.

"That's the second," whispered the priest harshly. Together they waited, staring out together through the tall, narrow window that looked towards Rye.

Then for the third time there rose against the far-off horizon, above that faint peak of luminosity that marked where Rye watched over her marshes, a thin line of white fire, slackening its pace as it rose.

Before it had burst in sparks, there roared out overhead a deafening voice of fire and thunder, shaking the air about them, bewildering the brain. Then another. Then another.

Beneath the two as they stood, shaking with the shock, silent and open-mouthed, staring at one another, in the courtyard a door banged; then another; and then a torrent of voices and footsteps as the servants and grooms poured out of the lower doors.

III

Two hours later the two ecclesiastics sat together, on either side of the large table in the Cardinal's room. The Cardinal passed over the sheets one by one as he finished them. One set was being brought straight up here from the little office at the end of the hall. Another set, they knew, was simultaneously being read aloud by Lord South-minster in the hall below.

The guns had aroused even the most drowsy; and the whole population, village as well as castle, had poured into the courtyard to hear the news.

Monsignor sat and read sheet after sheet after his chief, hopelessly trying to notice and remember the principal points of the report. Everything was recorded there—the assembling of the crowds, the difficulty that the later members found in getting through into the House at all; the breakdown of the police arrangements; and the storming of the wireless station by an organized mob, many of whom had been later put under arrest.

Then there was the Prime Minister's speech, recorded word by word in the machines, and translated later, by machinery instead of by human labor, into terms of dots and dashes, themselves transmitted again over miles of country, and retranslated again by mechanical devices into these actual printed sheets that the two were reading.

The speech was given in full, down to that tremendous scene when half the House, distracted at last by the cries that grew nearer and nearer, and the messengers that appeared and reappeared from outside, had risen to its feet. And then the Cardinal leaned back suddenly, with a swift in-drawing of his breath that was almost the first sign of emotion that he had shown.

Monsignor looked up. The last two sheets were still under the ringed hand that lay upon the table.

"Well, it's done," said the Cardinal softly, almost as if talking to himself. "But it needed his last card."

"Your Eminence?"

"The announcement as to the East," went on the other, with the same air. "I thank God it came in time."

"Your Eminence, I don't understand."

The Cardinal looked at him full.

"Why," he said, "the Holy Father was accepted as Arbitrator of the East by the united Powers this morning. The news was in the Prime Minister's hands at six o'clock. But I'm sorry he had to use it; it would have been stronger without. Don't you understand, Monsignor? The House would have refused to vote otherwise."

"But it's finished—it's finished, isn't it, your Eminence?"

"Yes, yes, it's finished. Or had we better say it's begun. Now the last conflict begins. Now, Monsignor, I'm afraid I must begin to dictate. Would you mind setting the phonographs?"

From the hall beneath rose a sudden confusion of cheering and stamping of feet.

✳ PART THREE ✳

CHAPTER I

I

"Monsignor," said the Cardinal, "I am afraid I shall have to ask you to go, after all. It is extremely important that the Catholic authorities in England should be represented in this scheme. And I think you will have to travel with the first batch. They leave Queenstown on the first of April."

"Certainly. And when shall I be back, your Eminence?"

"You must judge for yourself. It will not be more than a month or six weeks at the outside, and I dare say a good deal less. It will depend on the temper of the settlers. The American civil authorities will have the final arrangements. But it is exceedingly important that the emigrants should have someone to speak for them; and as, of course, the Church will be believed to be really responsible, it will be as well that an ecclesiastic should be their friend. Identify yourself with them as far as possible. The civil authorities are sure to be inclined to be hard."

"Very good, your Eminence."

The scheme had come to birth very rapidly. After the second reading of the Establishment Bill, it had been taken for granted, and rightly, that the rest was but a matter of time, and it was calculated that, considering the Government's attitude, the Bill would receive the royal assent before the end of the summer. Immediately, therefore,

the more peaceable Socialists had taken fright, and in every European
country had made representations that now that their last refuges in
Germany and England had been closed to them, some arrangement
ought to be made by which they could enjoy complete civil and religious liberty elsewhere. The idea had been in the air, of course, for a
considerable time. There had been complaints on all sides that public opinion was too strong, that Socialists, in spite of the protection
given to them, suffered a good deal in informal ways owing to their
opinions, and that some expedient would have to be found for their
relief. Then America had come to the rescue, openly and formally, and
had offered Massachusetts, which already had a large proportion of
Socialists in its population, as a colony which would be tolerated as
definitely socialistic. Christians would be warned that the new system
would, if the Powers agreed, be on definitely non-Catholic lines, and
that the emigration laws would be in future suspended with regard
to Massachusetts. There were, of course, innumerable details still to
be worked out, but by the end of February the understanding was
established, and from every European country emigrant parties were
arranged.

There was something almost attractive about the scheme to the
popular mind. It had been talked of for years before this arrangement
by which the Socialists should have an opportunity of working out
once more those old exploded democratic ideas to which they still
clung so pathetically. Every child knew, of course, how fifty years before
the experiment had been made in various places, and how appalling
tyranny had been the result—tyranny that is over those who, in the
Socialist communities, still held to Individualism. But what would
happen, the world indulgently wondered, in a community where there
were no Individualists? One of two things certainly would happen.
Either the scheme would work and every democrat be satisfied, or the
theory would be reduced to a practical absurdity and the poison would
be expelled forever from the world's system. Besides, if this asylum were
once definitely secured and guaranteed by the assent of the Powers, the
new heresy laws that were already coming to birth in Germany, that

were already enforced with considerable vigor in the Latin countries, and were (it was known) being prepared and adapted for England— these could now go forward and be applied universally, without any fear of undue severity. It would, once and for all, get rid of those endless complaints as to Christian injustice in silencing the free expression of infidel and socialistic ideas, and offer them a refuge where such things could not only be discussed, but put to the test of practice.

Monsignor Masterman himself was still in a state of personal indecision, but he certainly welcomed this solution of some of his interior troubles, and he had warmly supported the scheme at every opportunity he had.

But it was strange how he could not yet, in spite of his efforts, get rid of that deep discomfort which had been, for a time, lulled by his visit to Ireland. There was still, deep down in his mind, a sense that the Christianity he saw around him, and which he himself helped to administer, was not the religion of its Founder. There was still an instinct which he could not eradicate, telling that the essence of the Christian attitude lay in readiness to suffer. And he only saw around him, so far as the public action of the Church was concerned, a triumphant Government. He could not conceal from himself a fear that the world and the Church had, somehow or other, changed places.

However, this new scheme was, at any rate, an act both of justice and mercy, and he was very willing indeed—in fact he had actually proposed it more than once—to go himself with the first emigrants from England to Massachusetts.

II

In spite of all that he had seen on his journeys, he still found an extraordinary fascination in watching the scene at Queenstown, as the great Olympic-line volors each carrying three hundred passengers, one by one made ready and left. He himself was to leave in the last of the four.

From the stage erected at the end of the long headland to the south of the town, he could see the harbor on the right, closed in by the city itself, rising up from the water's edge to the huge cathedral, finished fifty years before; and on his left the open sea. It was a brilliant spring morning; the air, just charged with moisture and soaked by sunlight, was a radiant medium through which the city sparkled on one side and the long, low rollers shone on the other, discharging themselves against the foot of the rocks four hundred feet below where he stood. Sea-birds wheeled and screamed about him, tilting and sliding up the slopes of the fresh west wind; but he noticed that as the first volor detached itself and slid out over the sea, pausing for an instant to head around to the compass, as if by magic every bird was gone: he could see them far away, white dots skimming inland as if for protection.

These transatlantic volors were incalculably in advance of any he had seen before. He turned, as the first moved out, its long upper and lower decks lined with watching, silent faces—of whom the great majority were those of men—and asked for a little information from the genial Irish canon who had come from the cathedral with him, to see him start.

"They are eight hundred feet long," he said, "and limited to three hundred passengers. Of course there's the crew and stewards besides. The crossing varies from thirty-six to forty-eight hours…. Yes, transhipments are sometimes made during the voyage; but it's not usual. It involves a good deal of delay."

Monsignor listened as the talk went on, gathering a few facts here and there—the reason why Queenstown was still retained, as in the days of the old steamships, for a principal port, in spite of the transformation of Ireland; the total weight of the boats when the gas was out of them; above all, the incredible speed that could be attained and kept up, with a good following wind. He learned also how, by the very rigid laws of air-way, enforced now by all nations under very heavy penalties, the danger of collisions was practically abolished; and so forth. The canon talked fluently and well; but the mass of new information was so great, and the interest of watching so intense, that the inquirer's attention wandered a good deal.

He was watching the crowd of emigrants, two hundred feet below on the ground, seen through the spidery framework of the stage, railed off into a circle, surrounded by barriers that kept out the onlookers; and diminishing visibly as he watched, as the full platforms flew up to the embarking stage just below where he stood and the empty platforms descended again. The murmur of talking came up to him like the buzz of a hive.

He understood that he was assisting at an historical event. For today practically marked, in England at any rate, the practical recognition of the two principles which up to now had been found, from their mutual irreconcilability, the cause of practically all the wars, all the revolutions, all the incessant human quarrels and conflicts, of which history was chiefly composed—their recognition and their adjustment. These two principles were the liberty of the individual and the demands of society. On one side, every man had a certain inherent right to demand freedom; on the other, the freedom of one individual was usually found to mean the servitude of another. The solution, he began to think, had arrived at last from the recognition that there were, after all, only two logical theories of government: the one, that power came from below, the other, that power came from above. The infidel, the Socialist, the materialist, the democrat, these maintained the one; the Catholic, the Monarchist, the Imperialist maintained the other. For the two, he perceived, rose ultimately from two final theories of the universe: the one was that of Monism—that all life was one, gradually realizing itself through growth and civilization; the other that of Creation—that a Transcendent God had made the world, and delegated His sovereign authority downwards through grade after grade.

So he meditated, remembering also that the former thing was rapidly disappearing from the world. These Socialist colonies were not to be eternal, after all: they were but temporary refuges for minds that were behind the age. Probably another century or two would see their disappearance.

The second and third boats started almost simultaneously, each suddenly sliding free from either side of the stage. There was a ringing of bells; one boat, he saw, shot ahead in a straight line, the other curved out southwards. He watched the second.

It resembled to his eyes a gigantic dragonfly—a long gleaming body, ribbed and lined, blazing and winking in the spring sunlight, moving in a mist of whirling wings. From the angle at which he watched its curve, it seemed now to hang suspended, diminishing to the eye, now shooting suddenly ahead. There it hung again, already a mile away, as if poised and considering, then with increasing speed it moved on and on, like a line of brilliant light; little metallic taps sounded across the water; it met the horizon, rose above it, darkened, again flashed suddenly.

He turned to look for the other; but, so far as he could see, the huge blue arc was empty. He turned again; and the third, too, was gone.

A great ringing of bells sounded suddenly beneath him.

"You've got your luggage on board, Monsignor? Well, you'd better be going on board yourself. She'll start in five minutes."

The arrival at Boston harbor was one more strange experience, and the more strange because the man who had lost his memory knew that he was coming into a civilization which, although utterly unknown to him by experience, yet had in his anticipation a curious sense of familiarity.

They had met with westerly gales, and although the movement of the ship seemed wholly unaffected (so perfect was the balancing system), yet the speed was comparatively low, and it was not until shortly before dawn on the second day that they came in sight of the American coast.

Monsignor woke early that morning, and after lying and listening for half an hour or so to the strange little sounds with which the air was full—the steady rush of wind like a long hush; the shivering of some tiny loose scale in one of the planes outside his window; a minute inexplicable tapping beneath the floor of the cabin—all those sounds so unidentifiable by the amateur, and yet so suggestive—he got up, dressed, and went across to the oratory, where he had said

Mass on the previous morning, to say his prayers. When he had finished he came out again, went upstairs, and along to the end of the ship, whence from a protected angle he could look straight ahead. The lights were all on, as the sun was not yet up, and the upper deck, except for a patrolling officer, was entirely empty.

For a while he could make out little or nothing beyond the jutting prow beneath him, itself also illuminated, and various outlines and silhouettes of devices and rigging which even now he did not properly understand. Then, as his eyes grew accustomed to the dark, he began to see.

Beneath him flitted a corrugated leaden surface, flecked occasionally with white, which he knew to be water, eight hundred feet at least below, and once he caught a glimpse of a flattened-looking, fish-shaped object, which went again in an instant, lighted interiorly, which he guessed to be a coasting steamer. Before him nothing at first was visible except an enormous gulf of gloom, but presently, as the dawn came on behind, this gulf became tinged with a very faint rosy color in its upper half, enabling him to distinguish sea from sky, and almost immediately afterwards the sea itself turned to a livid pale tinge under the glowing light.

The next thing that he noticed was that the edge of the sea against the sky began to look irregular and blotted, a little lumpy here and there, and as he looked this lumpiness grew and rose higher.

He turned as the step of an officer sounded close to him.

"That's land, I suppose?" he said.

"Yes, Father; we shall be in by half-past five. Beg your pardon, Father, are you staying long?"

Monsignor shook his head.

"That depends on a hundred things," he said.

"Curious idea this colony; but I dare say it's best."

Monsignor smiled and said nothing.

Interiorly his heart had been sinking steadily during the journey. He had mixed freely with the emigrants, and had done his best to make friends; yet there was something not only in their attitude to him—for though they were respectful enough, they were absolutely impervious to any advances, seeming to regard him as independent but rather timid children might look upon a strange schoolmaster— but in their whole atmosphere and outlook that was a very depressing change from the curious, impassive, but alert and confident air to which he had grown accustomed among the priests and people with whom he mixed. The one thing that seemed to interest them was to discuss methods of government and the internal politics of their future life in Massachusetts. They asked a few questions about crops and soil; he even heard one group in animated conversation on the subject of schools, but the talk dropped as soon as he attempted to join in it. They all talked English, too, he noticed.

Yet though the atmosphere seemed to him very ungenial, it appeared to him not altogether new; there appeared, somewhere in the back of his mind, to be even an element of sympathy. He felt almost like one who, having climbed out of a pit to the fresh air, looks back at others who not only live in the pit, but are content to live there.

For the world in which he had now consciously lived for the last twelve months was, in spite of the sharp rigidity and certitude, an inexorable logic from which he shrank, undoubtedly a place of large horizons. In fact it seemed as if there were no horizons. On all sides there stretched out illimitable space, for eternity (with its corollaries) was fully as effective in it as was time. Those with whom he mixed, however little he might share their emotions, at any rate, talked as if death was no more than an incident in life. Secretly he distrusted the reality of this confidence; but at least it appeared to be there. But with these folks all was different. These frankly made their plans for this world, and this world only. Good government, stability, good bodily health, equality in possessions and opportunities—these were their ideas of good; and better government, greater stability, more perfect health, and more uniform equality their ideals.

So he pondered, over and over again, trying to understand why it was that he was at home with neither party. With his old friends he felt himself incapable of their certitudes and aspirations; with these new people, viewed for the first time *en masse,* he felt life resting on him like a stifling blanket. He told himself bitterly that he resembled the child's amphibian, which could not live on the land and died in the water.

He watched mechanically the vault of heaven broaden and brighten with the sunrise behind, and the waste beneath presently to show lines and patches and enclosures as they approached Boston harbor. And his heart sank as each mile was passed, and as presently against the clear sky there stood up the roofs and domes and chimneys of the Socialistic Canaan.

III

IT was three or four days before he could again form any coherent picture to himself of what this new life would mean when once it was really under way.

He was lodged in the Government buildings, adapted a few years before from the old temple of the Christian Scientists; and each day in the rotunda he sat hour after hour with keen-faced Americans, and the few Europeans who had accompanied the emigration boats that now streamed in continually.

He flung himself into the dreary work, such as it was, with all his power; for though he had little responsibility, he was there as the accredited agent of the English ecclesiastical authorities, and his business was to show as much alacrity and sympathy as possible.

The city was, indeed, a scene of incredible confusion, and a very strong force of police was needed to prevent open friction between the belated and aggrieved Catholics for whom Boston would in future be impossible as a home, and who not yet had faced the need of migrating, and the new very dogmatic inhabitants who already regarded the city as their own. All legal arrangements had, of course, been made before the first emigrants set foot on the continent; but the redistribution of the city, the sale of farms, the settling of intolerable disputes between various nationalities—all these things, sifted although they were through agents and officials, yet came up to the

central board in sufficient numbers to occupy the members for a full
nine hours a day.

It was at the end of the fourth day that Monsignor went around
the city in a car, partly to get some air, and partly to see for himself
how things were settling down.

Of course, as he told himself afterwards, he scarcely had a fair
opportunity of judging how a Socialist State would be when the
machinery was in running order. Yet it seemed to him that, making
all allowances for confusion and noise and choked streets and the
rest, underneath it all was a spirit strangely and drearily unlike that to
which he was becoming accustomed in Europe. The very faces of the
people seemed different.

He stopped for a while in the quarter to which the English had
been assigned—that which in old Boston had been, he learned, the Italian quarter. Here, in the little square where he halted, everything was
surprisingly in order. The open space, paved with concrete, was unoccupied by any signs of moving in; the houses were trim and neat, newly
painted for the most part; and people seemed to be going about their
business with an air of quiet orderliness. Certainly American arrangements, he thought, were marvelously efficient, enabling as they did
some fifteen hundred persons to settle down into new houses within
the space of four days. (He had learned something, while he sat on the
central board, of the elaborate system of tickets and officials and inquiry
officers by which such miraculous swiftness had been made possible.)

Here at least they were an orderly population, going in and out of
the houses, visiting in one corner of the square the vast general store
that had been provided beforehand, presenting their pledges, which,
at any rate for the present, were to take the place of the European
money that the emigrants had brought with them.

He halted the car here, and leaning forward, began to look around
him carefully.

The first thing that struck him was a negative emotion—a sense
that something external was lacking. He presently perceived what this
was.

In European towns, one of the details to which he had become by
now altogether accustomed was the presence, in every street or square
at which he looked, of some emblem or statue or picture of a religious
nature. Here there was nothing. The straight pavements ran around
the square; the straight houses rose from them, straight-windowed
and straight-doored. All was admirably sanitary and clean and whole-
some. He could see through the windows of the house opposite the
clean walls within, the decent furniture, and the rest. But there was
absolutely nothing to give a hint of anything beyond bodily health
and sanitation and decency. In London, or Lourdes, or Rome there
would at least have been a reminder—to put it very mildly of other
possibilities than these: of a Heavenly Mother, a Suffering Man; a
hint that solid animal health was not the only conceivable ideal. It was
a tiny detail; he blamed himself for noticing it. He reminded himself
that here, at any rate, was real liberty as he had conceived it.

He began to scrutinize the faces of the passersby, sheltering himself behind his elbow that he might not be noticed—appearing as if he
were waiting for someone. Women passed by, strong-faced and business-like; men came up and passed, talking in twos or threes. He even
watched for some while a couple of children who sat gravely together
on a doorstep. (That reminded him of the meeting of tomorrow, when
certain educational matters had to be finally decided; he remembered
the proposed curriculum, sketched out in some papers that he had
to study this evening—an exceedingly sound and useful curriculum,
calculated to make the pupils satisfactorily informed persons.)

Again and again he told himself that it was fancy that made him
see in the faces of these people—people, it must be remembered, who
were not commonplace, but rather enthusiasts for their cause, since
they preferred exile to a life under the Christian system—that made
him see a kind of blankness and heaviness corresponding to that
which the aspect of their streets presented. Many of the faces were
intellectual, especially of the men—there was no doubt of that; and
all were wholesome-looking and healthy, just as this little square was
sensibly built and planned, and the houses soundly constructed.

Yet, as he looked at them *en masse,* and compared them with his general memories of the type of face that he saw in London streets, there was certainly a difference. He could conceive these people making speeches, recording votes, discussing matters of public interest with great gravity and consideration; he could conceive them distributing alms to the needy after careful and scientific inquiry, administering justice; he could imagine them even, with an effort, inflamed with political passion, denouncing, appealing. But it appeared to him (to his imagination rather, as he angrily told himself) that he could not believe them capable of any absolutely reckless crime or reckless act of virtue. They could calculate, they could plan, they had almost mechanically perfect ideas of justice; they could even love and hate after their kind. But it was inconceivable that their passion, either for good or evil, could wholly carry them away. In one word, *there was no light behind these faces,* no indication of an incomprehensible power greater than themselves, no ideal higher than that generated by the common sense of the multitude. In short, they seemed to him to have all the impassivity of the Christian atmosphere, with none of its hidden fire.

He gave the signal presently for the driver to move on, and himself leaned back in his seat with closed eyes. He felt terribly alone in a terrible world. Was the whole human race then utterly without heart? Had civilization reached such a pitch of perfection—one part through supernatural forces, and the other through human evolution—that there was no longer any room for a man with feelings and emotions and an individuality of his own? Yet he could no longer conceal from himself that the other was better than this—that it was better to be heartless through too vivid a grasp of eternal realities, than through an equally vivid grasp of earthly facts.

As he reached the door of the great buildings where he lodged, and climbed wearily out, the porter ran out, hat in hand, holding a little green form.

"Monsignor," he said, "this arrived an hour ago. We did not know where you were."

He opened it there and then. It contained half a dozen words in code. He took it upstairs with him, strangely agitated, and there deciphered it. It bade him leave everything, come instantly to Rome, and join the Cardinal.

CHAPTER II

I

THERE was dead silence on the long staircase of the Vatican, leading
up to the Cardinal Secretary's rooms, as Monsignor toiled up within
half an hour of his arrival at the stage outside the city. A car was waiting for him there, and had whirled him first to the old palace where he
had stayed nine months ago with Father Jervis; and then, on finding
that Cardinal Bellairs had been unexpectedly sent for from the Vatican, he had gone on there immediately, according to the instructions
that had been left with the *majordomo*.

He knew all now; wireless messages had streamed in hour after
hour during the flight across the Atlantic. At Naples, where the
volor had first touched land, the papers already mentioned full and
exhaustive accounts of the outbreak, with the latest reports; and by
the time that he reached Rome he was as well informed of the real
facts of the case as were any who were not in the inner circle of those
who knew.

The Swiss guard presented his fantastic halberd, as he passed in,
panting after his climb; a man in scarlet livery took his hat and cloak;
another preceded him through the first anteroom, where an ecclesiastic received him; and with this priest he passed on through the
second and third rooms up to the door of the inner chamber. The
priest pushed the door open for him and he went in alone; the door
closed noiselessly behind him. The room was the same as that which
he remembered, all gold and red damask, lighted from the roof, with
the great brass-inlaid writing table at the farther end, and the broad
settee against the right-hand wall, but it seemed to him in his apprehensiveness that the solemnity was greater and the hushed silence

even deeper. Two figures sat side by side on the settee, each in the scarlet ferraiuola of ceremony. One, Cardinal Bellairs, looked up at him and nodded, even smiling a little; the other stood up and bowed slightly, before extending his hand to be kissed. This second figure was a great personality—Italian by birth, an extraordinary linguist, a very largely made man, both stout and tall, with a head of thick and perfectly white hair. He had been a "rapabile" at the last election; and, it was thought, was certain of the papacy someday, even though it was unusual that a Secretary of State should succeed.

He had a large, well-cut face, rather yellowish in color, with very bright, half-veiled black eyes.

Monsignor kissed the ring without genuflecting, as the custom was in the Vatican, and sat down on the chair indicated.

No one spoke for a moment.

"How much have you heard, Monsignor?" asked Cardinal Bellairs abruptly.

"I have heard that the Socialists have seized Berlin and the Emperor; that the city is fortified; that there have been two massacres; and that the Emperor's life is threatened unless the Powers grant all the terms asked within four days from now."

"Have you heard of the death of Prince Otteone?"

"No, your Eminence."

"Prince Otteone was executed last night," said the Cardinal simply. "He begged to go as the representative of the Holy Father to treat for terms. They said they were not there to treat, but to grant terms. And they say that they will do the same for every envoy who does not bring a message of complete submission. That will be known everywhere by midday."

Again there was silence. The Cardinal Secretary glanced from one face to the other, as if hesitating. Monsignor made no attempt to speak. He knew that was not his business.

"Can you guess why I have sent for you, Monsignor?"

"No, your Eminence."

"I am leaving for Berlin myself tonight. The Holy Father kindly allows me to do so. I wish to leave some instructions about English affairs before I go."

For a moment the priest's mind was unable to take in all the significance of this. The Cardinal's air was of one who announces that he is going into the country for a few days. There was not the faintest sign even of excitement in his manner or voice. Before the priest could speak the Cardinal went on.

"Your Eminence, I have told you what confidence I rest in Monsignor Masterman. He has all the affairs of the English Church in his hands. And I desire that, if possible, he should be appointed Vicar-Capitular in the event of my death."

The Secretary of State bowed.

"I am sure—" he began.

"Your Eminence," cried the priest suddenly, "it's impossible…it's impossible."

The Englishman looked at him sharply.

"It is what I wish," he said.

Monsignor collected himself with a violent effort.

He could not, even afterwards, trace the exact process by which he had arrived so swiftly at his determination. He supposed it was partly the drama of the situation—the sense that big demands were in the air; partly nervous excitement; partly a certain distaste with life that was growing on him; but chiefly and foremost a passionate and devoted affection for his chief, which he had never till this instant suspected in himself. He only perceived, as clearly as in a vision, that this gallant old man must not be allowed to go alone, and that he—he who had criticized and rebelled against the brutality of the world—must go with him.

"Your Eminence," he said, "it is impossible, because I must come with you to Berlin."

The Cardinal smiled and lifted his hand, as if to an impetuous child.

"My dear fellow—"

Monsignor turned to the other. He felt cool and positive, as if a breeze had fanned away his excitement.

"You understand, your Eminence, do you not? It is impossible that the Cardinal should go alone. I am his secretary. I can arrange everything with the Rector of the English College here, if there is no one else. That is right, is it not, your Eminence?"

The Italian hesitated.

"Prince Otteone went alone—" he began.

"Exactly. And there were no witnesses. That must not happen again."

There was an obvious answer, but no one made it. Cardinal Bellairs stood up, lifting himself with his stick.

"It is very good of you," he said quietly. "I understand why you make the offer. But it is impossible. Monsignor, will you talk with His Eminence a little? There are one or two things he wishes to tell you. I have to see the Holy Father, but I will be with you again soon."

The priest stood up, too.

"I must come with you to His Holiness," he said. "I will abide by his decision."

The other shook his head, again smiling almost indulgently. Monsignor turned swiftly to the Italian.

"Your Eminence," he said, "will you get this favor for me? I must see the Holy Father after Cardinal Bellairs has seen him, since I may not go with him."

The English Cardinal turned with a little abrupt movement and stood looking at him. There was a silence.

"Well—come," he said.

II

THE contrast between these two great Princes of the Church and their Lord and Master struck Monsignor very strongly, in spite of his excitement, as he followed his chief into the Pope's room, and saw an almost startlingly commonplace man, of middle size, rise up from the table at which he was writing.

He was a Frenchman, Monsignor knew, and not an exceptional Frenchman. There was nothing sensational or even impressive about his appearance, except his white dress and insignia; and even these, upon him, seemed somehow rather tame and ordinary. His voice, when he spoke presently, was of an ordinary kind of pitch, and his speaking rather rapid; his eyes were a commonplace gray, his nose a little fleshy, and his mouth completely undistinguished. He was, in short, completely unlike the Pope of fiction and imagination; there was nothing of the Pontiff about him in his manner. He might have been a clean-shaven businessman of average ability, who had chosen to dress himself up in a white cassock and to sit in an enormous room furnished in crimson damask and gold, with chandeliers, at a rather inconvenient writing-desk. Even at this dramatic moment Monsignor found himself wondering how in the world this man had risen to the highest office on earth. (He had been the son of a postmaster in Tours, the priest remembered.) The Pope murmured an unintelligible greeting as the two, after kissing his ring, sat down beside the writing-table.

"So you have come to take your leave, your Eminence?" he began. "We should all be very grateful for your willingness to go. God will reward you."

"Plainly it must be a Cardinal this time, Holy Father," said the Englishman, smiling. "We have still four days. And one of my nationality has affinity with the Germans, and yet is not one of them, as I remarked to your Holiness last night. Besides, I am getting an old man."

There was nothing whatever of the gallant *poseur* in his manner, whatever were the words. Monsignor perceived that somehow or another these persons stood in an attitude towards death that was beyond his comprehension altogether. They spoke of it lightly and genially.

"Eh, well," said the Pope, "it is decided so. You go tonight?"

"Yes, Holy Father, it is absolutely necessary for me to arrange my affairs first. I have chartered a private volor. One of my own servants has volunteered to drive it. But there is one more matter before I receive your Holiness' instructions. This priest here, my secretary, Monsignor Masterman, wishes to come with me. I ask your Holiness to forbid that. I wish him to be Vicar-Capitular of my diocese, if possible, in the event of my death."

The Pope glanced across at the priest.

"Why do you wish to go, Monsignor? Do you understand to what you are going?"

"Holy Father, I understand everything. I wish to go because it is not right that the Cardinal should go alone. Let there be a witness this time. The Rector of the English College here can receive all necessary instructions from His Eminence and myself."

"And you, Eminence?"

"I do not wish him to go because there is no need why two should go, Holiness. One can carry the message as well as two."

There was silence for a moment. The Pope began to play with a pen that lay before him. Then Monsignor burst out again.

"Holy Father, I beg of you to let me go. I am afraid of death; that is one reason why I should go. I am crippled mentally; my memory left me a few months ago; it may leave me again, and this time helpless and useless. And it is possible that I may be of some service. Two are better than one."

For a moment the Pope said nothing. He had glanced up curiously as the priest had said that he was afraid of death. Then he had looked down again, his lips twitching slightly.

"Eh, well," he said. "You shall go if you wish it."

III

THERE was only a very small group of people collected to see the second envoy leave for Berlin. The hour and place of starting had been kept secret, on purpose to avoid a crowd; and beyond three or four from the English College, with half a dozen private friends of the Cardinal, a few servants, and perhaps a dozen passers-by who had collected below in curiosity at seeing a racing-volor attached to one of the disused flying stages on the hill behind the Vatican, no one else, in the crowds that swarmed now in the streets and squares of Rome, was even certain that an envoy was going, still less of his identity.

Monsignor found himself, ten minutes before the start, standing
alone on the alighting-stage, while the Cardinal still talked below.

As he stood there, now looking out over the city, where beneath
the still luminous sky the lights were already beginning to kindle, and
where in one or two of the larger squares he could make out the great
crowds moving to and fro—now staring at the long and polished sides
of the racing boat that swayed light as a flower with the buoyancy
of the inrushing gas—as he saw all these things with his outward
eyes, he was trying to understand something of the new impulses and
thoughts that surged through him. He could have given little or no
account of the reasons why he was here; of his hopes or fears or expec-
tations. He was as one who watches on a sheet shadow figures whirl
past confusedly, catching a glimpse here of a face or body, now of a
fragmentary movement, that appeared to have some meaning—yet
grasping nothing of the intention or plan of the whole. Or, even better, he was as one caught in a mill-race, tossed along and battered, yet
feeling nothing acutely, curious indeed as to what the end would be,
and why it had had a beginning, yet fundamentally unconcerned. The
thing was so: there was no more to be said. He knew that it was necessary that he should be here, about to start for almost certain death,
as that his soul should be inhabiting his body.

But even all these recent happenings had not as yet illuminated
him in the slightest as to the real character of the world that he found
so bewildering. He felt, vaguely, that he ought to have by now all the
pieces of the puzzle, but he was still as far as ever from being able
to fit them into a coherent whole. He just perceived this—and no
more—that the extraordinary tranquillity of these Catholics in the
presence of death was a real contribution to the problem—as much
as the dull earthliness of the Socialist colony in America. It was not
merely Dom Adrian in particular who had been willing to die without
perturbation or protest; his judges and accusers seemed just as ready
when their turn came. And he—he who had cried out at Christian
brutality, who had judged the world's system by his own and found it
wanting—he feared death; although, so far his fear had not deterred

him from facing it. He took his place in the narrow cabin in the same mood, following the Cardinal in after the last goodbyes had been said. It was a tiny place, fitted with a single padded seat on either side covered with linen and provided with pillows; a narrow table ran up the center; and strong narrow windows looked directly from the sides of the boat. A stern platform, railed in and provided with sliding glass shutters, gave room to take a few steps of exercise; but the front of the boat was entirely occupied with the driver's arrangements. It was a comparatively new type of boat, he learned from someone with whom he had talked just now, used solely for racing purposes; and its speed was such that they would find themselves in Berlin before morning.

The stern door was swung to by one who leaned from the stage. Still through the glass the Cardinal smiled out at his friends and waved his hand. Then a bell struck, a vibration ran through the boat, the stage outside lined with faces suddenly swayed and then fell into space.

The Cardinal laid his hand on the priest's knee.

"Now let us have a talk," he said.

IV

THE air that breathed down from the Alps was beginning to cloud the windows of the cabin before they had finished talking.

The man who had lost his memory, under the tremendous stress of an emotion of which he was hardly directly conscious at all—the emotion generated by the knowledge that every whistling mile that fled past brought him nearer an almost certain death—had experienced a kind of sudden collapse of his defenses such as he had never contemplated.

He had told everything straight out to this quiet, fatherly man—his terrors, his shrinking from the unfamiliar atmosphere of thought to which he had awakened, it seemed, a few months before, his sense that Christianity had lost its spirit, and, above all, the strange absence of any definite religious emotion in himself. He found this difficult to put into words; he had hardly realized it even to himself.

The Cardinal put one question.

"And yet you are facing death on the understanding that it is all true?"

"I suppose so."

"Very well, then. That is faith. You need say no more. You have been to confession?"

"This afternoon."

The old man was silent for a moment.

"As to the unreality, the feeling that the Church is heartless, I think that is natural. You had a violent mental shock in your illness. That means that your emotions are very sensitive, almost to the point of morbidness. Well, the heart of the Church is very deep, and you have not found it yet. That does not greatly matter. You must keep your *will* fixed. That is all that God asks. I think it is true that the Church is hard, in a certain sense; or shall we call it a divine strength? It is largely a matter of words. She has had that strength always. Once it nerved her to suffer; now it nerves her to rule. But I think you would find that she could suffer again."

"Your Eminence!" cried the priest lamentably. "I am beginning to see that. Yourself. Prince Otteone."

The Cardinal lifted his hand.

"Of myself we need not speak. I am an old man, and I do not expect to suffer. Prince Otteone was another matter. He was a young man, full of life; and he knew to what he was going. Well, does not his case impress you? He went quite cheerfully, you know."

The priest was silent.

"What are you thinking of, my son?"

The priest shivered a little.

"Tell me," said the Cardinal again.

"It is the Holy Father," burst out the other impulsively. "He was terrible: so unconcerned, so careless as to who lived or died."

He looked up in an agony, and saw a look almost of amusement in the old man's eyes fixed on him.

"Yes, do not be afraid," murmured the old man. "You think he was unconcerned? Well, ought he not to be? Is not that what we should expect of the Vicar of Christ?"

"Christ wept."

"Yes, yes, and his Vicar, too, has wept. I have seen it. But Christ went to death without tears."

"But...but this man is not going," cried the priest. "He is sending others. If he went himself—" He stopped suddenly; not at a sound, but at a kind of mental vibration from the other.

Up here in these heights, under the pressure of these thoughts, every nerve and fiber seemed stretched to an amazing pitch of sensitiveness. It seemed to him as if he had never before lived at such a pitch.

But the other said nothing. Once his lips opened but they closed again. He waited.

The priest said nothing.

"I think no one would expect the Holy Father to go himself under such circumstances," said the Cardinal gently. "Do you not think that it might be harder for him to remain?"

Monsignor felt a wave of disappointment. He had expected a revelation of some kind, or a vivid sentence that would make all plain.

The old man leaned forward again smiling.

"Do not be impatient and critical," he said. "It is enough that you and I are going. That should occupy us. Come, let us look through these papers again."

It was an hour later that they swept down into the French plains. The glass cleared again as they reached the warmer levels, and Monsignor became conscious of an overpowering weariness. He yawned uncontrollably once or twice. His companion laughed.

"Lie down a little, Monsignor. You have had a hard day of it. I must have some sleep, too. We must be as fresh as we can for our interview."

Monsignor said nothing. He stepped across to the other couch, and slipped off his shoes, took off his cincture, and lay down without a word. Almost before he had finished wondering at the marvelous steadiness of this flying arrow of a ship, he had sunk down into complete unconsciousness.

<h1 style="text-align:center">V</h1>

HE awoke with a start, coming up, as is common after the deep sleep of exhaustion, into a state in which, although the senses are awake, the intellect is still in a kind of paralysis of slumber. He threw his feet off the couch and sat up, staring about him. The first thing which he noticed was that the cabin was full of a pale morning light, cold and cheerless, although the shaded lights still burned in the roof. Then he saw that the Cardinal was sitting at the farther end of the opposite couch, looking intently out; that one of the glass shutters was slid back, and that a cold, foggy air was visibly pouring in past the old man's head. Then he saw the head of the driver through the glass panes in the door; his hand rested on the grip of some apparatus connected with the steering, he believed.

But beyond this there was nothing to be seen through the windows opposite, of which the curtains had been drawn back; he saw nothing but white driving mist. He tore back the curtains behind him, and there also was the mist. It was plain then that they were not at rest at any stage; and yet the slight humming vibration, of which he had been conscious before he fell asleep, and even during one or two moments of semi-wakefulness during the night, this had ceased. The car hung here, like a floating balloon, motionless, purposeless—far up out of sight of land, and an absolute silence hung around it.

He moved a little as these things began to arrange themselves in his mind, and at the movement the Cardinal turned around. He looked old and worn in this chilly light, and his unshaven chin sparkled like frost. But he spoke in his ordinary voice, without any sign of discomposure.

"So you are awake, Monsignor? I thought I would let you have your sleep out."

"What has happened? Where are we?"

"We arrived half an hour ago. They signaled to us to remain where we were until they came up."

"We have arrived!"

"Certainly. We passed the first Berlin signaling light nearly three-quarters of an hour ago. We slowed down after that, of course."

The priest turned his head suddenly and made a movement with it downwards. The Cardinal leaned forward again and peered through the open shutter.

"I think they are coming up at last," he said, drawing his head back. "Hush! Listen, Monsignor."

The priest listened with all his might. At first he heard nothing except the faint whistle of the wind somewhere in the roof. Then he heard three or four metallic noises, as if from the depths of a bottomless pit, faint and minute; and then, quite distinctly, three strokes of a bell.

The Cardinal nodded.

"They are starting," he said. "They have kept us long enough."

He slipped along the seat to where his scarlet cincture and cap lay, and began to put these on.

Monsignor sprang across and lifted down the great Roman cloak from its peg.

"You had better get ready yourself," said the Cardinal. "They will be here in a moment."

As the priest slipped on his second shoe, a sound suddenly stopped him dead for an instant. It was the sound of voices talking somewhere beneath in the fog. Then he finished, and stood up, just as there slid cautiously upwards, like a whale coming up to breathe, past the window by which the Cardinal was now standing cloaked and hatted, first a shining roof, then a row of little ventilators, and finally a line of windows against which a dozen faces were pressed. He saw them begin to stir as the scarlet of the Cardinal met their eyes.

"We can sit down again," said the old man, smiling. "The rest is a matter for the engineers."

It seemed strange afterwards to the priest how little real or active terror he felt. He was conscious of a certain sickly sensation, and of a sour-ish taste on his lips, as he licked them from time to time; but scarcely more than this, except perhaps of a sudden shivering spasm that shook him once or twice as the fog-laden breeze poured in upon him.

He sat there watching through the windows in a kind of impassivity, as much as he could see of the method by which the racing-boat was attached by long, rigid rods to the steady floating raft that had risen from beneath. (He was even interested to observe that these rigid rods were of telescopic design, and were elongated from their own interiors. One of them pushed forward once to within a foot of the windows; then the tapering end seemed to fall apart into two hooked ends, singularly like a lean finger and thumb with roughened surfaces. This, in its turn, rose out of sight, and he heard it slide along the roof overhead, till it caught some projection, and there clenched.)

So the process went on, slowly and deliberately.

The driver still remained at his post, answering once or twice questions put to him from some invisible person outside. The Cardinal still sat, motionless and silent, on the opposite seat. Then, after perhaps ten minutes' delay, a sensation of descending became perceptible.

His fear, such as it was, took a new form, as presently through the thinning fog he became aware that the earth was approaching. The first clear indication of this was the sound of a clock striking. He counted the strokes carefully, and immediately forgot what it was that he had counted. Then, as he watched with straining eyes for buildings or towers to make their appearance, the movement stopped; there was a faint jarring sensation, then the sound of tramping feet, then a heavy shock. He had forgotten that stages were used.

The Cardinal stood up.

"Come, Monsignor," he said, and gave his hand to him.

So the two stood a moment longer. Then the footsteps sounded on the boat; a shadow fell across the glass of the stern-door. The door opened, letting in a rush of foggy air, and two men in uniform came swiftly inside.

"Your name and your business, gentlemen," said the foremost shortly, in excellent English.

"I am come on behalf of the Holy Father," said the Cardinal steadily. "My name is Cardinal Bellairs. This is my secretary, Monsignor Masterman. He is not an envoy."

"Exactly," said the man. "That is all in order. You were seen by our guard-boats. Will you step this way?"

A bridge had been thrown across from the raft to the racing-boat, and the latter was now attached to an immense stage whose sides ran down into the fog. The stage-platform was crowded with men, some in official uniform, some in blouses; but a way was kept clear for the visitors, and they passed across without any actual show of hostility or resentment. Monsignor noticed but one detail—that no salutation of any kind was given; and as they took their seats in the lift, with the two officials close beside them, he heard guttural conversation break out, and, he thought, one loud laugh. The doors were latched, and the lift dropped.

The speed was so great that it would have been impossible to see anything of the town into which they descended, even had the fog been absent. As it was, Monsignor saw nothing except the sudden darkening of the air around them. Then as the speed slackened he saw the side of some great building not twenty yards away. Then the lift stopped and the doors were opened.

A group of men stood there, with something of an expectant air in their stolid faces. All these were in uniform of some description; one stood a little in advance of the rest and held a paper in his hand.

"Cardinal Bellairs?" he said, also in English. "And Monsignor Masterman?"

The Cardinal bowed.

"We had information from Rome last night. I understand you have a communication from the Powers?"

"From the Holy Father, whom the European Powers have appointed to represent them."

"It is the same thing," said the man brusquely. "The Council is waiting to receive you. Kindly follow me."

The official who had brought them down stepped forward.

"I understand, sir, that this gentleman" (he indicated the priest) "is not an envoy."

"Is that so?" asked the other.

"It is."

"Very good. I only have authority to introduce the envoy. Monsignor Masterman will be good enough to follow the other gentleman. Your Eminence, will you come with me?"

VI

On looking back afterwards on the whole experience, that which stood out as most shocking in it all, to the priest's mind, was the abominable speed with which the tragedy was accomplished. It was merciful, perhaps, that it was so, for even the half-hour or so which elapsed before the priest had any more news dragged itself to an intolerable length.

He walked up and down the little furnished room—some kind of parlor, he understood, attached to a government building seized by the revolutionaries, guarded, he knew, by a couple of men in the passage, whose voices he occasionally heard—in a sort of dull agony, far more torturing than positive objective fear.

He tried to comfort himself by retelling to himself the story of the last few days; reminding himself how, after the first outburst, when the police had been shot down by those new weapons of which he understood nothing, and the palace had been taken, and the city reduced to a state of defenseless terror—the revolutionaries had sternly repressed the second attempted massacre in a manner not unworthy of real civilization.

A great deal of the whole story was unintelligible to him. He just knew the outlines. First, it was obvious that the revolution had been planned in all its details months before. There had been, soon after the Emperor's conversion, a great access of other converts, accompanied by a dispersal to other countries, notably America, of innumerable people of the lower classes who were known as Socialists. All this was looked upon by the authorities as natural, and as actually reassuring.

There had been a few protests against the new proposals with regard to legislation; but not enough to rouse any suspicion that violence would be attempted. Finally, when the organized emigration was beginning, and even the most pessimistic politicians were beginning to regard the situation as saved, without the slightest warning the blow had been struck, obviously by the directions of an international council whose very existence had not been suspected.

As to the details of the revolution itself he was even more vague, for the understanding of it depended on an acquaintance with the internal arrangements of Berlin, by which a kind of interior citadel, not outwardly fortified in any way, yet held in its compass all those immense "power-stations" by which, in the present day, every town was defended. (He did not know exactly what these "power-stations" were, beyond the fact that they were the lineal successors of the old gunforts, and controlled an immense number of mines both within the city and without it, as well as some kind of "electric ray," which was the modern substitute for cannon.) Well, it was this "citadel," including the Emperor's palace, that had been suddenly seized by the revolutionaries, obviously by the aid of treachery. And the thing was done. It was impossible for the other Powers, or even for the German air-navy itself, to wipe the whole place out of existence, since it was known that the Emperor himself was in the hands of the rebels. (It was a bald story, as he had heard it; yet he reflected that great *coups* usually were extremely and unexpectedly simple.)

Finally, there were the terms demanded—terms which the Powers were unanimous in rejecting, since they included the formal disestablishment of the Church throughout Europe and the complete liberty of the Press, with guarantees that these should continue. The alternative to the acceptance of these terms was the execution of the Emperor and formal war declared upon Europe—a war which, of course, could have but one ending, but which, until that end came, would mean, under the new conditions of warfare, an almost unimaginable destruction of life and property, especially since (as was known) the Socialists repudiated all the international laws of warfare. The defiance was, of course, a ridiculous and a desperate one, but it was the defiance of a savage child who held all modern resources in his hands and knew how to use them. There was also possible, as some said, a rising all over the civilized world, should the movement meet with success.

So much, in brief, was what Monsignor Masterman knew. So much, indeed, was now public property all the world over, and it was not reassuring. Certainly he feared death for himself; yet, as he passed up and down, he could honestly and sincerely tell himself that this was not foremost in his mind. Rather it was a sense of bewildered shock and horror that such things could have broken in upon that orderly, disciplined world with which he had become familiar. It was this horror that hung over him—its impression deepened by the bleak April morning, the nervous strain under which he suffered, the brusque discourtesy of the men who had received him, and the knowledge that scarcely thirty-six hours before an envoy who had come alone and peaceably had been put to death in this silent city. And the horror also centered for him now, as in a symbol, in the old Cardinal whom he was learning to love.

He framed, as men do when the imagination is stimulated to the highest pitch, a dozen possible events—each seen by him mentally, clear, in a picture. He constructed for himself the Cardinal's return with news of a compromise, with an announcement at least of delay. (He knew a few of the proposals that were to be made by sanction of the Pope.) Or he saw him coming back, anxious and perturbed, with nothing decided. Or he imagined himself being sent for in haste.

And there were other pictures, more terrible; and against these he strove with all his will, telling himself that it was inconceivable that such things should be. Yet not one of his imaginings was as terrible as the event itself.

It came swift and sudden, without the faintest sign of premonition.

As he turned in his endless pacings, down at the farther end of the room, his ears for the instant filled with the clatter of some cart outside the open, barred windows, a figure came swiftly into the room, without the sound of a footstep to warn him. Behind he could make out two faces waiting.

It was the Cardinal who stood there, upright and serene as ever, with a look in his eyes that silenced the priest. He lifted his hand on which shone his great amethyst, and at the motion, scarcely knowing what he did, the priest was on his knees.

"*Benedictio Dei omnipotentis, Patris et Filii et Spiritus Sancti, descendat super te, et maneat semper.*"

That was all; not a word more.

And as the priest sprang up with a choking cry, the slender figure was gone, and the door shut.

CHAPTER III

I

ALL day long there had hung a strange silence over the city, unlike in
its quality that ordinary comparative quiet of modern towns to which
the man who had lost his memory had become by now accustomed.
He knew well by now the gentle, almost soothing hum of busy streets,
as the traffic and the footsteps went over the noiseless pavements, and
the air murmured with the clear subdued notes of the bells and the
melodious horns of the swifter vehicles; all this had something of a
reassuring quality, reminding the listener that he lived in a world of
men, active and occupied indeed, but also civilized and self-controlled.

But the silence of this inner quarter of Berlin was completely
different. Its profoundness was sinister and suggestive. Now and again
came a rapid hooting note, growing louder and more insistent, as
some car, bound on revolutionary work, tore up some street out of
sight at forty miles an hour and away again into silence. Several times
he heard voices in sharp talk pass beneath his window. Occasionally
somewhere overhead in the great buildings sounded the whir of a
lift, a footstep, the throwing up of a window. And to each sound he
listened eagerly and intently, ignorant as to whether it might not mark
the news of some fresh catastrophe, the tidings of some decision that
would precipitate his world about him.

As to the progress of events he knew nothing at all.

Since that horrible instant when the door had closed in his face
and the Cardinal had gone again as mysteriously as he had come—
now three days ago—he had heard no hint that could tell him how
things developed. He had not even dared to ask the taciturn servant
in uniform who brought him food as to the fate of the old man. For

he knew with a certainty as clear as if he had seen the dreadful thing done, that his friend and master was dead—dead, as the Revolutionary Committee had said he would be, if he came with any message other than that of submission. As to the manner of his death he dared not even conjecture. It would be swift, at least.

Ten thousand thoughts, recurring and recurring, like pictures thrown on a wall, ran past his attention as the hours went by. He saw the gathering of armaments—the horizon tinged by the gathering war-vessels of the air—the advance, the sudden storm of battle, the gigantic destruction from these vast engines of power of which he had learned nothing but their ghastly potentialities. Or he saw the advance of this desperate garrison, dispersing this way and that for their war upon the world—silent vessels, moving in the clouds, to Rome, to London, to Paris and Versailles, each capable of obliterating a city. Or he saw, again, the submission of the world to the caprice of these desperate children who feared nothing—not even death itself—who crouched like an ape in a powder-magazine, lighted match in hand, careless as to whether or no themselves died so long as the world died with them.

He formulated nothing; concluded nothing; he rejected every conjecture which temporarily constructed itself in his almost passive mind. He did not even yet fully understand that the question he had asked of himself months before—the question that had tortured him so keenly—as to whether these Christians who ruled had not forgotten how to suffer—had been answered with dreadful distinctness. He just perceived that the young Roman prince had been gallant; that the old man had been more gallant still, since those to whom he came had already proved that they would keep their word. And now the third day was drawing to an end, and by midnight suspense would be over.

The fog still hung over the city; but towards sunset it lifted a little, and he raised his heavy head from his breast as he lay, half sitting, half lying, on the tumbled sofa and blankets on which he had slept, to see the red sunlight on the wall above him. It was a curious room to a man who had grown accustomed to modern ways; there was a faded carpet on the floor, paper on the walls, and the old-fashioned electric globes hung, each on its wire, from the whitewashed ceiling. He saw that it must be a survival, or perhaps a deliberate archaism.

The sunlight crept slowly up the wall.

Then the door was unlocked from the outside, and he turned his head to see James Hardy come smiling towards him.

II

"GOOD evening, Monsignor. I am ashamed that I have not paid you a visit before. But we have been very busy these days."

He sat down without offering to shake hands. The priest saw, with one of those sudden inexplicable intuitions more certain than any acquired knowledge, two things: first, that his having been left alone for three days had been by deliberation and not carelessness and second, that this visit to him only a few hours before the time of truce expired was equally deliberate. His brain was too confused for him to draw any definite conclusion from these facts; but he made at least one provisional decision, as swift as lightning, that he must hold his tongue.

"You have had an anxious time, I am afraid," went on the other. "But so have we all. You must bear no malice, Monsignor."

The priest said nothing. He looked between his half-closed eyelids at the heavy, clean-shaven, clever face of the man who sat opposite him, the strong, capable, and rather humorous mouth, his close-cut hair turning a little gray by the ears, watching for any sign of discomposure. But there was none at all.

The man glanced up, caught his eye, and smiled a little.

"Well, I am afraid you're not altogether pleased with us. But you must bear in mind, Monsignor, that you've driven" (he corrected his phrase) "you drove us into a corner. I regret the deaths of the two envoys as much as you yourself. But we were forced to keep our word. Obviously your party did not believe us, or they would have communicated by other means. Well, we had to prove our sincerity." (He paused.) "And we shall have to prove it again tonight, it seems."

Again there was silence.

"I think you're foolish to take this line, Monsignor," went on the other briskly. "This not speaking to me, I mean. I'm quite willing to tell you all I know, if you care to ask me. I've not come to bully you or to triumph over you. And after all, you know, we might easily have treated you as an envoy, too. To be quite frank, it was I who pleaded for you. Oh, not out of any tenderness; we have got past that. You Christians have taught us that. But I thought that so long as we kept our word we need not go beyond it. And it's proved that I'm right. Aren't you curious to know why?"

The priest looked at him again.

"Well, we are going to send you back after midnight. You will have to witness the last scene, I am afraid, so that you can give a true account of it—the Emperor's death, I mean."

He paused again, waiting for an answer. Then he stood up, at last, it seemed, pricked into impatience.

"Kindly come with me, Monsignor," he said abruptly. "I have to take you before the Council."

III

It was a large hall, resembling a concert-room, into which the priest came at last, an hour later, under the escort of James Hardy and a couple of police, and he had plenty of time to observe it, as he stood waiting by the little door through which he stepped onto the back of the platform.

This platform stood at the upper end of the hall, and was set with a long semicircle of chairs and desks, as if for judges, and these were occupied by perhaps thirty persons, dressed, he saw, in dull colors, all alike. The dresses seemed curiously familiar; he supposed he must have seen them in pictures. Then he remembered a long while ago Father Jervis' telling him that the Socialists resented the modern developments in matters of costume.

The President's desk and seat were raised a little above the others, but from behind the priest could see nothing of him but his black gown and his rather long iron-gray hair; he seemed to be answering in rapid German some question that one of his colleagues had just put to him.

The rest of the hall was almost empty. A table stood at the foot of the platform, and here were three or four of the usual recording machines; a dozen men sat here, too, some writing, some listening, leaning back in their chairs. In the middle, on the opposite side of the table, stood a structure resembling a witness-box, ascended by two steps, railed in on the three other sides. A man with a pointed gray beard was leaving the box as the priest came in. Standing about the hall also were perhaps twenty other persons apparently listening to the President or waiting their turn. There were tall doors at the end of the hall, closed and guarded by police, and in the middle of each of the long sides two other doors, also closed, communicating with other rooms and passages, in one of which the priest had waited just now until the Council could see him.

Except for the rapid, heavy voice of the President the hall was very quiet, and from the very silence and motionlessness of those present there exhaled a certain air of tenseness. It would have been impossible for any intelligent person not to notice it, and for the priest, his nerves strung as they now were to an extreme pitch of sensitiveness and attention, the atmosphere was overwhelmingly significant. Of what it signified he had no idea, beyond the knowledge he already possessed—that the hours were running out, and that midnight would see a decisive event which, though it must mean ultimately the ruin of every person present, might, for all that, change the line of the world's development. A protest so desperate as this could not but have a tremendous effect upon human sentiment. He had caught a glimpse an hour before, as he whirled through the streets, far up against the luminous sky westwards, of a string of floating specks, which he knew to be the guard-boats, strung out now, night and day, in a vast circle around the city. At midnight they would surely move.

Dark had already fallen outside, but the hall was as light as day with the hidden electric burners above the cornices, and he could see not only the faces, but the very expressions that characterized them. One thing at least was common to them all—a silent, fierce excitement.

It would be about ten minutes before the priest's turn came to face the Council. It seemed that the member to whom the President was speaking was not satisfied, and question and answer, all in rapid, unintelligible German, went on without intermission. Once or twice there was a murmur of applause, and more than once the President beat his hand heavily and emphatically upon the desk before him to enforce his point. The priest guessed that the unanimity was not perhaps as perfect as the world had been given to believe. However, guessing was useless. The President leaned back at last, and Hardy stepped forward to his chair and whispered. The President nodded, and the next moment, at a sign from Hardy, the two police urged the priest forward by the arms across the platform, down the steps, and so around to the right up into the witness-box. Then the President, who had still been whispering behind his hand, turned abruptly in his chair and faced him.

Monsignor related afterwards what an extraordinary moment that had been. His nerves were already tight-stretched and his expectation was at the highest; but the face of this man who now looked at him (tremendous though he knew such a personality must be, which could conceive and drive through such a revolt as this), the face of him was beyond all imagining.

In the fashion of the day it was clean-shaven, and the absence of hair, except where that of his head framed the face, increased the impressions of those lines and shadow. It was a priestly face, saw Monsignor, with all the power and searching-ness of one who can deal with living souls; but the face of a fallen priest. In complexion it was sallow, but the sallowness of health, not of weakness; full-shaped, but without being fat; the lips were straight and thin, the nose sharp and jutting and well curved, and the black eyes blazed at him with immense power from beneath heavy brows. His hair was brushed straight back from the forehead, and fell rather long behind. The face resembled a carefully modeled mask, through the eyes of which alone the tremendous life was visible.

The priest met those eyes straight for an instant, then he lowered his own, knowing that he could not be wholly himself if he looked that man in the face.

He was surprised to hear words of English uttered. He looked up again, and there was Hardy speaking, from beside the President's chair.

"Monsignor, you would not answer me just now. Now that I am speaking in the Council's name, will you consent to do so?"

"I will answer what I think right to answer."

There was a touch of amusement in Hardy's voice as he went on.

"You need not be afraid, Monsignor. We do not extort answers by the rack. I only wished to know if you would be reasonable."

The priest said nothing.

"Very good, then. First we will tell you our intentions. At midnight, as you know, we keep our word, and the Emperor will have to go the way of the others. It is regrettable, but the Christians do not seem to understand even yet that we are in earnest. You will have to be present at that scene, I am sorry to say; but you can comfort yourself by ministering to your co-religionist. He has not had a priest admitted to him since his arrest. Immediately afterwards you will be set at liberty, and put on board the air-boat on which you traveled from Rome, with the same driver who brought you here, on one single condition. That condition is that you go straight to the Holy Father, tell him all that you have seen, and take with you one or two little objects."

He paused and beckoned to some one behind. A man came forward with a little box which he laid on the table. Hardy opened it.

"This is the box you are to take. Yes, I see that you recognize them. They are the biretta, the skull-cap, the cross, and the ring of the late Cardinal Bellairs. There are also in this box the ring and a medal belonging to the late Prince Otteone…. You will take these with you as pledges of what you say. Will you consent to do this?"

The priest bowed. For the moment he was unable to speak.

"You will also tell the Holy Father," went on the other, replacing, as he spoke, the things in the box, "what you have seen of our dispositions. You will say that you saw us entirely resolute and unafraid. We do not fear anybody, Monsignor—not anything at all; I think you understand that by now.

"You will have a letter, of course, to take with you. It will contain our final terms. Because (and I assure you that you are the first of the outside world to hear this news)—because we have decided to extend our patience for one more week. We shall, during that week, in order to prove the genuineness of our intentions, make a raid upon a certain city and, we hope, destroy it. (Naturally, I shall not inform you where that city stands.) And if, at the end of that week, our former terms are not accepted, we shall carry out our promises to the full. You may also add," he went on more deliberately, "that our party is represented in every capital of Europe, and that these may be expected to act in the same way as that in which we have acted, as soon as the week expires. We have no objection to telling you this: our plans are completely made, and no precautions on your side can hinder them. Is that clear, Monsignor?"

"Yes," said the priest.

"You are satisfied that we mean what we say?"

"Yes."

Hardy's manner changed a little. Up to now he had been speaking coldly and sharply, except where once or twice a slightly ironical tone had come into his voice. Now he bent forward a little with his hands upon the table, and his tone became a trifle friendly.

"Now there are just one or two questions that the Council wish me to put to you."

Monsignor glanced up at the circle of watching faces, and as he looked at the President, he could have sworn that a look of displeasure came over the man's face.

"Well, our first question is this (I dare say you will not answer it; but if you will oblige us, we shall be grateful): Can you tell us whether, when you left Rome, the Holy Father, or the European Powers, showed any signs of yielding?"

The priest drew a breath.

"I am absolutely sure," he said quietly, "that they had no idea of yielding, and that they never will."

"Why did they send envoys then?"

"They were willing to make other concessions."

"What were these concessions?"

Monsignor hesitated.

"I am not an envoy; I have no power to say."

"Do you know what they were?"

"Yes."

"Why will you not say? Is it not the wish of the Powers to come to terms?"

"It was their wish."

"Do you mean that it is so no longer?"

"I cannot imagine it being their wish any longer."

"Why?"

"Because you murdered the two envoys they sent," said the priest, beginning suddenly to shake all over with uncontrollable nervous excitement.

"Have you any reason for saying that?"

"I know what I would do myself under such circumstances."

"And that is—"

The priest straightened himself, and seized the rail before him to steady himself.

"I would wipe out of existence every soul that was concerned in those murders. I would have no more civilized dealings with savages."

There was a sudden movement and murmur in the circle on the platform. From the intentness with which they had followed the questions and answers, Monsignor saw that they understood English well enough. One man sprang to his feet. But simultaneously the President was on his own, and with a gesture and a sharp word or two restored order.

"That is very deplorable violence," said Hardy. "But it is most Christian."

"I am beginning to think so myself," said the priest.

"Well, well," said the other, tapping the table irritably, "we must get on—"

A door behind him, communicating with the offices behind the hall, opened suddenly as he spoke these words, and he broke off. Monsignor followed the direction of his eyes, and saw a man enter who was plainly in a state of extreme excitement. He was across the platform in three or four quick steps, and laid a paper before the President, pushing by Hardy to do so. Then he stood back abruptly and waited. The President took up the paper deliberately and read it. Then he laid it down again, and a question, too, was asked smartly in the same rapid German, and answered smartly.

Then he turned, and creasing the paper between his fingers as he spoke, uttered a sentence that brought every man to his feet.

IV

IN the confusion that followed Monsignor stood for a while disregarded. The man who had brought the message, had, after one more sentence snapped at him over the President's shoulder, vanished once more. For the rest—they were up now, forming into groups, talking excitedly, dissolving again, and reforming. Only two remained quiet—Hardy and the President; the latter still in his chair, staring out moodily, with the Englishman whispering into his ear. Then Hardy, too, stood back and stared about him. One or two men came up, but he waved them aside. Then his eyes fell upon the priest, still waiting: he slipped away from the chair, came down the steps, and beckoned to him.

Monsignor was in a whirl, but he turned and came obediently out of his place into the corner by the steps. He noticed that even those who guarded the lower doors were talking.

"There's news," whispered Hardy sharply. "Another envoy is coming. Who is it?"

The priest shook his head.

"I have no idea."

"He'll be here in ten minutes," said Hardy. "He passed the line of guard-boats five minutes ago. Monsignor—"

"Yes."

"Just come behind here a moment. I want to have a word with you."

As they crossed the platform he slipped off again to the President's chair, whispered a word to him, and returned.

"Come through here," he whispered.

Together they passed through the door at the back, and so into one of the little rooms through which they had come together half an hour before. There he closed both doors carefully and came up to the priest.

"Monsignor," he said, and hesitated.

The priest looked at him curiously. He began to see that a disclosure was coming.

"Monsignor, I have not been hard on you. I came as soon as I could."

"Well?"

"I…I don't know what's going to happen. The envoy's coming at the last hour. The Council is in a very divided state of mind. You saw that?"

"Well?"

"They're wavering. It's no use denying it. They'd accept almost anything. It's perfectly desperate. They see that now."

He was fingering the priest's sleeve by now, and his eyes were full of a pitiable anxiety.

"What do you wish me to do?"

"Well, they'll say I was responsible—if the negotiations come to anything, I mean. They'll say I urged them on. They'll sacrifice me— me and the President. They'll say they never would have gone to such lengths—what's that noise?"

Monsignor jerked his head impatiently. He began to see light.

"Well," went on the other nervously, "I want you to speak for me, if necessary—*if necessary,* you understand? You're a Christian, Monsignor. You'll stand by me."

The priest waited before answering; as the situation took shape before his eyes, he began to understand more and more clearly; and yet...

A voice called out sharply beyond the door, and Hardy leapt to the handle, beckoning with his head; and as the priest obediently followed, he gave him one more look of entreaty and opened the door.

The President stood there. The great man, more impressive than ever now, as his great height showed itself, ran his eyes slowly over the two.

"Come back to the hall," he said, so slowly that even the priest understood it, and turned.

"The envoy's coming," whispered Hardy breathlessly, as he paused before following. "You'll remember, Monsignor."

It was hardly a minute since they had left, and yet all confusion had vanished. Every man was back in his seat, with that same impassive and yet attentive air that they had worn when Monsignor first saw them. Yet, with his new knowledge, it seemed to him as if he could detect, beneath all that, something of the indecisiveness of which he had just learned. Certainly they were under admirable discipline; yet he began to see that discipline had its limitations.

The President was already in the act of sitting down, Hardy was stepping up behind him, and the priest was still hesitating by the door, when down at the lower end of the hall there was a movement among those who guarded it, the great doors opened, and a figure walked straight in, without looking to right or left.

He came on and up; and as he came the hush fell deeper. It was impossible even to see his face; he was in a long traveling cloak that fell to his feet; a traveling cap covered his head; and about his throat and face was thrown a great white scarf, such as the air-travelers often used. He came on, still without looking to right or left, walking as if he had some kind of right to be there, straight up to the witness-box, ascended the steps, and stood there for an instant motionless.

Then he unwound his scarf, lifted his cap and dropped it beside him, threw back his cloak with a single movement, and stood there—a white figure from head to foot, white capped. There was a great sigh from the men on the platform; two or three sprang to their feet, and sat down again as suddenly. Only the President did not move. Then there fell an absolute silence.

V

"Eh, well," said the Pope in delicate French. "I am arrived in time then."

He looked around from side to side, smiling and peering—this little commonplace-looking Frenchman, who had in his hand at this period of the world's history an incalculably greater power than any living being on earth had ever before wielded—Father of Princes and Kings, Arbiter of the East, Father as well as Sovereign Lord of considerably more than a thousand million souls. He stood there, utterly alone, with a single servant waiting out there, half a mile away, at the flying-stage, in the presence of the Council who in the name of the malcontents of the human race had declared war on the world of which he was now all but absolute master. No European nation could pass a law which he had not the right to veto; not one monarch claimed to hold his crown except at the hands of this man. And the East—even the pagan East—had learned at last that the Vicar of Christ was the friend of peace and progress.

And he stood here, smiling and peering at the faces.

"I come as my own envoy," said the Pope presently, adjusting his collar. "The King said, 'They will reverence My Son,' so I am come as the Vicar of that Son. You have killed my two messengers, I hear. Why have you done that?"

There was no answer. From where the priest stood he could hear labored breathing on all sides, but not a man moved or spoke.

"Eh, well, then, I have come to offer you a last opportunity of submitting peacefully. In less than an hour from now the armed truce expires. After that we shall be compelled to use force. We do not wish to use force; but society must now protect itself. I do not speak to you in the name of Christ; that name means nothing to you. So I speak in the name of society, which you profess to love. Submit, gentlemen, and let me be the bearer of the good news."

He spoke still in that absolutely quiet and conversational tone in which he had begun. One hand rested lightly on the rail before him; the other gently fingered the great cross on his breast, naturally and easily, as the priest had seen him finger it once before in his own palace. It was unthinkable that such a weight in the world's history rested on so slight a foundation. Yet for a few frozen moments no one else moved or spoke. It is probable that the scene they witnessed seemed to them unsubstantial and untrue.

Then, as the priest still stood, fascinated and overwhelmed, he noticed a movement in the great chair before him. Very slowly the President shifted his position, clasping his hands loosely before him and bending forward a little. Then a dialogue began, of which every word remained in the priest's mind as if written there. It was in French throughout, the smooth delicacy of the Pope's intonation contrasting strangely with the heavy German accent of the other.

"You come in as an envoy, sir. Do you then accept our terms?"

"I accept no terms. I offer them."

"And those?"

"Absolute and unconditional submission to myself."

"You received our notice as to the treatment of such envoys?"

(There was a rustle in the hall, but the other paid no attention.)

"But certainly."

"You come armed then—protected in some manner?"

The Pope smiled. He made a little opening gesture with his hands.

"I come as you see me; no more."

"Your armies are behind you?"

"The European air-fleets start from every quarter at midnight."

"With your consent?"

"But certainly."

"You understand that this means immeasurable bloodshed?"

"But certainly."

"You defend that?"

"My Master came bringing not peace, but a sword. But I am not here to teach theology."

"But until midnight—"

"Until midnight I am in your hands."

Again the silence fell, deeper than ever. Monsignor took his eyes off the Pope's face for an instant to glance around what he could see of the circle. All were staring steadily, some half sunk down in their seats, others stretched forward, clasping the outer edges of the desks with strained hands, all staring at this quiet white figure who faced them. He looked again at that face. If there had been in it, not merely agitation or fear, but even unusual paleness, if there had been in those hands, one of which bore the great Papal ring, not merely trembling, but even a sign of constriction or tenseness, it might well have been, thought the priest afterwards, that the scene would have ended very differently. But the naturalness and ease of the pose were absolute. He stood there, the hands lightly laid one upon the other, his face pale certainly, but not colorless. There was even a slight flush in his cheeks from his quick walk up the long hall. It was a situation in which the weight of a hair would turn the scale.

Then the President lifted his head slightly, and a tremor ran around the circle.

"I see no reason for delay," he said heavily. "Our terms are clear. This man came with the full knowledge of them and the consequences of disregarding them—"

The Pope lifted his hand.

"One instant, Mr. President—"

"I see no reason—"

"Gentlemen—"

A murmur of consent rolled around the thirty persons sitting there, so unmistakable that the man who up to now had ruled them all with a hint or gesture dropped his head again. Then the Pope went on.

"Gentlemen, I have really no more to say than that which I have said. But I beg of you to reconsider. You propose to kill me as you have killed my messengers. Well, I am at your disposal. I did not expect to live so long when I set out from Rome this morning. But, then, what will you gain? At midnight every civilized nation is in arms. And I will tell you what perhaps you do not know—that the East is supporting Europe. The Eastern fleets are actually on their way at this moment that I speak. You propose to reform society. I will not argue as to those reforms; I say only that they are too late. I will not argue as to the truth of the Christian religion. I say only that the Christian religion is already ruling this world. You kill me? My successor will reign tomorrow. You kill the Emperor; his son, now in Rome, at that moment begins to reign. Gentlemen, what do you gain? Merely this— that in days to come your names will be foul in all men's mouths. At this moment you have an opportunity to submit; in a few minutes it will be too late."

He paused a moment.

Then, to the priest's eyes, it seemed as if some subtle change passed over his face and figure. Up to now he had spoken, conversationally and quietly, as a man might speak to a company of friends. But, though he had not noticed it at the time, he remembered later how there had been gathering during his little speech a certain secret intensity and force like the kindling of a fire. In this pause it swept on and up, flushing his face with sudden color, lifting his hands as on a rising tide, breaking out suddenly in his eyes like fire, and in his voice in passion. The rest saw it, too; and in that tense atmosphere it laid hold of them as with a giant's hand; it struck their tight-strung nerves; it broke down the last barriers on which their own fears had been at work.

"My children," cried the White Father, no longer a Frenchman now, but a very Son of Man. "My children, do not break my heart! So long and hard the labor—two thousand years long—two thousand years since Christ died; and you to wreck and break the peace that comes at last; that peace into which through so great tribulations the people of God are entering at last. You say you know no God, and cannot love Him; but you know man—poor willful man—and would fling him back once more into wrath and passion and lust for blood?—those lusts from which even now he might pass to peace if it were not for you. You say that Christ is hard—that His Church is cruel, and that man must have liberty? I, too, say that man must have liberty—he was made for it; but what liberty would that be which he has not learned to use?

"My children! Have pity on men, and on me who strive to be their father. Never yet has Christ reigned on earth till now—Christ who Himself died, as I, His poor servant, am ready to die a thousand times, if men may but themselves learn to die to self and to live to Him. Have pity, then, on the world you love and hope to serve. Serve it indeed as best you can. Let us serve it together!"

There was an instant's silence.

He stood there, his hands clasped in agony upon his cross. Then he flung his hands wide in sudden, silent appeal.

There was the crash of an overturned desk; the crying out of desperate voices all together, and as from the great tower overhead there beat out the first stroke of midnight, the priest, on his knees now, saw through eyes blind with tears, figures moving and falling and kneeling towards that central form that stood there, a white pillar of royalty and sorrow, calling for the last time all the world unto him.

But the President sat still at his desk, motionless.

CHAPTER IV

I

THE sight on which the watcher's eyes rested, as he sat, hung here in motionlessness above Westminster, a hundred feet higher than the great St. Edward's Tower itself, was one not only undreamed of, but even inconceivable to me of earlier days.

For it seemed as if some vast invisible air-way had been flung straight from the midst of London, down away to the southwest horizon, where it ran into the faint summer haze thirty miles away. So level was the line held by the waiting volors on either side—vast barges, shining like silver, hung with the great state-cloths of modern days—that it appeared as if the eye itself were deceived, as if there were indeed a pavement of crystal, a river of glass, so clear as itself to be unseen, on whose surface floated this navy of a dream such as the world itself had never imagined.

Now and again, like a fly on water, there darted from one side to the other a tiny boat, in the blue and silver of the city guards, or dropped, ducked, and vanished; now and again it wheeled, and came whirling up the line, vanishing at last in the long perspective. But, for the rest, the monsters waited motionless in the sunlight, their state-cloths, hung as from the old barges, from stem to stern, as motionless as themselves, except when now and again the summer breeze stirred from the southwest, lifting the lazy streamers, wafting softly the heavy embroideries, and stirring, even as the wind stirs the wheat, the glittering giants that waited to do their Lord honor.

Opposite the air-barge where the watcher sat, perhaps a hundred yards away, floated the royal boat, between a pair of warships, one blaze of scarlet, blue, and gold, flapping out the Royal Standard of

England, and flashing the glass of the stern-cabin as the great creature
rocked gently now and again in the breeze; and upon its deck rose up
the canopy where the king and his consort sat together, and the line of
scarlet guards visible behind. On the warships on either side the crew
waited, the ship itself dressed as for a review, every man motionless
at his post, with the crash of brass sounding from the lower decks.
And so down the line the eye of the watcher went again and again,
fascinated by the beauty and the glory, down past where the great
ducal barges hung, each in order, past the officers of state, past the
Parliament barges, down to where the boats, in numbers beyond all
reckoning, faded away into the haze.

To those who looked across to where the man himself sat the
sight must have been no less amazing. For he sat here, in his new dress
of Cardinal's scarlet, on the throne of ceremony beneath his canopy
with his attendants about him, on a wide deck laid down with scarlet,
its prow crowned by the silver cross—a silent watching figure, with a
splendor of romance about him more suggestive even than the material glory that showed his newly won dignity.

There was not a soul there in those astounding crowds, whether
among those who hanging here between heaven and earth, awaited
for the ceremonial reception, the coming of him who was Vicar of one
and Lord of the other, or even among those incalculable multitudes
beneath, who packed the streets, crowded the flat roofs and looked
from every window. It was this man they knew, this tiny red figure,
sitting solitary and motionless, who, scarcely three months before had
stood before the revolutionary Council of Berlin, of his own will and
choice—who had gone there and faced what seemed a certain death,
for love of the old man whose body now lay beneath the high-altar
of the tremendous cathedral beneath, and to whose office and honors
he had succeeded, and for the sake of the message he had carried. It
was this man, alone of the whole Christian world, who after looking into the face of death, not for himself only, but for one who was
dearer to him and to that Christian world than life itself, had seen
in one moment the last storm roll away from human history forever;

who had seen with his own eyes, Christ in this Vicar—*Princeps gloriae* come at last—take the power and reign.

He, too, was conscious of all this, at least subconsciously, as he sat motionless, a figure carved in ivory, a man who had found peace at last. Here, in the contemplating train, as with his eyes he looked over the vast city of London, enormous and exquisite beyond the dreams of either the reformers or the artists of a century ago, seen as through the crystal of the summer air, as he lifted his eyes now and again to the solemn barges opposite with all that that dignity meant; above all as he looked down that immeasurable line, that roadway of a god, along which presently at least the Vicar of a God should come—all this and a thousand memories more—memories of events such as few experience in a lifetime, crowded into twelve months—passed in endless defile, coherent and consistent at last under the pointing finger of Him who had directed and evolved them all.

First, then, he saw himself, a child in knowledge, beginning life at a point where many leave it off, plunged into a world that was wholly strange and bewildering, a world which though Christian in name, seemed brutal in nature—brutal as the pagan empires were brutal, yet without the excuse of their ignorance and passion.

Yet his intellect had seemed unable to refute the conclusion of that march of events, that adherence of all ideals in a reasoned whole, that fulfillment of instincts, that play of forces, upon which, as upon a tide, Catholicism had floated to final victory in the history of mankind. Not one element had seemed wanting; and, as if to convince by sensible visions that the brain that shrank from merely argued logic, one by one he had seen for himself as in a picture lesson, and at Versailles the social problem of an individual kingdom had once more submitted to monarchy—that faulty mirror of the divine government of the world; how at Rome the stability of rival kingdoms, had found itself once more in an arbiter whose kingdom was not of this world; how finally, at Lourdes, in the widest circle of all, the very science of the world itself had found itself not confronted or opposed, but welcomed and transcended by a school of thinkers whose limitations lay only in the Infinite.

Once more then he had returned. Yet he found that the head
and the imagination are not all; that man has a heart as well; and that
this has its demands no less inexorable than those of intellect. And
it was this heart of his that had seemed outraged and silenced. For
he had found in Christianity a synthesis of ideas—a coincidence of
knowledge—which, while satisfying that head, emerged in a system
to which his heart could be no party. He had learned that "Christian
society must protect itself"; and he had seemed in this to find a denial
of the essential Christian doctrine that success comes only by defeat,
and triumph by the Cross. It had seemed to him that Christ had
accepted the taunts at last, had come down from that Cross and won
the homage only of those who did not understand Him. He had been
quieted indeed for a time, under the power of men who, whatever the
rest of the world might do, still thought that suffering was the other
part. Yet he had been quieted; not convinced.

Then he had sought a glimpse of the reverse of the picture—of
that which now seemed the sole alternative to that faith which he
feared—a glimpse only, yet full of significance. For he had seen men
to whom the better part of themselves seemed nothing; men who
walked with downcast eyes, piling mud and stones together, and fan-
cying the heap to be a very City of God.

Then, swift as grace itself, had come his answer.

He had seen men who had already all that the world could give,
men who, he had thought lusted only for power, go to an unknown
and yet a certain death for the sake of a world for which he had
thought they cared only to reign—and go with smiles and cheer-
fulness. And while he still hurried in indecision, still hesitated as to
whether this or that was the Kingdom of God—this shrinking dream
of a world sufficient to itself, or this brightening vision—then the last
light had come, and he had seen as the augur by sheer self-abnigation,
by contempt of his own life, by the all but divine power of an ordinary
man walking in grace. There had been no rhetoric in that triumph,
no promises, no intoxication of phrases, no overwhelming personality such as that which had faced him. There had been nothing but a

little quiet personage with a father's heart, who by his very fidelity to his human type, by the absolute simplicity of his presence had first climbed to the highest point that man could reach, and then by that same fidelity and simplicity, had cast himself down, and in the very hour that followed the unconditional surrender which his enemies had made, had granted them a measure of liberty such as they had never dreamed of. In the name of the Powers, whose super-lord and representative he was, he had abolished the death-penalty for opinions subversive of society or faith, substituting in its place deportation to the new American colonies; he had flung open certain positions in Catholic states hitherto tenable only on a profession of the Christian religion to all men alike; and he had guaranteed to the new colonies in America a freedom from external control and a place among civilized power such as they had never expected or asked.

This then was the new type of man who had at last conquered the world. It was not a superman that had been waited for so long, not a demigod armed with powers of light; not a man raising himself above his stature, building towers on earthly foundations that should reach to heaven; not just a man, utterly true to himself and his instincts, walking humbly before his God; looking for a city that has no foundations, coming down to him out of heaven. It was a supernature, not a superman; grace and truth transfiguring nature; not nature wrenching itself vainly towards the stature of grace. It was man who can suffer, who can reign; since he only who knows his weakness, dares to be strong. *Vicisti Galilae!*

II

SLOWLY then he had come to see that, as had been told him long before, the kingdoms of this world were already passing into the hands of a higher dominion—and this was the significance of this microcosm of those kingdoms that now lay before his bodily eyes.

There, opposite to him, in the blaze of sunlight, stood the throne that for a thousand years had faced the throne of the Fisherman, now as a Suzerain, now as a rebel—stable and fixed at last in its allegiance.

Here beneath him lay London, the finest city in the world, where, if ever anywhere, had been tried the experiment of a religion resting on the strength of a national isolation instead of a universal supernationalism; it had been tried, and found wanting. Beneath him lay his own cathedral, already blazing within like a treasure-cave, ready for its consummation, without, tranquil and strong; behind him the ancient Abbey once again in the hands of the children; far away to the right, seeming strangely near in this lucid atmosphere, hung, like a bubble, the great dome below which, as he knew, stood the first basilican altar in London, newly consecrated as a sign of its papal dignities and privileges. And beyond that again London; and yet again London, a wonderful white city, gleaming at a thousand points with cross and spire and dome and pinnacle, patched with green in square and park and open space—London come back again at last to her ancient faith and her old prosperity.

But this was not all.

For he knew and his imagination circled out wider and wider that he might take it in—he knew that Europe itself at last dwelt again with one mind in her house. There beyond the channel—across which ten minutes ago, as the thunder of guns had told him, the Arbiter of the World had come at last with his train of kings behind him—there lay the huge continent, the great plains of France, the forests of Germany, the giant tumbled debris of Switzerland, the warm and radiant coasts, the ancient world-stage of Italy, passionate Spain which never yet had wholly lost her love. There all lay, at one at last, each her own, with her own liberties and customs and traditions, yet each in the service of her neighbor, since each and all alike lay beneath the peace of God.

Still wider fled his thought. He saw to the southwards and far away westwards across the seas, how now this country, now that, flew its flag and administered its laws, yet how those flags all together saluted the Crossed Keys; how those laws, however diverse, bowed all together before the law of liberty; and how there, farther yet, already the gates of the East had rolled back, and how there peered out across half the world the patient seeking forces of those old children of earth, awakened at last to destinies greater than their own—awakened, not as men had once feared, by the thunder of Christian guns, but by the call of the Shepherd to sheep that were not of His Fold.

So there the vision lay before him—this man who had lost his memory and had found a greater gift instead.

An old priest in the white fur of a canon came gently up the deck from behind.

"Your Eminence," he said, "they have signaled up the line. I thought, perhaps—"

The new Cardinal started as one from a dream.

"What is it, Father Jervis?"

The old man looked at him closely; then he laid his hand on his arm.

"Your Eminence, the King is waiting. Do you not remember? Your Eminence was to give the signal."

Beneath, like huge voices speaking a single word all at once, roared the old guns from the Tower and Greenwich and the palaces.

The Cardinal shook his head.

"I…I forget," he said. "I was thinking. What am I to do?"

The old priest looked at him again earnestly, without speaking. Then he leaned forward closer still.

"Will your Eminence authorize me to give the signals?"

"Yes, yes, Father…anything. What am I to do? Have I to say anything?"

His eyes had a look of dawning terror in them as he glanced from side to side. The priest once again laid his hand on the lace-covered wrist and held it there steadily.

"Nothing at all, your Eminence. You have simply to sit still. I will arrange everything."

Still standing there, he turned slightly and made a sharp gesture behind the throne with his left hand. A bell sounded instantly. There was a moment's silence. Then once again a bell; and a chorus answered it.

Very slowly the Cardinal lifted his head, and saw before him the royal barge sway ever so slightly, conscious himself that through his own vessel a vibration was beginning to run as the huge engines beneath moved into action. Again roared the guns far down the river, and, as the bellow ceased, from a thousand steeples broke out the clamor of brazen tongues.

He sat still; he knew at least that this he must do. Surely this obscurity of brain would pass again in a moment. He was going to meet the Holy Father, was he not? Down there, down that road of light and air, along which now his great barge floated side by side with the King's. That was it. He remembered again now as his memory flickered in glimpses. This was the great progress around the world of the new Arbiter of the World, the Vicar of the Prince of Peace, come into his kingdom at last.

He kept his eyes steadily before him, scarcely seeing the flash of the river as it swept beneath him and away, or on all sides the dipping flags, the monstrous gilded prows, the bravery of color, down this broad road on which he went, scarcely conscious that, as he passed, the great barges wheeled behind him to follow to the meeting; scarcely hearing the tremendous music that, sweeping up from the crowded streets below, wafted up to him the adoration of a free people who had learned at last that the law of liberty was the law of love.

Ah, there at last they came!

Far down, rising every instant higher above the summer haze, outlined against a heaven of intensest blue, approached a cloud that sparkled as it came, that broke into a thousand points of color—a long, flat cloud, seen at first as a streamer stretched across the sky, curving down behind, as it seemed, into the haze from which it came. On and up it came, growing every instant, widening and deepening, ever more and more clear in color and form and depth.

It could be seen now of what elements it was made—a throng of tiny specks, moving like stately birds, which, even as the eye watched, seemed to spread their wings upon the breeze that followed; to expand their bulk, and to grow, as the distance lessened, into the separate colors of each.

Then once again bellowed the guns, heard now like the voice of articulate thunder five miles behind, rolling up the river as if to speed this fleet upon its way; and still he kept his eyes upon those who came so swiftly.

There in front moved the great guard-ships, monsters of polished steel, decked at prow and stern with the huge banners that stood out straight behind in the swiftness of their coming, but which, even as he looked, flapped and bellied to this side and that as the speed decreased. Then, wheeling outwards, disclosing as they wheeled the insignia that each bore, the eagles of Germany, the lilies of France, and the rest, the guard of thirty giants fell once more into line, half a mile apart, as those that followed came on, and waited, beating the air with the shimmer of their netted wings.

Then ship after ship came up, each wheeling in its turn and waiting, building now up with the speed of thought a vast semi-circle, expanding ever more and more swiftly, as the watcher looked—himself halted now, with the royal barge on his right and his train of boats behind. There each in its turn passed the air-navies of the Great Powers, come to bring their Lord with honor on his progress through the world—vast armaments of inconceivable war, enrolled at last in the service of the Prince of Peace.

Then when the movement was complete, and there lay there across the burning blue of the sky, five hundred feet in air, this vast curve of glittering splendor, ten miles from horn to horn, on came the great fleet that they had escorted.

There, then, the watcher saw two by two, first the barges of the Papal Orders, the Order of the Holy Sepulcher with its five-fold cross, and the Golden Spur, leading—huge medieval galleons, carved at prow and stem, each bearing its insignia; then came couple after couple bearing the Papal Court, followed closely by great barges, each with its canopy and throne, and the coat of the Cardinal whom each bore flying overhead.

And then a glorious sight.

For, moving alone in a solid phalanx, each vessel separated only by the space necessary for close maneuvering, came the royal barges of Europe, flanked on either side by a line of guard-boats—France, Austria, and Germany, then Belgium and Holland, then the Scandinavian kingdoms, then a crowd of lesser States from the Balkan, Greece, and the Black Sea; then the black-eagled barge of Russia, and finally the great galleons of Spain and Italy: and on each sat a royal figure beneath a canopy of state. And last of all moved a huge vessel, in scarlet and white, with a banner of white and gold and cross-keys at the prow; scarcely seen at first through the crowding craft, with a squadron of guard-ships coming after.

There, then, the man who had lost his memory sat motionless, and watched it all—this astounding display of inner grace transformed into glory at last, that royalty which, since first the Fisherman took his seat in Holy Rome, had little by little, through reverse and success, forced its way outwards on the world—the leaven hid in the meal till all was leavened. And it seemed to him as he looked, as if through the splendor of the mid-day sun, the glitter of that sea of air-craft—through the pealing of the bells beneath and the shock of the guns and the shrill crying that filled the air—there moved other presences, too, in yet a third medium than those of air and earth; as if diffused throughout this material plane was a world of more than matter and mind, more than of sense and perception—a world where all was reconciled and made at one—this clash of flesh and spirit— and that at last each answered to each, and spirit inspired flesh, and flesh expressed spirit. It seemed to him, for one blinding instant, as if at last he saw how distance was contained in a single point, color in whiteness, and sound in silence, as at the very word of Him who now at last had taken His power and reigned, whose Kingdom at last had come indeed, to whom in very truth all power was given in heaven and earth.

EPILOGUE

THE white-skirted, clean-looking doctor came briskly and noiselessly into the little room that opened off ward No. IV in the Westminster Hospital as the clock pointed to nine o'clock in the morning, and the nursing-sister stood up to receive him.

"Good morning, sister," he said. "Any change?"

"He seemed a little disturbed about an hour ago by the bells," she said. "But he hasn't spoken at all."

Together they stood and looked down on the unconscious man. He lay there motionless with closed eyes, his unshaven cheek resting on his hand, his face fallen into folds and hollows, colorless and sallow. The red coverlet drawn up over his shoulder helped to emphasize his deadly pallor.

"It's a curious case," said the doctor. "I've never seen coma in such a case last so long."

He still stared at him a moment or two; then he laid the back of his hand gently against the dying man's cheek, then again he consulted through his glasses the chart that hung over the head of the bed.

"Will he recover consciousness before the end, doctor?"

"It's very likely; it's impossible to say. Send for me if there's any change."

"I mayn't send for a priest, doctor?" she said hesitatingly. "You know—"

He shook his head sharply.

"No, no. He distinctly refused, you remember. It's impossible, sister. I'm very sorry."

When he had gone, she sat down again, and drew out her beads furtively upon her lap.

It was a horrible position for her. She, a Catholic, knew now pretty well the history of this man—that he himself was a priest who had lost the faith, who had associated himself with an historian who was writing a history of the Popes from what he called an impartial standpoint, who had, so the doctor said, distinctly and resentfully refused the suggestion that another priest should be sent to help him to make his peace before he died. And, for her, as a convinced Catholic, the position had a terror that is simply inconceivable to those of a less positive faith.

She could do nothing more. She said her beads.

There was a curious mixture of silence and sound here on this Easter Sunday in this bare, airy little ward, with the door closed, and the windows open only at the top. The room had a remote kind of atmosphere about it, obtained perhaps partly by the solidity of the walls, partly by the fact that it looked out onto a comparatively unfrequented lane, partly by the suggestiveness of a professional sick-room. The world was all about it; yet it seemed rather to this nurse, sitting alone at her prayers and duties, as if she had a window into the common world of life rather than that she actually was a part of it. Even the sounds that entered here had this remote tone about them; the footsteps and talking of strayed holiday-makers, occasional fragmentary peals of bells, the striking of the clock in high Victoria Tower—all these noises came into the room delicately and suggestively rather than as interruptions, yet distinct and noticeable because of the absence of the usual rush of traffic across the great square outside.

The nurse dozed a little over her beads. (She had been on duty since the evening before, and would not be relieved for another hour yet.) And it seemed to her, as so often in that half-sleep, half-wakefulness when the drowsy brain knows all necessary things and awakes alert again in an instant at any unusual movement or sound, as if these sounds began to take on tones of other causes than those of themselves.

It seemed, for example, as if the steady murmur were the shouting of phantom crowds at an immeasurable distance, punctuated now

again by the noise of distant guns, as, somewhere around a corner a
vehicle passed over a crossing of cobblestones; as if the bells of the
churches rang with a deliberate purpose, to welcome or rejoice over
some event...some entry of a king, she fancied, in a far-off city. Once
even, so deep grew her drowsiness, she fancied herself looking down
on some such city, herself up in the sunlight and air, floating on the
cloudy vessel of her own sleep.

"Pray for us sinners," she murmured, "now and in the hour of our
death."

Then she awoke in earnest, and saw the eyes of the patient fixed
intelligently upon her.

"Fetch a priest," he said.

"Father," said the dying man an hour later, "is that all? Have you
finished?"

"Yes, my dear Father—thank God!"

"Well, sit down a minute or two. I want to talk to you."

The young priest, sent for nearly an hour ago in haste from the
Cathedral, finished putting up again into his little leather case the tiny
stocks of holy oil with which he had just anointed the dying man. He
had heard his confession; he had returned again to fetch the *Viaticum*
and the oils; and now all was done; and the old priest was reconciled
and at peace. The young man was still a little tremulous; it was his first
reconciliation of a dying apostate, and it seemed to him a marvelous
thing that a man could come back after so long, and so simply—and
an apostate priest at that! He had heard this man's name before, and
heard his story.

But he was intensely anxious to know what it was that had
wrought the miracle. The sister had told him that until this moment
the patient had steadily refused even the suggestion to send for a
priest. And then when he had come, there had been no preliminaries.
He had simply slipped on his stole as the sister went to the door, sat
down by the bedside, heard the confession and undertaken one or two
little acts of restitution on his penitent's behalf.

He sat down again now and waited.

The man in the bed lay with closed eyes, and an extraordinary peace rested over him. It was almost impossible to believe, so white were the reflections of these clean walls, so white the linen, that there was not a certain interior luminosity that shone over his features. His chin and lips and jaws were covered with a week's stubble, his eyelids were sunk in the sockets, and the temples looked shrunken and hollow; yet there was a clearness of skin, not yet dusky with the shadow of death, that appeared almost supernatural to this young man who looked at him.

"The sign of the Prophet Jonas," said the dying priest suddenly. "Resurrection."

"Yes?"

"That is what I have seen," he said.

"No, I know it was a dream. But it is possible; the Church has the power within her. It may happen some day; or it may not. But there is no reason why it should not?"

The other leant over him.

"My dear Father—" he began.

The old priest smiled.

"It is a long time since I heard that," he said. "What's your name, Father?"

"Jervis…Father Jervis. I come from the Cathedral."

The eyes opened and looked at him curiously.

"Eh?"

"Father Jervis," said the young priest again.

"Any relations?"

"Some nephews—children. That's all of my name."

"Ah…well… Perhaps—" he broke off. "Did they tell me your name, before I became unconscious?"

"It's very likely. I'm the visiting chaplain here."

"Ah, well! Who knows—? But that doesn't matter…. Father, how long have I to live?"

The young priest leaned forward and laid his hand on the other's arm.

"A few hours only, Father," he said gently. "You are not afraid?"

"Afraid?"

His eyes closed, and he smiled naturally and easily.

"Well, listen. Lean closer... No... Call the sister in. I want her to hear, too."

"Sister—"

She came forward, her eyes heavy with sleep, but they were bright, too, with an immense joy.

"Can you wait up a little longer, sister?" said Father Jervis. "He wants us both to hear what he has to say."

"Why, of course."

She sat down on the other side of the bed.

Still the sounds from outside went on—the footsteps and the voices and the bells. They were beginning to ring for the Easter morning service in the Abbey; and still, within this room, was this air of silence and remoteness.

"Now, listen carefully," said the dying man....

THE END

CLUNY MEDIA

Designed by Fiona Cecile Clarke, the CLUNY MEDIA *logo
depicts a monk at work in the scriptorium,
with a cat sitting at his feet.*

*The monk represents our mission to emulate
the invaluable contributions of the monks
of Cluny in preserving the libraries of the West,
our strivings to know and love the truth.*

*The cat at the monk's feet is Pangur Bán, from the
eponymous Irish poem of the 9th century.
The anonymous poet compares his scholarly
pursuit of truth with the cat's happy hunting of mice.
The depiction of Pangur Bán is an homage to the work
of the monks of Irish monasteries and a sign
of the joy we at Cluny take in our trade.*

"Messe ocus Pangur Bán,
cechtar nathar fria saindan:
bíth a menmasam fri seilgg,
mu memna céin im saincheirdd."